The Return
of the
Raven Mocker

Books by Donis Casey

The Alafair Tucker Mysteries
The Old Buzzard Had It Coming
Hornswoggled
The Drop Edge of Yonder
The Sky Took Him
Crying Blood
The Wrong Hill to Die On
Hell With The Lid Blown Off
All Men Fear Me
The Return of the Raven Mocker

The Return
of the
Raven Mocker

An Alafair Tucker Mystery

Donis Casey

Poisoned Pen Press

First Edition 2017

10 9 8 7 6 5 4 3 2 1

Library of Congress Catalog Card Number: 2016949022

ISBN: 9781464207549   Hardcover
       9781464207563   Trade Paperback

Poisoned Pen Press
6962 E. First Ave., Ste. 103
Scottsdale, AZ 85251
www.poisonedpenpress.com
info@poisonedpenpress.com

Printed in the United States of America

Cast of Characters

Alafair Tucker—Takes care of everyone even if they don't ask

Shaw Tucker—Her husband, in charge of everything, more or less

Their children:

Martha McCoy—age 27, President of Boynton Red Cross Chapter
Major Streeter McCoy—her husband, in Washington D.C., winning the war

Mary Lucas—age 25, keeping quarantine
Sergeant Kurt Lucas—her husband, in Washington D.C., translating German documents
Judy Lucas—age 33 months, their daughter

Alice Kelley—age 24, feeling poorly
Walter Kelley—her husband, also feeling poorly
Linda Kelley—age 27 months, their daughter

Phoebe Day—age 24, Alice's twin, taking care of her father
John Lee Day—her husband, running the farm
Zeltha Day—age 4, their daughter
Tucker Day—age 26 months, their son

Lt. George W. Tucker, also known as Gee Dub—age 22, in France

Ruth Tucker—age 19, taking care of her mentor
Seaman Trenton Calder, Ruth's intended, somewhere in the North Atlantic

Private Charlie Tucker—age 17, driving trucks in England, whether he ought to be or not

Blanche Tucker—age 13, wrangling babies

Sophronia Tucker—age 12, causing trouble

Grace Tucker—age 6, or close enough to make no difference

Members of the family:

Chase Kemp—age 8, Alafair's nephew and ward, a talented spy

Scott Tucker—the law in Boynton, Oklahoma, Shaw's cousin

Hattie Tucker—Scott's wife

Slim Tucker—their son, Scott's deputy

No relation, but God's children all the same:

Wesley M. Cotton—prosecuting attorney, District Court of Muskogee County

Doctor Emmett Carney—doing the best he can against long odds

Ann Addison (Mrs. Doc)—the local midwife, pressed into service

Nola Thomason—Alice's neighbor

Homer Thomason—Nola's husband

Dorothy Thomason—their daughter, Sophronia's friend

Lewis Hulce—Nola's son from a previous marriage

JoNell Reed—Lewis' beloved

Mrs. Gale—Alice's neighbor

Old Man Escoe—Mrs. Gale's father, loves cats and children

Animals:

Sweet Honey Baby—a horse often involved in criminal activity

Bacon, Charlie Dog, Big Fella, Buttercup, Crook—the family dogs

A half-grown yellow kitten—may be magic

Prologue

Wesley M. Cotton, prosecuting attorney for the District Court of Muskogee County, Oklahoma, looked up from the deposition on his desk to study the couple seated before him. Mr. and Mrs. Shaw Tucker, currently residing on a farm located outside of Boynton in the western part of the county.

They were a middle-aged pair, middle forties, he thought. Cotton knew from the deposition that they were farmers, but he would have known that without being told. They were both well-dressed, but weathered and brown as nuts from a life lived outdoors. Mr. Tucker was a tall man, maybe six feet, with straight black hair, a floppy mustache, deep, hazel eyes and bold cheekbones that bespoke Indian ancestry.

The wife, who was called Alafair, according to the statement, was middle-sized at best. She was clad in a plum-colored suit with a full skirt, and a trim white cotton blouse. Her plum silk hat with a dark purple ribbon and wreath of small flowers around the crown was set squarely on top of wavy dark hair that was slipping out of an untidy bun at the back of her head.

"Thank you for taking time to travel all the way back here to Muskogee to answer some questions about the changes in your statement, Mrs. Tucker."

It was Shaw who responded. "Yes, sir, we're glad to do it. Mr. Hughes told us that you are the one who will decide whether to bind Mr. Thomason over for trial."

"That's right." Cotton looked at Alafair, who looked right back. "Mrs. Tucker, according to Deputy Hughes, you now believe that the wrong person has been arrested in connection with the murder that took place in Boynton on October 12, 1918. However, you are the party who originally provided the evidence which led to Mr. Thomason's arrest in the first place. When you were interviewed by Deputy Sheriff Hughes in Boynton on October 16, you were entirely convinced that Mr. Thomason was guilty."

Alafair nodded, but Shaw responded for her. "That is true. But my wife has come into possession of some new information that you should hear."

Shaw Tucker was doing the talking, but Cotton had no illusions that the reason was because Alafair Tucker was shy or demure. Ever since she had set foot in his office, Cotton was aware that she had been evaluating his every move, judging his every word. He resisted an urge to straighten his tie and adjust his waistcoat. Instead, he folded his hands on his desktop and leaned forward. "If that is the case, I would appreciate it if you would relate this new information to me in your own words, Mrs. Tucker."

Her sharp, dark eyes gave him a final once-over. Cotton decided that he had passed inspection when she relaxed back into her chair and said, "Mr. Cotton, what I told Mr. Hughes is the truth, and I know it looks real bad for Mr. Thomason. But at the time, I wasn't aware of everything that led up to that day. You have the wrong man, Mr. Cotton, and I aim to tell you how I found out."

Chapter One

How it Was That Alafair Tucker's Youngest Started School

People die all kinds of ways. Some die in war, some die of sickness, and some people die because of the hatred of others. But on the fine soft Sunday morning of September 1, 1918, Alafair Tucker was not thinking of all the ways that people die. She was thinking that when Monday came, her youngest child, Grace, was going to start the first grade.

On that day, the congregation of the first Christian Church of Boynton, Oklahoma, prayed for a speedy end to the Great War in Europe. The new preacher, Mr. Huster, didn't ask that the enemy be annihilated and crushed into dust, as did many of his flock in their private prayers, but that the better angels of human nature would prevail and peace and goodwill be restored between nations.

Alafair Tucker prayed for an end to hostilities as hard as anyone. But she didn't hold out much hope that reason would prevail any time soon. She hadn't seen any evidence of reason in her fellow man for some time now.

Five years earlier, when the war in Europe had begun, Alafair had expressed her compassion for the poor people who were living in the midst of the fighting. Otherwise she had had no opinion on the reasons for the war or even on its outcome. After all, the conflict was taking place five thousand miles away from Muskogee County, Oklahoma. How could it touch her family?

She should have known better. When it came to a scrap, no government run by men could leave well enough alone. The United States had now been involved in the conflict for more than a year, and many of her loved ones were in harm's way.

Alafair and Shaw Tucker were the parents of ten children living and the grandparents of four. Alafair had spent her life raising up her children and now most of them were off on their own pursuits. In fact some were likely to get themselves widowed or killed or maimed, and there was not one thing in the world she could do about it but try and be prepared to pick up the pieces of a shattered life.

Her two sons and three of her sons-in-law had been called to the service of their country. Her oldest boy, Gee Dub, was somewhere in France now. He had been called up right after his twenty-first birthday and sent to Camp Funston, in Kansas. Since he had some college education, had been in the National Guard, and could shoot the eyelashes off of a gnat, he was tapped for officer training within the first two weeks. Afterwards he had spent a few months training inductees in riflery, which, he wrote his parents, was a pretty frightening proposition considering he had to show most of the recruits which end of the rifle the bullet came out of.

Alafair's younger boy, Charlie, shouldn't have gone to war at all. After Gee Dub was called up, Charlie stowed away on a troop train leaving out of Boynton in October of '17, so eager to do his bit that he never gave a thought to the fact that he was breaking his mother's heart. But since he was only sixteen years old at the time, he had been turned away from nearly every recruiting office in the eastern part of the state.

So he hitched a ride to Oklahoma City, where he still had no luck. The Marines told him he had flat feet, which he didn't. The Navy doctor told him his chest sounded weak. Which it didn't. Charlie figured that they were making excuses not to take him because he still had fuzz on his cheeks. But the Army recruiter surveyed the young man's considerable height and his well-nourished frame and decided that since he had a quota to fill, the armed services could find a use for Charlie Tucker.

Shaw spent several weeks hunting in vain for his prodigal child, until Charlie finally wrote his folks from boot camp at Camp Pike in Little Rock, Arkansas. Shaw immediately got on the train and headed out, meaning to have Charlie mustered out for being underage. His solemn intent was to fetch the boy home by the ear and turn him over to his mother. But after an exchange with Charlie that was half argument and half abject begging, and a long heart-to-heart with Charlie's commander, Shaw had returned home alone. Alafair pressed him to go back, or she would go herself. But Shaw convinced her that it was useless. The boy would just run away again. Besides, when Charlie had finally gotten to training camp, the sergeant had taken one look at his youthful mug and assigned him to the motor pool.

Charlie spent three months learning to drive trucks and motorcycles and repair engines, and that suited him fine. While Charlie was in Arkansas learning the vagaries of the internal combustion engine, he had turned seventeen and the draft age had been lowered to eighteen. He wrote to his mother that as time went on he would just naturally become legal. He was in England now, carrying messages, repairing trucks, and scheming ways to get to France before the war was over.

◇◇◇

As the summer of 1918 progressed and her sons-in-law went, one by one, to do their duty, Alafair had had her moment of weeping for each one in turn. Then she wiped her eyes, squared her shoulders, and went about her business.

In fact, over the past several weeks she had seemed happy, as though nothing was troubling her. Shaw thought this was exceedingly odd. If any of her young ones were in danger, or suffering in any way, and there was anything Alafair could do about it, she would move heaven and earth to see that it was done.

Sometimes her efforts turned out well, and sometimes they didn't, but no matter the outcome, Alafair could never rest content until she was sure that she had done everything that could possibly be done to save her children pain.

Which was why Shaw Tucker was worried about Alafair's state of mind. Several of the brood were in danger of suffering at the moment, yet Alafair appeared to be untroubled. Cheerful, even.

How could her happy demeanor be real when every sunrise brought the possibility of a telegram from the War Department telling them that one of their daughters was a widow or that one of their boys had lost a limb, or his life, in France?

Shaw tried to let it go. Everyone coped with the unthinkable in their own way. Perhaps he was even a little envious. The rumor was that the war would be over soon, but Shaw couldn't stop gnawing on the awful possibilities, and he had to admit that dwelling on his fear and dread did not make his life any easier.

At the moment, Alafair's attention was focused on the fact that Grace was going to start first grade. At not-quite-six, she was still a couple of months shy of the cut-off age for first grade, but Grace had grown up with nine much-older siblings who had taken it upon themselves to be her teachers. Especially twelve-year-old Sophronia, child number nine, who had loved to play school with her baby sister since Grace had been old enough to toddle about on her own two feet.

All the family attention had paid off handsomely. At least that's how Alafair explained the fact that Grace could already read and figure, write, and draw like a much older child.

As the summer wound down, Grace was wild to start school and could talk of nothing else. At first Alafair was worried about starting her too early, even if she was advanced for her age. Shaw had pointed out that if they waited until the next year, after Grace turned six at the end of October, she would be older than most of her classmates and so far ahead of them that it would create even bigger problems for her.

So Alafair had taken Grace to town before school started and asked the primary teacher, Miss Graham, to interview her.

Miss Graham was impressed, though not pleased that Grace was going to have to "unlearn the bad habits" she had picked up from her sisters and brothers. Alafair pointed out that a few of Grace's older siblings had been taught by Miss Graham, so if Grace had any bad habits when it came to reading and writing, Miss Graham could look to herself.

The upshot was that Grace would start first grade on September second. She already knew many of her prospective classmates, including her own cousin, Katie Lancaster. That was the nice thing about living near a small town and being related in one way or another to most of the population.

Alafair was as excited as Grace about her adventure. In August, she made first-day dresses for Grace, Sophronia, and thirteen-year-old Blanche, the only three of her offspring who were still in school, and a fancy striped shirt for her eight-year-old nephew and ward, Chase Kemp. She and the children made a holiday out of a trip into town to buy new shoes and school supplies. On the Sunday before school started, Alafair prayed for a speedy end to the war and an auspicious beginning for Grace's first foray into the world without her mother.

On the morning of September second, Alafair tied a big white bow into Grace's black hair and handed her a little tin pail packed with her favorite cold chicken sandwich and a cookie. On Grace's very first day Alafair drove the youngsters into town in the buggy, rather than making them walk.

The older children jumped out as soon as they spotted their friends, waving acknowledgement when Alafair called after them to be sure and keep an eye out for Grace through the day. Alafair had intended to escort her youngest to her classroom, but Grace would have none of it. She was a big girl now and knew where she was supposed to go. She threw her arm around her mother's neck and gave her a hurried kiss on the cheek. Then she was gone without a backward glance.

Alafair stood in the road beside the buggy and watched the children meet and greet their friends, until the bell rang and the horde of children ran and skipped and walked and dragged themselves to their classrooms. She stood there until the school-yard was empty and the only sound she could hear was the flapping of the flag at the top of its pole.

Then Alafair burst into tears. Her last chick had fledged and was taking her first flight. Alafair felt ridiculous, standing there in the road, sobbing as though she had lost her last friend. She had already been through this rite of passage more often than most mothers. She always felt a bit low when any of the children started school for the first time. It wasn't the end of the world. After all, Grace wasn't even six years old. She'd be living at home for at least another decade. It was all a natural thing, part of God's plan. We're born, we grow up, we get married, we raise our families. We die.

Alafair's attempt to reason with herself caused her to sob even harder.

She stood on the road beside her buggy, staring at the empty schoolyard and weeping, for how long she couldn't tell. She felt like an idiot, and tried to stay out of sight of anyone who passed by. She had finally taken herself in hand and was dabbing her swollen eyes with a handkerchief when she felt a hand on her arm and turned to face a tall, fair-haired young woman holding the hand of a dark-eyed toddler.

"Howdy, Ma."

"Alice!" She gave her third-oldest daughter a quick hug and opened her arms wide to envelop her granddaughter. "And my darlin' Linda! Come over here, baby, and let me love on you."

Linda ran into her embrace and Alice gave her mother a mischievous grin. "We figured we'd walk over to the school this morning and see how you were feeling about…the state of the world and such."

Alafair stood up with Linda in her arms. "Oh, honey, I was feeling sad until I saw your shining face and my baby girl here. I was just about to drive over to your house before I go to the post office…" She hesitated when Alice turned and beckoned to a woman who had been standing behind her. Alafair hadn't even noticed her.

"Mama, this is my next-door neighbor, Miz Thomason. Her daughter went back to school today, too. Every Monday afternoon Miz Thomason and I walk down to the armory together to do Red Cross work and let Martha boss us around." Alafair's eldest, Martha McCoy, was the organizer and guiding light of the local Red Cross Chapter.

Mrs. Thomason had a pleasant look about her. Her eyes were a translucent light gray color, and the hair that peeked out from under a shady straw bonnet was the pale golden-brown hue of maple wood. She was older than Alice, about the same age as Alafair herself. She was also a substantial woman, thirty pounds heavier and half a head taller than Alafair.

"Alice told me that your youngest is off to school for the first time," Mrs. Thomason said. "I swear, when my baby first went out into the world without me, I felt lower than a gopher hole."

Alafair smiled. "I didn't even realize I was so blue about it until she walked away from me without a care in the world."

"I do know your pain, though my youngest will be out of grammar school before long." The woman held out a hand. "Call me Nola. I feel like we already know one another, thanks to Alice, here. My husband is Homer Thomason of the Muskogee Tool and Die Company. Your husband and mine have done business."

Ah, yes, Alafair was acquainted with Homer Thomason. He had been out to the farm once or twice, and Shaw had indeed bought a few farm implements from him. Alafair had served the men coffee and pie at her kitchen table while they talked about harrows. She did not recollect ever meeting Mrs. Thomason.

She shifted Linda to one arm and took the proffered hand. "I'm Alafair. Pleased to meet you. What grade is your young'un in?"

"Dorothy is starting sixth grade this year. I can hardly believe it."

"I have a girl in the same class as yours. In fact I believe I've heard Sophronia talk about her friend Dorothy."

"Fronie and Dorothy are friends, Ma," Alice said. "Last year the girls would walk up to my house or to Miz Thomason's house over the luncheon break."

Nola nodded. "Once or twice Sophronia has come home with Dorothy for a snack during recess, too. Dorothy asks me right along if she can bring one playmate or another. She's my only daughter, and sometimes she gets lonely for a girlfriend. Nothing makes me happier than when Dorothy brings her little friends over. I love watching all the girls play, and listening to their chatter is like listening to birdsong to me. Sophronia is a real polite little gal, and smart, too. She always has some story to tell to make Dorothy laugh."

Alafair tried not to look too proud at the unsolicited praise. "Yes, Fronie can talk the legs off a chair, don't I know it. I'm sorry I've not met Dorothy. Our farm is way out yonder north and west, so it's not so easy for the children's friends to drop in."

"Do y'all have to get on home right now? If you have a minute to spare, I'd be pleased if y'all would come by my house for a glass of tea and a morsel of gingerbread."

Alice cheerfully accepted, but Alafair almost demurred out of habit. For the past quarter-century, her philosophy had been that when you have a farm and a home to run, and children galore to raise, you don't have the time to think about a social life. The farm and home still had to be run and she still had children to be raised. But today there would be no human soul besides herself in her house until Shaw, along with whichever of the farmhands he decided to invite, showed up at her kitchen door for dinner at one o'clock. She had convinced herself that she had been looking forward to the unheard-of freedom to work uninterrupted. But the sudden realization that she could make time for a visit with someone not directly related to her gave her pause.

"Why, I suppose I could spare a few minutes. I aim to go to the post office before I have to get home and fix dinner, but I was going to drop in on Alice first, anyway. I'd admire to sit a spell and make your better acquaintance, Miz Thomason."

Chapter Two

How Alafair Made a Friend

The Thomason house was long and low, with a deep front porch that Nola had covered with potted plants and comfortable lounging furniture. A perfect place for sitting outside to watch the children play on a summer evening, with a cold, sweet drink on the side table and your crocheting in your lap. Nola ensconced Alafair and Alice in cushiony wicker chairs and plied them with iced tea and gingerbread. Under her mother's watchful eye, Linda happily explored the porch.

The women spoke of little things, mostly having to do with their children and their homes. They spoke of their war work, but once they had told one another about which of their relatives were in the service, they had nothing to say about the war itself. The older women were amazed that they had never crossed paths, considering how many people they knew in common. Nola was acquainted with all three of Alafair's town-dwelling daughters, Martha, Alice, and Ruth. She knew Martha through the Red Cross chapter. Alice was her next-door neighbor, and Dorothy took piano lessons from the middle Tucker girl, Ruth.

Nola Thomason and her family had lived in Boynton for almost five years. They were originally from Nixa, Missouri, just south of Springfield. Oh, yes, Alafair was familiar! She had a cousin who lived in Ozark, just a hop, skip, and a jump from Nixa. No, the Thomasons were Baptists, so had never attended services at the new location of the First Christian Church of Boynton, where the Tuckers worshiped.

Alafair only lingered for twenty minutes, but when she and Alice finally left, she was feeling much better. It had been pleasant to enjoy the company of another woman her own age and chat about insignificant things like the weather and flowers and trying to bake a cake without eggs.

Before she left to run her errands, Alafair walked next door to Alice's house with Linda in her arms.

As they strolled, Alafair said, "Miz Thomason seems like a real nice lady, Alice. How long has she lived next door?"

"Oh, they moved into that house right after the Grants left two years ago."

"It's good that you have an older woman so near to go to if you need something."

The corner of Alice's mouth twisted upwards and she shot her mother a glance along her shoulder. She knew Alafair would be comforted to think Alice had a surrogate mother to watch over her, since the real thing couldn't be with her twenty-four hours a day. "Yes, we visit quite a lot. I used to visit with the Widow Gale in the house to the back of me, but since her old daddy, Mr. Escoe, came to live with her, Miz Gale don't get out much and doesn't much like company, either. So I was glad when Miz Thomason and them moved in. I like her, and Dorothy is crazy as a bedbug about Linda...." Alice paused to tickle the chin of the child in question. "Dorothy comes over two or three times a week and volunteers to help me weed my flowers or do some sewing, but truth is she wants to play with the little honey bee here."

They reached Alice's house and paused the conversation long enough to mount the steps and go inside. Alafair put Linda on the floor and sat down in an armchair. Alice took off her hat before resuming where she left off.

"Homer Thomason is Nola's second husband, Ma. Her first husband died of the lockjaw back in aught-aught, leaving her with a young son. She was a widow for years before she married Mr. Thomason and Dorothy came along."

"She has a nice house," Alafair observed.

"The farm machinery business is good, and they only have one measly child to support." Alice delivered the comment with a hint of irony.

"I thought you said she had a child with her first husband."

Alice retrieved Linda's hand from the dirt around the potted ficus before she sat down with the tot on her lap. "Oh, Lewis is a grown man, now. He must be about my age."

"Is he in the service?" Alafair hadn't noticed a blue star flag in the Thomasons' window.

"No. I'm guessing he couldn't go because he wears spectacles as thick as the bottom of a pop bottle. He's a Four-Minute Man, though, and has been on all the Liberty Bond Drive committees. You probably know him, Ma. He works for Junia Williams over at Williams' Drug."

Lewis…Lewis… Alafair was wracking her brain. She patronized Williams' Drug Store often, and had at least a nodding acquaintance with all of Mr. Williams' employees. Suddenly the image a of thin, dark-haired young man in glasses, standing behind the pharmacy counter, popped into her mind.

"Lewis Hulce? That skinny fellow with a nose like a knife?"

"That's him. I don't see him around his mother's house much. Him and his stepdaddy don't get along. I know him well enough to exchange pleasantries when I go to the drug store, if you want to call it an exchange. He's so quiet and polite I doubt he'd bite a biscuit."

Alafair said, "Why, I always found him to be friendly enough." But she knew why a young man might be reticent in the presence of a young woman as pretty as Alice.

There was a pause in the conversation when Linda screeched her displeasure at being restrained. "All right. Mercy! You're as wiggly as an eel." Alice put the girl down and she streaked away as fast as her little legs would take her.

"How is Walter?" Alafair asked more to be polite than out of concern for her son-in-law's well-being. Walter Kelley, a barber, had registered when the draft age was raised from thirty-one to forty-five, but had not yet been called up and hadn't volunteered. Alafair had no desire to see Alice left alone for the duration. Or worse, widowed and Linda orphaned. But secretly she thought that a little hardship would probably do Walter some good.

She had never warmed to Alice's husband. She thought him glib and insincere, and was not convinced that he was as attentive to his wife as he ought to be. Alice didn't complain, though, so Alafair kept her mouth shut.

"He's fine. Business has been slow. Too many men have left town lately. He said sometimes he sits and twiddles his thumbs for an hour between customers." Alice smiled, but her gaze skittered away. That tiny evasive movement gave Alafair a rush of inexplicable anger at Walter Kelley. Before she could say anything, Linda reappeared at a run with a stuffed animal in her hand and thrust it into her grandmother's face.

Alafair melted at once. "Whatever is this? Do you have a new bear? Where is the bear's nose? Can you say 'nose'?"

After a few minutes of a giggly recitation of bear body parts, Alafair extricated herself from the game and stood. "I've got to go to the post office and then get home and get dinner started, darlin'," she said to Alice, as she unwound Linda from her leg. "It's such a treat to visit with you like this. Maybe I'll carry Chase and the girls back and forth to school for a week or so, at least while it's still hot in the afternoons. Take a few minutes to visit with all you town girls for a spell, at least until y'all get sick of me."

"I'll warn Ruth and Martha," Alice said brightly.

Alafair had driven halfway up the long drive from the road to the house before she saw that two more of her grown daughters, Mary and Phoebe, both of whom lived on adjoining farms, were sitting together on the porch, waiting for her. Three of her grandchildren were in the front yard; sweet Zeltha, bubbly Judy, and sturdy Tucker, the only boy, always noisy and sticky and into something. Shaw met her at the gate, which surprised her. Now that he had a contract to sell mules to the U.S. Army and had lost much of his unpaid family work crew to the service, his labor was relentless. He looked bedraggled and dusty from spreading hay since five o'clock that morning, but he gave her a sympathetic smile and handed her down from the buggy when she came to a halt in front of the house. She felt embarrassed, afraid that her eyes still bore evidence of her unseemly weeping.

"We don't have any more babies, Shaw." She sounded resigned.

The words were barely spoken when the grandchildren swarmed through the front gate and clamored for Alafair's attention. Shaw said nothing, but raised an eyebrow as Alafair hoisted Judy and Tuck and settled one on each hip. Even Alafair, bereft as she was, had to laugh at the irony. Shaw led the horse and rig toward the barn and Alafair started for the house with her arms full of children and four-year-old Zeltha grasping her skirt.

Mary and Phoebe stood when she mounted the porch steps. "What are y'all girls doing here?"

Mary put an arm around Alafair's shoulder. "We figured you could use your family around you right about now, Ma."

Mary's German-born husband, Kurt, had endured such prejudice when the war started that he had waived his "protected occupation" exemption as a farmer and enlisted to show his one-hundred percent unadulterated Americanism. On top of which he and Mary had legally changed their last name from "Lukenbach" to "Lucas," which Alafair could never remember to save her life. Or maybe she just didn't want to remember the ugliness that had led to such a drastic move.

Now Mary Lucas and her little Judy were on their own in their pretty white farmhouse half a mile west of the family homestead. When Kurt left for Washington City to translate German documents for the U.S. Army, Mary's parents had tried to talk her into moving home until the war was over. Mary wouldn't hear of it. Alafair admitted to herself that it wasn't a logical move, since Mary's house was bigger than hers and was inhabited by many fewer people. But she couldn't stand the idea of Mary and her tot in that big house all by themselves and at the mercy of anti-immigrant night riders. In the end Shaw had given Mary a slobbery, overprotective mastiff the size of a small horse, and Chase Kemp had moved to Mary's house to provide company and a willing hand.

At least Phoebe, Alice's fraternal twin, still had her husband with her, and for a good reason. John Lee Day had a game leg and a bad eye, the result of his barn collapsing on him during a tornado two years earlier.

"Girls, did your daddy ask y'all to come by today?" Alafair's tone was accusatory. She was aware that in spite of her efforts to appear cheerful, Shaw knew she was feeling low. But she bristled at the idea that he thought she needed distracting. "I'm sure y'all are too busy to be cosseting me."

"Don't be like that, Ma," Phoebe said. "We knew you'd be busy this morning so we decided to fix dinner over here. We're all hungry, too. Now, dinner's on the table. Let's eat."

Alafair was touched by their concern, but the littlest bit disturbed that her children thought they should be taking care of her now, instead of the other way around.

Chapter Three

How Alafair Saw Trouble Coming

Back in the spring, Gee Dub had written to his mother from his base in Kansas that he had suffered from a mild case of the flu that had gone like wildfire through Camp Funston. That bit of news had caused Alafair to harvest and store more of her medicinal herbs than usual that year. She knew how influenza worked. It would reappear in the fall, and she intended to be ready for it.

It was a good thing, too. Since early August, a virulent outbreak of the disease had been running rampant through big, East Coast cities like Boston and Philadelphia. They were calling it Spanish influenza. Then came the word that the flu had spread to California and the West Coast. The newspapers were reporting the bare fact of the spreading illness. The Boynton Town Council, like all the other government organizations, was mum about the danger.

But Alafair knew influenza. It was only a matter of time until it came to Boynton.

Still, she wasn't overly frightened. Her brood was healthy and strong and had lived through every childhood illness known to man with no lasting effects. In fact, by the end of August, the news from the United States Health Commission was that the worst was over and the country should be seeing a reduction in the number of cases soon. Just take normal precautions. It was only the flu. Don't let anything interfere with war production, especially now that Germany was on her knees and influenza had helped put her there. It just showed that God was on our side.

Alafair was a competent doctor of childhood illnesses and injuries, and had a store of homemade pharmaceuticals at the ready. She knew how to waylay trouble, as well. Good, simple food, sleep, fresh air, and cleanliness.

Through the first week in September, Alafair would bring the children to school in the morning and stop by Alice's house for a visit afterwards. Then she would unhitch her mare, Missy, from the shady spot beside Alice's house and drive the two blocks to the post office to pick up her mail. She was disappointed that there were no letters from the boys that week, but not surprised. Alafair's sons wrote regularly, but the letters tended to come in bundles that spanned several weeks.

After the post office stop, she made a point to check in with her other town-dwelling daughters, hungry for any word of their menfolk and anxious to offer what comfort she could to her lonely girls. The eldest, Martha McCoy, was working full time, keeping up with Red Cross projects and running the McCoy Land and Title Company while her husband, Streeter, was in Washington D.C., attached to the procurement office of the War Department. Middle daughter Ruth's intended, Trenton Calder, was on the *U.S.S. Baltimore*, currently at sea somewhere around Scotland. Ruth was still boarding at Rebecca MacKenzie's big house north of town, giving piano lessons as well as working part-time with the Red Cross chapter. Since Alice Kelley had two-year-old Linda to watch out for, she had taken it upon herself to run a makeshift day care center out of her house when the Red Cross ladies had a special project to finish.

Gee Dub was a fairly good correspondent. He had always been a considerate youngster, and would not want his mother and father to suffer from not knowing how he was doing. For a while his parents held out hope that the war would be over before he was sent overseas, but newly promoted Lieutenant George

Washington Tucker had shipped out for France on the tenth of August. They had received a letter he had written while he was still on board ship, so they knew that he must have arrived in Europe. That was all.

Charlie wrote even more often, much to his mother's surprise. "Considerate" was not a word that Alafair would have readily applied to her good-hearted-but-thoughtless son. Alafair figured that Charlie probably felt guilty about the way he had run off without a word and caused his parents endless trouble and worry.

It was out of her way, but on Thursday, Alafair drove by the big, red brick schoolhouse before she left town for home. Even though it had been days since Grace had started school, Alafair was still strangely blue about it. She expected to see nothing more than an empty yard, but to her surprise, the schoolyard was full of children at play. Was it already time for recess? She knew she should hurry home, but she caught sight of Grace, along with three or four other little girls, jumping rope and making a contest over who could jump the longest without getting her feet tangled up. Their piping voices chanted out their jump rope rhyme in unison.

Down by the river, down by the sea,
Johnny broke a bottle and blamed it on me.
I told Ma, Ma told Pa,
Johnny got a spanking so ha ha ha.
How many spankings did Johnny get?
One, two, three, four….

Grace and her friends were already expert rope-jumpers, so the counting went on for quite a long time before someone squealed and the game ended in peals of laughter, only to start up again at once.

Cinderella, dressed in yella
Went upstairs to kiss a fella
Made a mistake and kissed a snake
How many doctors did it take?
One, two, three, four…

Alafair snapped the reins and headed out of town at a trot before she could start crying again.

Alafair spent her first few childless afternoons working herself to distraction, harvesting and canning vegetables, washing and mopping, sewing and mending. Alafair's country-dwelling daughters, Mary and Phoebe, had taken to walking over to help with dinner and bringing a child or two with her to keep Alafair company through part of the afternoon, leaving for home just in time for Alafair to put on her blue gingham sun bonnet, hitch Missy to the buggy, and drive back into town to pick up the children from school.

As the first week came to a close, Alafair pulled up in front of the schoolhouse as the final bell rang and youngsters poured out of the building and scattered like a flock of startled birds. Chase was first to appear and clambered up into the shotgun seat. Chase Kemp was two years older than his cousin Grace, and a boy, but since he had come to live with Alafair's family a couple of years earlier, the children had not paid much attention to either fact. He was bursting with news about his schoolday, and Alafair leaned over the dashboard to listen to him, enjoying his excitement. Blanche appeared next, then Grace, her slate under her arm and her hair bow bedraggled. Grace was so full of chatter that it took a moment for Alafair to notice that Sophronia was standing next to the buggy with a friend at her side, waiting for an opportunity to butt in.

Sophronia was a small for her age, suntanned and freckled, stick-thin, and scabby-kneed from her rough and tumble ways. She wore dresses for school and church, but the moment she was free from her obligation to be neat, she changed into a pair of her brother Charlie's outgrown overalls and a flannel shirt, and would have run barefoot summer and winter if Alafair had allowed it. The relatives thought her tomboyish, but Sophronia had no desire to be a boy. She was a girl, and felt no compulsion to alter her behavior because of that fact. Some of the aunts thought Alafair should insist that she act more like her sister,

Blanche, a delicate, ladylike creature who at thirteen was already using her considerable beauty and charm to have her way.

But Alafair liked Sophronia just the way she was—a free and unfettered spirit. She would realize what the world expected of her soon enough.

Alafair put a hand on Grace's head to pause her narrative and cocked an eyebrow. "And who's this, Fronie?"

"Ma, this is my best friend Dorothy." Sophronia grasped the girl's arm and thrust her forward. "Her desk is right in front of mine because both our last names begin with a 'T'."

"Why, hello, Dorothy! I met your mama when I brought Sophronia and them to school on the first day. In fact, here comes your mama now…"

Nola Thomason was hurrying down the road toward them, her cheeks red from exertion. She was dressed in a plain brown shirtwaist dress and a long white bib apron emblazoned with a red cross in the middle of the breast.

"Oh, hello, Miz Tucker." Nola wiped a strand of hair out of her eyes. "Dorothy, honey, I almost forgot you! Howdy, Sophronia. I say, Alafair, you've got yourself a passel of youngsters, there. Dorothy, how was your day? Did your teacher give you homework?"

Alafair handed Grace up into the backseat. "You look frazzled, Miz Thomason. Did you just get out of a Red Cross meeting?"

"It's still going on. Martha called a special meeting this afternoon. She got a telegram today from the National Headquarters telling all chapters to establish an influenza committee. They said that if the flu hits, each community is going to have to depend on itself to deal with it. We're trying to make as many gauze masks as we can today. Martha said she's going to try and get Miz Addison to give us first aid lessons so we'll know the best way to nurse anybody who gets sick. Dorothy, baby, I'm sorry but I have to go back to the armory as soon as I take you home. You and your father will have to have a bite at the café downtown."

"I could come and help you make masks," Dorothy said.

Sophronia immediately volunteered, followed in short order by all the other children in the buggy.

Nola shook her head. "You have to eat supper, Dorothy, or I'd say all right. I didn't have time to make good plans tonight."

If Alafair and her many charges weren't expected at home shortly, she would have driven directly to the armory and offered their services as mask-makers. "I wish we could help tonight. Tell Martha that I'll talk to her at church on Sunday. After school lets out Monday, perhaps we can all take an hour to pitch in with whatever task needs doing."

Nola liked the idea. "We'd all be happy as can be for the extra help." She took Dorothy's hand. "But right now..."

Sophronia spoke up "Ma, can Dorothy come out to the house and have supper with us?"

"Oh, I couldn't impose..." Nola said, at the same time Alafair said, "I'd be proud to have her, but I'm afraid I don't know how she'd get home."

The thought of going home with her friend energized Dorothy and she tugged her mother's skirt. "Please, Mama! Papa doesn't want to babysit me. Couldn't you motor out and get me after your meeting is over?"

Alafair and Nola locked eyes, each woman judging the other's feelings on the matter.

"You have a conveyance?" Alafair asked.

"Homer's truck. He can bring me if he's not busy, or I can drive it myself pretty well. You know, I told Martha that after we finish with the masks, I'd like to go with her to search out a place where the influenza committee can headquarter."

Alafair could tell that Nola was torn. "Nola, we have plenty of food and places at the table. We won't even notice another young'un."

"Well, it would be a relief, I admit. Thank you so much. I promise that me or her papa will come fetch her before dark." She pushed Dorothy forward. "Now, you behave," she said, and took off down the road before anyone could think better of the plan.

Any other woman who had an unexpected child thrust upon her without warning might have felt used. But Alafair was grateful for the chance to do something helpful, and children, unexpected or not, were always welcome in her home. Besides, a busy person had no time to brood.

◇◇◇

There were chores to be done before supper, so Blanche went to her room to change before heading to the garden. Since Sophronia was entertaining a guest, Alafair invited the two girls into the kitchen for a snack first. Grace tagged along, unwilling to miss anything.

Alafair wiped her hands on her apron. "Y'all girls sit down and have a glass of milk while Dorothy tells me all about herself. Then y'all can go outside and play for a spell before Fronie has to do her chores. You can help her, if you want, Dorothy." The three girls were seated side by side with their hands folded neatly on the tabletop. They all looked so sweet and prim in their school dresses that Alafair almost laughed. She didn't know Dorothy, but she was quite aware that her two youngest were more tart than sweet, and hardly prim.

The girls filled her in on how much they loved school and how they *adored* their teachers, then they polished off their milk and biscuits with honey lickety-split and went outside to play jump rope. Alafair grabbed Grace by the collar when she tried to follow. It was chore time and Dorothy wasn't Grace's guest. Grace's after-school job was to feed the chickens. She hated the task and thus begrudged her sister's fun when she had to suffer. Alafair listened with amusement to Grace grumbling on the back porch as she measured out parched corn into an old dishpan, but offered no comfort. Blanche was already in the garden cutting okra and green beans for supper, so if she had any complaints, Alafair didn't have to hear them.

Alafair stood over the counter slicing potatoes, all the doors and windows open to the mild late summer day, listening to the sixth-graders chat and play.

Dorothy and Sophronia played *Mabel, Mabel, set the table* on their jump ropes until they tired, then sat down on an upturned tub with their heads together. Their plan was to have a private conversation, but they were situated right under the kitchen window and Alafair could hear every word.

Dorothy began with a hefty sigh. "I like it here, Fronie. It's so nice and peaceful. I like your sisters and your mama, too."

"I like it, too," Sophronia admitted, "even if nothing much happens out here. I like the animals and I like going off into the woods by myself to read. There isn't anything I like better than to read books and take care of animals."

"I wish I lived on a farm. When you live in town there's no place to get away by yourself. Mama won't even let me have a dog. She says it's too much trouble."

Sophronia was shocked. "I couldn't do without our dogs! Why old Charlie Dog is almost as old as me. Him and Bacon and Buttercup and Crook are part of the family."

"Y'all get along with each other, too. My papa and my brother, Lewis, get their backs up every time they see one another. My papa isn't Lewis' father, so they fight a lot. A lot, a lot. I hate it when they yell at each other. Mama tries to keep the peace and get in between them, but it's got so they don't even act like she's there. Papa always apologizes to her afterwards, but I can tell it makes her real sad. I wish they'd stop it. One time my papa even slapped Lewis in the face. It was awful, but then Lewis didn't come around for a couple of weeks. At least there wasn't any fighting while he stayed away."

"I hate to hear that." Sophronia's tone was sympathetic. "You ought to come spend the night out here whenever they get to going at one another. Me and my sisters holler at each other sometimes, but it don't mean anything and we get over it right quick."

"I wish I could. I could use a rest from their wrangling sometimes."

"Well, why can't you?"

"I don't like to leave Mama on her own when Lewis and Papa are fighting. Besides, I doubt if your mother would want me hanging around."

"Oh, pshaw. One of us always has somebody or the other

staying overnight. I have a bunch of baby nieces and nephews and near to a thousand cousins. Ma never minds a bit."

Dorothy sounded wistful when she answered. "Maybe I could ask my mother about it."

The back of Sophronia's auburn-haired head appeared in the window when she stood up. "Hey, you want to meet my horse?"

"You have your own horse?" Dorothy was awed.

Sophronia tugged her friend to her feet. "I do. Well, he's my brother Charlie's horse, really, but I'm taking care of him while Charlie's over in England. He's the best horse in the world. His name is Sweet Honey Baby."

The girls' voices faded as they ran together toward the barn. Alafair resumed slicing potatoes.

Early in the evening, Chase Kemp came running up the path that led from Mary's front door to Alafair's, looking for Grace and an hour of play before supper. Alafair sent her nephew off to the chicken yard to help Grace with her chores, and called in Sophronia and her friend to go to the back porch and clean the cream separator.

When supper was finally over and the shadows were growing long, Alafair began to wonder if she was going to have to ask Shaw to take their visitor back to town. He was saved the trip when Grace slammed into the house and bellowed, "Ma, Dorothy's mama is here."

Alafair followed the girl out the front door. Nola was standing in the yard on the flagstone path that threaded through the herb garden, holding Dorothy by the hand and having a conversation with Chase Kemp. She was red-cheeked and dusty after driving her husband's truck over the unpaved country roads. Alafair strode down the porch steps, extending her hand.

"Howdy, Nola. Gracious, you look wore out. Why don't you come on in and sit a spell? Take your shoes off and rest your feet. I've got some tea chilling in the icebox."

"Good evening, Alafair. I apologize for being so late. After we finished with the masks, Martha talked us into rolling six more boxes of woolen socks for the troops. And then her and me and Hattie Tucker went over to inspect the fellowship hall in the Methodist Church to maybe be our influenza headquarters. I didn't mean for you to have to babysit my girl till the cows come home."

"I declare. Well, Martha's quite the persuader. And don't fret, I don't mind at all. Dorothy pitched right in and helped with supper." She was leading Nola up the steps as she spoke.

"Now, I don't aim to impose on you any longer," Nola said as Alafair guided her into the parlor with a firm hand on her back.

"Never you mind about that. Y'all can drive back into town in just a little bit. But first, you must be parched. Have a seat, and I'll bring you a glass of tea."

Mrs. Thomason made another token protest, but Alafair could tell that she was grateful for the chance to rest after her dusty, bouncing ride over the rutted dirt road from town. She removed her hat, took a long swig of cold, sweet tea, and sat back into the cushions with a sigh. "Homer is still at the office, so I figured I could just drive myself out to fetch Dorothy. I admit I had forgot how far a piece it is out here."

The evening was warm, with a fair light breeze billowing the curtains at the open windows, and the whirr of cicadas starting up as the day wound down. The two women chatted over the sound of the children playing on the front porch. Chase had joined the girls in a game of jacks. Dorothy, being the guest, was allowed to go first. Judging by the laughter and exclamations, she made it through fivesies before the children's long-legged young mutt, Bacon, could no longer restrain himself from snatching the bouncing rubber ball and taking off across the yard. They managed to catch the pup and pry the ball from his jaws before he swallowed it, and resumed their game on the porch. Grace was next. Unbothered by the slobbery ball, she began singing to the bouncing rhythm before she had even finished onesies.

This old man, he play one,
He play knick-knack on my thumb.
With a knick-knack paddy whack,

Give a dog a bone.
This old man come rolling home.

Lulled by the children's hypnotic chanting, Alafair and Nola Thomason fell into an desultory conversation. It had been a long time since Alafair had had a friend. Oh, she knew many of the citizens of Boynton, mostly from church and volunteer war work. But her social circle consisted almost entirely of relatives and revolved around Sunday dinners, family celebrations, holiday get-togethers. The rest of the time there were chores that needed doing, or a child who needed attention—a story to be told, a skinned knee to be kissed, a task to be taught, a game to be played.

Alafair took some time to list her many offspring and their spouses and children, and what each did for a living. Yes, she told Nola, she was kin-by-marriage to Hattie, wife of the town constable, Scott Tucker. Scott was her husband Shaw's first cousin. They were also related to Peter McBride, Shaw's stepfather, and the two Tucker uncles on the town council.

Alafair finished reciting her kinship connections, then said, "Shaw tells me that Homer is a real good salesman, honest and helpful."

"He loves working for Muskogee Tool and Die. It's a good living, too, though it does take him away from home a lot. He thinks that there's enough of a future in the field that he'd like to start his own business, but it'll be a long while before we have enough money for that."

"Alice tells me that Lewis Hulce over at Williams' Drug is your son." Alafair paused, giving Nola the opportunity to elaborate or not, as she wanted.

Nola hesitated, and for a moment Alafair figured she would skirt the topic.

But she turned back toward Alafair with a sigh. "Lewis is my first husband's son. It was hard on him when I married Homer. He was only six when his father died, and I expect he had gotten used to having me to himself. Him and Homer never much warmed to one another. That's a hard thing to bear, for my boy Lewis is the apple of my eye. He saved me," she said, "when my first husband died. If I hadn't had Lewis, I would have had nothing to live for. After his father passed, he was so careful of my feelings, so concerned about my well-being, it was almost like he was the parent and I was the child. He's still that way. Still looking after his mother, and Dorothy as well. It's just Homer he can't bear, and I fear the feeling is mutual."

Alafair nodded. "That's a hard thing. Well, now that Lewis has grown up and has his own interests, don't you expect relations between them will improve by and by?"

Nola glanced away, which told Alafair that she was about to slide around the truth.

"Lewis has been renting a room next to Burrows' Café for the last two years. He has a young lady friend now. JoNell Reed, her name is. Her father works for the refinery. I think Lewis could do better, but that's neither here nor there. He still comes around the house regular. Whenever Homer is out of town, Lewis bunks in with us overnight. Maybe once a week he comes for supper. I like seeing him, but him and Homer always end up bumping heads. Homer doesn't like it when Lewis criticizes the way he takes care of us, but Lewis thinks he's looking out for me." That was all she said about that.

Alafair did not press her. What went on in families was a private affair. She had not had enough dealings with Lewis Hulce to form an opinion of his character. He seemed pleasant enough when he waited on her over the counter at the drug store. She knew Homer Thomason a little better. He didn't appear to be a man whose wife would need protection from him, but appearances could be deceiving.

"You know, it's good that Sophronia has such a dear friend in Dorothy," Alafair said. "If she'd like to come out for a sleep-over now and then, that would be a fine thing."

Chapter Four

How It Was That the Blue Death Came to Boynton, Oklahoma

In the middle of the cold, cold winter of 1917-1918, somewhere in the far reaches of western Kansas, Ernest Clinton received a letter from the President of the United States. He had been called by his country do his bit and help defeat the Hun. So Ernest packed a change of underwear, and caught the train to Camp Funston, just outside of Junction City, Kansas, and took his place in the ranks of the U.S. Army.

Ernest's family had survived the winter all right, but the breeding sow had gone off her feed. She was a good breeder and a good mother, for a sow, and the family income was greatly supplemented by her regular production of piglets. It would have been a tragedy if she died. When she developed a fever and a barking cough, Ernest and his dad had kept a close watch on her. They had even taken turns sleeping in the barn next to her pen.

She didn't die, but she hadn't quite recovered her usual vigor before Ernest had to report for training at Camp Funston.

Private Ernest Clinton of the 356th Infantry Regiment was feeling funny when he boarded the ship taking him and his comrades to France. When he didn't show up for breakfast on the morning of the first full day at sea, his sergeant found him in his berth, burning with fever.

For two days Clinton shook with ague. He emptied his guts into a bucket until the bucket was full, then he used the floor, as did everybody else in the berthing quarters. He expected he'd feel better when he could put his feet on dry land again, but it didn't happen that way.

When they got to Le Havre, Private Clinton had to be carried off the ship on a stretcher. He spent his first month in France in a Red Cross base hospital along with half the other soldiers in his unit. La Grippe, the nurses called it, which Clinton thought was a pretty fancy name for the ordinary old flu. It was the flu, all right, but hardly ordinary. By the time Private Clinton was well enough to join his unit on the front, six of the fellow sufferers in his unit had died, including the man in the cot to his right. It had been a horrible death. The guy's face grew mottled as he struggled to breathe, and by the time he finally departed this life, his skin had turned as blue-black as a fresh bruise.

That scared Clinton worse than any bullet or bayonet the Bosche might send his way. But Clinton recovered.

On the morning he was to be released, he sat on his cot, buttoning his tunic and thanking God that he hadn't come all the way over here to France just to die for nothing. "Can't wait to get into the action," he said.

"So you're heading out to the front?" asked the hospital orderly, Beau Dupree. "Good luck, buddy. It's a sad thing to have to go from a nice clean bed to sleeping in a mud hole while the Heinies try to blow you up or gas you to death."

Dupree was not much older than Clinton, but he looked like a piece of cured leather that had been left out in the rain for about a month. Ernest looked him up and down. "You've been up there already?"

"Naw. I've been carting you poor devils back and forth on stretchers for the last year. My enlistment was up two weeks ago. If my replacement hadn't got the crud I'd have been out of here by now." He drew a tobacco pouch out of his tunic pocket and rolled a cigarette. "Besides, I've seen all of France I care to. All I want is to get back to Lafayette, Louisiana, and my *maman*."

Clinton asked the orderly if he too had suffered through the illness.

"I'm a Cajun," Dupree said with a laugh. "I eat so much cayenne that even Madame La Grippe don't dare come near me."

"Well, good luck to you, Corporal, and I hope you don't get it." And with that, Clinton and Dupree went their separate ways.

Hospital Orderly Beau Dupree was practically the last man standing when his troop ship docked in New York. The trip across the Atlantic had been hellish. The thousands of soldiers who were going home had been sealed into their quarters to try to keep a shipboard epidemic at bay. Dupree had never been particularly claustrophobic, but after they had been at sea for less than a day he was about to crawl up the walls. Even so, Dupree would have understood the reason for quarantine—if it had worked.

By the second day at sea, so many men had reported to sick bay with the flu that they were practically stacked on top of one another. One by one the doctors and nurses succumbed, and Dupree, and the few others who were still uninfected, volunteered for nursing duty.

After a week at sea, twenty-five or thirty men a day were dying. There was no room to keep the bodies. So soldiers who had survived all those months in Europe, dug into the dirt like moles, died and were sent to their final resting place at the bottom of the sea.

After his ship finally tied off at New York Harbor, and he and his exhausted comrades had carried down the gangplank all the stretchers of those who were still alive, Beau Dupree shouldered his kit and caught a train for New Orleans.

It took Dupree another two days to hitch his way to Lafayette, then hoof several miles to his mother's house on the bayou. She rushed out on the porch when she recognized the wiry figure straggling up the path with his duffel flung over his shoulder.

"*Ma fils! Ma petit!*" she cried, and wrapped her arms around him.

Dupree sagged into his mother's embrace. "Maman, I don't feel so good."

Cayenne pepper had failed Beau Dupree in a big way. He thought for a while that he might die, or maybe it was just that he figured death was preferable to the way he felt. His brother, Jean, had not been there when Beau arrived at their mother's house, since he worked for the railroad and had been on his usual run from New Orleans to Houston to Oklahoma City. But when Jean did get home, he was as tender a nurse to his only brother as was their mother.

Maman was a pretty good *traiteur* and knew her herbs and all the right prayers, so within a couple of weeks, Dupree was up and about, even if he still wasn't much use around the farm.

"Now that you are beyond the worst," Jean told him, "I must take up my route again. The mail must go through, you know, *mon frere.*"

Jean felt fine when he boarded the mail car in Lafayette. Just outside Denton, Texas, he suddenly took ill. When the train pulled into the station at Oklahoma City, the baggage handler opened the boxcar to find a blue corpse draped over the mail bags.

So Jean Dupree met his end alone in a boxcar somewhere outside of Oklahoma City. It was too bad and everyone felt terrible about it. But the mail bags were removed from the car and distributed to trains going all over the Southwest, because no matter what happened, the mail had to go through.

Chapter Five

How Alafair Prepared to Do Battle with the Spanish Influenza

Shaw came into the house and placed the mail on the kitchen table. Alafair didn't bother to dry her hands before rushing over to inspect the pile.

"No letters from the boys today," Shaw said, before she could get her hopes up. He waved a copy of the latest *Boynton Index* in her direction. "I won't be going to a Co-op meeting today, either. But I do have news. I stopped in to see Scott before I went to the post office. Seems the town council met this morning. They've decided to try and keep the flu epidemic from spreading to Boynton. They've banned public meetings from today on. There will be no school starting tomorrow."

Alafair felt her heart speed up. "For how long?"

"Until further notice. Says here in the paper that passenger train service is cut off for thirty days, too. Nothing or nobody gets on or off at the Boynton station, except for the mail. Scott told me that some of the other towns around here have instituted the same policy."

"What about church?"

"Well, Scott is notifying each local congregation and asking them to suspend services. He told me that Preacher Huster has already agreed not to hold services at the Christian Church next Sunday. As for the shops and businesses, Scott says that's up to them. I did see that Mr. Khouri has a sign in his window saying that his market will stay open for awhile. Until he thinks better of it, I reckon."

"So the town council is aiming to quarantine Boynton? That can't be done, can it? What about folks coming in and out by road?"

"Scott said he's putting road blocks on the main roads in and out of town, just to warn folks if there is an outbreak here. I don't think anybody expects they can cut the town off from the world altogether."

"I know that the epidemic is still raging on the East Coast, but are things really that bad here? There has hardly been any news about the grippe in Oklahoma. The local papers haven't said anything."

Shaw poured himself a glass of cool water from the pitcher in the window and sat down at the table. "According to Isaac Kirby over at the *Index*, the flu is spreading like wildfire in Tulsa. Last week there was no sign of it, and this week they've had to open a special hospital in an abandoned warehouse just to have some place to put all the extra cases."

Alafair's eyes widened. "That doesn't sound good. Maybe we'd better warn Mary and Phoebe to keep their little ones close to home as well."

◇◇◇

Alafair was trying to brush the tangles out of Grace's hair when she heard a woman's voice calling from the drive. "Mama, Mama…"

She exchanged a puzzled glance with Grace and went to the front door to peer through the screen. Martha McCoy was standing in the drive that ran beside the house and to the barn, dressed in her blue Red Cross uniform. She had ridden from town on Streeter's motorcycle.

Alafair opened the screen and came out onto the porch. "Martha, what in the world…?"

Martha halted her mother with a gesture. "Don't come down, Ma. I just rode out to tell you that Miz Fluke the postmistress has come down with the Spanish flu. When she didn't open up the post office this morning Scott went to check on her and she's sick in bed. After I heard that, I went by her house to take her some soup. She's real sick, Ma. She couldn't even hardly sit up. I wanted you to know that the flu has finally made it to Boynton. Y'all better stay away from town for awhile."

Alafair's heart fluttered and fell. Blanche and Grace had both slipped out onto the porch behind her. She felt a child's hand grasp hers. "Martha, honey, what about you? What about Alice and Ruth?"

"I've already told both of them to stay home for a spell, at least until we see what's going to happen. Maybe it won't go any farther than Miz Fluke, though I'm fretted that the first person to get it in Boynton is the postmistress. There isn't anybody in this part of the county that hasn't come in contact with Miz Fluke. Now, Ma, don't worry about me. I'll take every precaution. But somebody has to help poor Miz Fluke. Since her boy went away to the army she doesn't have a soul to take care of her. I've already told Ruth that if I get sick she should ride out and let you know. But even if I do get sick, Ma, don't get all discombobulated. I'd have twenty-three nurses from my Red Cross chapter to take care of me. It's only the grippe. I've had it before." She flashed her mother an ironic smile.

"But, honey…" Alafair attempted.

Martha didn't let her finish. "Oh, before I forget, Alice is bringing Linda out here this evening to stay with you and Daddy for a spell. She and Walter would just as soon have that child out of town until this epidemic passes."

Alafair was relieved to hear that her granddaughter would be out of harm's way. "Maybe I can talk Alice into staying here, too, at least for a while."

Martha felt a stirring of sympathy for her mother. She could tell by Alafair's expression that she was plotting ways to get all her girls to return to the nest, safe under her wing.

Sophronia came skipping around the side of the house and broke into a run when she spied Martha. "Stop!" Martha hollered, and Alafair cried, "Fronie, come here!" Sophronia stopped so quickly that she nearly pitched forward onto her face. Her sisters burst into laughter.

Sophronia didn't know whether to laugh or cry or be insulted, and Alafair shot Blanche and Grace a withering look. "Fronie, come here," she repeated. "It's all right. Martha has just come from her friend's sickbed and she doesn't want to infect anybody." As Sophronia climbed up onto the porch from the far end, Alafair turned back to Martha. "Now, honey, as soon as you get home you scrub down your rooms with disinfectant and take a hot bath. Don't get chilled, now. And drink some hot lemonade. Are you taking the garlic and honey every day, like I told you? Do you have some butterfly weed at home? Elderberry flowers? Boneset? I can put some in a bag for you to take with you. Nothing is better for fever."

"Yes, Mother, dear." Martha's voice bubbled with a mix of affection and exasperation. "I have dried herbs and tinctures galore in my pantry because you gave them to me, if you'll remember."

◇◇◇

By the time Alice drove up in Walter's Ford with Linda beside her, supper was over and it was nearly dark. But the news she brought was grim. Nadine Fluke was no longer the only flu victim in Boynton.

"I've never seen anything like it, Ma. This morning I didn't know a single person with the grippe, and this evening there's at least a dozen just that I've heard tell of. Walter says that over the past few days the influenza has gotten real bad in Haskell. I've kept Linda inside all day, and she hasn't appreciated it much, either. I'd feel a lot better if she was out here in the country with y'all."

Shaw and Alafair exchanged a worried glance. "Alice, it'll be plumb dark directly," Shaw said. "Why don't you stay over? In fact, why don't you and Linda just stay out here until this thing passes?"

Martha had warned Alice of their parents' intention to gather as many of their daughters home as they could persuade. One corner of her mouth twitched. "Walter is expecting me back tonight, Daddy. Besides, I couldn't leave him on his own, and Martha and the rest of the Red Cross ladies are going to need all the help they can get."

JoNell Reed chugged down Main Street at a steady clip, full of purpose. Had she not been wearing a gauze mask, passers-by would have seen a petulant expression on her round face. She was on her way to confront her beau, Lewis Hulce, at Williams' Drug Store, and no quarantine was going to deter her. JoNell was a pretty creature, all rosy lips and pink cheeks. She was plump enough to be warm in winter and shady in summer, but it was expected that she would thin out when she lost her baby fat. Lewis was JoNell's first sweetheart, and her romantic ardor was spectacular to behold. Since JoNell was only sixteen years old, this fire of love did not surprise her mother, who had endured the youthful passions of two older daughters. Lewis Hulce was a bit flummoxed by it all.

JoNell marched into the drug store, past the soda fountain, past the candy bins and the glass cases of cigars and cheap jewelry, scarves, and pocket knives, all the way to the drug counter at the rear of the store. She pounded the bell on the counter a few times and Lewis appeared at the curtained door that led into the small compounding pharmacy in the back.

His bespectacled eyes widened. "JoNell, what in blazes are you doing here? Didn't you get my note?"

"I did." Her voice was high and piping like a little girl's, but had a musical, bell-like quality that Lewis found enchanting. "I was really looking forward to you coming over to our house for supper tonight. Mama was going to let me cook the whole meal. I was going to fix all your favorite things to eat. Mama let me buy a beef roast! I made a cake and used real eggs!"

"Well, Homer is out of town tonight and I'm going over to my mother's house, JoNell. I just found out this morning. He'll be gone for days. I can't leave my poor ma and Dorothy on their own all that time, you know that."

"But you do this all the time. What about our plans? What about me?" JoNell sagged. "Oh, Lewis. I swear you're downright fixilated on your mama. I wish you could stop thinking about her all the time and think about your little lovey-bird every once in a while."

Lewis couldn't see her mouth, but he could hear the pout in her voice. "I don't want to argue about this again. I've told you about the awful way that man treats her and I aim to provide her as much aid and comfort as I can, whenever I can. So don't keep going on about it. Besides, ain't you heard that men who do good by their mothers make the best husbands? Now, I'm sorry to mess up your plans, but you just keep hold of that cake with the real eggs for a couple more days and I promise I'll make it up to you."

JoNell's big brown eyes filled with tears. "Please, Lewis. I've just worked and worked to make you the most delicious meal. I've even sewed a beautiful new runner for the table and Mama is letting me use her wedding china. Please don't disappoint me. Oh, please, please."

As she spoke, JoNell slowly leaned in toward Lewis so far that he feared that she would end up draped over the counter like a human tablecloth. He gritted his teeth and sighed. JoNell was the most exasperating female; an exasperating, enchanting, sweet and fluffy froth of a girl. She was almost more trouble than any sane man would put up with. But then maybe he wasn't that sane, at least when it came to JoNell. She certainly did drive him crazy. Yet she was totally devoted to him. It was hard to resist a woman who would literally do anything you asked of her.

"Oh, all right, JoNell, get up off the counter. I'll put off going over to my mother's house until after your fancy supper."

JoNell squealed with delight and began skipping back and forth, clapping her hands. Lewis shushed her, red with embarrassment. "JoNell, for the love of Mike, stop that." But he laughed in spite of himself.

As far as Alafair was concerned, one of the more worrisome things about the epidemic was that she couldn't go into town to fetch her mail without the risk of bringing the plague back to her loved ones. But she couldn't stand the thought that a letter from one of her boys might arrive and she would not be able to retrieve it.

Alafair and her daughters came up with a makeshift solution whereby Alice would drive out every evening in her Model T Ford. She would stand at the gate and Alafair would stand at the front door and they would exchange reports. For the first few days, Alice would relate who else in the area had fallen ill and how her sisters were doing. Alafair was amazed at how fast the plague spread. Six people in town were sick, then a dozen. Then scores. They were all down with it at the Ross farm, then the Barlows'. Angela Phillips got sick one morning and died that evening. That was a shock. Angela was only twenty, and in the bloom of health.

Alice reported that Martha could hardly keep up with coordinating the care of whole families who were too ill to care for themselves. Alice herself developed dark smudges under her eyes from fatigue, and Alafair took to leaving fresh bread and jars of soup and medicinal teas in a box by the gate for her to take back to town for herself and her sisters.

Whenever Alice brought mail to the farm, she would open it and read it aloud to her parents. She never left the letters with her mother, in case they were contaminated. In return, Alafair gave Alice a detailed report on Linda's well-being while Alice leaned eagerly over the gate to catch every word. She was desperate to see her darling while she was there, but Linda never understood why she couldn't hug her mother, and it was a wrench for both of them when Alice had to leave Linda behind. It would take Linda an hour to stop crying after Alice left, and Alice wept nearly as long, herself. After two or three days, Alice asked her mother to be sure Linda was occupied elsewhere when she came.

It was hard for her to decide which was worse—seeing her baby or not seeing her.

Alice's husband, Walter, closed his barber shop. In the service of public health, men could do without haircuts for a while.

Then one day, Alafair waited for the familiar chug of the Ford's engine at the accustomed hour, and waited, and waited, and it didn't come. She was pacing up and down the drive in a panic, almost ready to saddle her mare and gallop into town, when she caught sight of a slight, auburn-haired woman on a bicycle toiling up the drive from the main road.

"Ruth!" she cried. She ran toward the figure but halted reluctantly just as her middle daughter came to a stop a couple of yards away from her. "Is Alice sick?"

Ruth raised her hands in a comforting gesture. "Yes, she came down with the headache and the ague this morning…." She hesitated when her mother gasped, then plowed on. "But Martha and I are taking good care of her, Ma, and Walter is with her. Try not to worry, now. She said that she doesn't feel that bad and you should try not to worry."

"I'm going back into town with you."

"No! Mama, now, listen, Alice doesn't want that. Miz Doc Addison has been by and she says her case isn't too bad. If you come into town you'll just get exposed and bring the flu back to all the little ones. I promise I'll let you know everything that's going on. I'll ride out twice a day, if you want. Alice will be all right, Mama. It's just the grippe. It's no fun but we've all had the grippe before and got over it."

Chapter Six

How Alafair Won the Day

The ceiling of Alafair's shaded back porch was covered with suspended bunches of drying herbs. When Shaw walked through from the backyard to the kitchen, his head brushed the tips of the dried leaves and set up a quiet susurration and released a deep, sweet, woodsy aroma that reminded him of a walk through the woods on an autumn day. He washed up at the basin next to the back door and took his time drying his face and hands on a cotton hand towel. The herbal smell on the porch was such a comfort that he lingered with his eyes closed and his hand on the kitchen door for the length of a couple of deep breaths before he went inside.

He expected to find the usual small remnant of his family getting ready for supper that evening, so he stopped short when he saw that every chair around the huge kitchen table was filled. Mary, along with Chase, Judy, and Linda were seated together at one end of the table. John Lee Day was at the other end, with Phoebe and their children at his side. The table was set, and all the children were at their places, wide-eyed and quiet. Alafair was sitting in a chair beside the back door, dressed in a crisp white shirt and blue serge skirt. All eyes turned in Shaw's direction when he paused in the door. Something was amiss, and everyone was aware of it, except for Judy and Linda, both of whom ran happily to their grandfather and demanded to be picked up.

"What is happening?" His voice was heavy with dread. Had a letter come from France?

Alafair stood up and relieved him of a toddler. "Ruth came by this afternoon and told me that Alice is down."

"How bad is she?"

"Ruth says she's not that sick yet, but you know how the flu is. Besides, I'm afraid Walter doesn't know how to take care of her. Ruth told me that so many folks in town are sick that her and Martha are run off their feet. Honey, I'm going into town to take care of Alice. I've already settled things with Mary and Phoebe. Mary is taking all the children home with her tonight. Blanche and Fronie are going with her to help her look after the little ones. Phoebe's sending her young ones over there, too. Her and John Lee are going to stay here with you so she can look after the house and you men."

Shaw shot his son-in-law an incredulous glance. He expected a display of male solidarity, but he didn't get it. "The women didn't tell me their plan until an hour or so ago, Pa," John Lee said. "But once Phoebe explained their thinking to me, I have to say I agree with them. I'll miss my young'uns, but I'll feel a lot better knowing they're quarantined until this plague passes over." Shaw blinked, trying to take it in. He handed Judy to her mother and faced Alafair. "So you've got it all arranged, have you?"

"We have, Shaw. You don't worry about a thing. Me and the girls have it in hand."

Shaw turned aside and gestured toward the back porch. "I need a word with you, Alafair."

"Don't you want some supper?"

"Later," he said, in a tone that brooked no discussion.

Mary began busily ladling rice onto the plate of the nearest child. Alafair stiffened her spine before she put Linda down in a chair and preceded Shaw into the relative privacy of the screened-in back porch.

Alafair started talking before Shaw could draw the door closed behind him. "Honey, we've thought and thought about it, and this is the best thing to do."

"I'm not going to allow this," Shaw said.

Alafair continued as though he had not spoken. "Alice needs me. Martha and Ruth need me. I know what to do. I have to help. If Alice dies, and I hadn't done everything I could do to prevent it, I'd never get over it."

Shaw bit his lip, torn. If anyone could nurse Alice back to health, it was Alafair. He couldn't stand the thought of something happening to Alice, his beautiful, hotheaded, blue-eyed girl. Yet… "What if you get the influenza, Alafair?"

"I have no intention of getting the influenza, Shaw." Her tone was so forceful that Shaw nearly laughed, which made him angry, because this was no laughing matter. He seized her by the shoulders. "Alafair, no matter how much you think Jesus bends to your will, I guarantee that you can get sick and die just like everybody else on this green earth. Don't you dare put yourself in harm's way when you don't have to. You still have young children who need their mother."

Alafair wasn't having it. "What about you and John Lee, Shaw, always gallivanting off to the livestock sales or meeting with buyers and suppliers? I know that everybody keeps their distance from one another these days, but y'all can bring the flu back home to us just as quick as anybody else. And what would happen to us if you did? That's one reason I want to send the children to Mary's until this passes. I'm worried about Blanche's weak chest. Mary can hole up out there at her place with the youngsters, and you and John Lee and your hired men can run her farm along with y'all's. What else can we do, Shaw? Seal ourselves up in the house and mortar shut all the doors and windows and not come out until this is over? We've got to live. We can do our best to try and stay healthy, but we've got to live and we've got to help each other as best we can."

Shaw heaved a sigh. He was not at all happy that she had made her arrangements without consulting him, but he had to admit that the plan made sense. The children would be quarantined, and he could conduct business without worrying overmuch about bringing influenza home to his family. It would be a relief to know that his town-dwelling daughters would be looked after by their mother. But with her eyes wide open, Alafair was putting herself at risk. What would I do if she died, he thought, though he didn't say it aloud. The idea caused the hair on the back of his neck to rise.

Alafair's expression had lightened. She could tell he was softening.

"So the children are going to Mary's this evening?" he asked.

"Yes, I packed their clothes this afternoon."

"Well, if you can wait until I have a bite of supper, I'll carry you to Alice's in the buggy."

She grinned. "I was counting on it."

After supper was done, Alafair quietly helped Phoebe clear the table. She donned her second-best hat with the cherries on the band, then went around and gave each child a lingering hug. The grandchildren were too small to know what was going on, but Alafair's own daughters were very much aware of why their mother was leaving and why they were being banished from the family home.

She gathered her three youngest to her. "Now, Mary is going to need your help with all these babies. When I get back, I don't expect to hear anything but good reports on all of you."

"What about Sweet Honey Baby? How will he get along without me?" Sophronia was anxious about all her animals, but the high-strung gelding was her special favorite.

When Charlie ran off to join the Army, Sophronia had more or less inherited his roan gelding with the white mane and tail. A tall Standard Thoroughbred, the roan had a high-stepping gait and arching neck. He was a beautiful animal, and he knew it. He also had a screw loose. Most of the time he was affectionate and easy to handle and ride, but sometimes, out of the blue, he would take a notion to go crazy. When that happened, it was wise to get out of his way, for the roan was capable of killing. But the roan loved Sophronia. With her he was gentle as a kitten, puffing and nodding and nosing her affectionately as she groomed him. It was Sophronia who had named him Sweet Honey Baby, which was a perfectly unsuitable name for such a fine specimen of horseflesh. But it was the only name to which the gelding responded, and the only name that would calm him down when his eyes began to roll and his head to toss. Sophronia had explained that he had had enough violence to do him and now required a name that expressed his desire for a life of gentle refinement.

"Don't you worry about Sweet Honey Baby, Fronie. Daddy and John Lee will take good care of him, and think how happy he'll be to see you when you come home."

Grace was anxious to comfort her sister. "Mary says we can bring Bacon. Him and Mary's dog Big Fella get along real well. Charlie Dog and the hounds will protect Daddy and Phoebe and John Lee."

"Keep with your lessons. School will start back up as soon as this sickness burns itself out, and I don't want any of you to fall behind." Alafair put a hand on Blanche's head. "You're the oldest, now, so Mary will be counting on you. And so will I. Don't forget. Honey with garlic in it, and Miz Carrizal's tea every day. I don't care if you don't like it, you take some every day." Esmeralda Carrizal was the talented *curandera* from Arizona who had cured Blanche's chronic bronchitis a couple of years earlier with her own brand of kitchen medicine.

Blanche was struggling to keep her composure. "Don't worry about us, Mama. You just take care of yourself."

Alafair picked up her little cardboard suitcase and joined Shaw at the back door.

"Ma, you take good care of yourself, now." Mary's affectionate, chiding tone sounded so much like Alafair's own that Shaw had to smile. "And tell Alice I'm praying for her. Send word every day on how she's feeling. On how all of you are doing."

"We'll do just that, Mary, honey. I hope all these young'uns don't drive you right 'round the bend."

"Oh, I plan to sit around and eat bonbons while Grace and ol' cousin Chase here watch the babies, and Blanche and Fronie do all the cooking and cleaning."

While the youngsters hooted with mock indignation, John Lee struggled up out of his chair and drew his father-in-law aside. "I hope this don't take more than a couple weeks." He glanced at the children. "I'm glad the young'uns will be safe, but I had a notion you'd say no to this scheme."

Shaw said nothing for a long moment. His eyes moved from John Lee's face to take in the sight of the women and children laughing and chattering. His mouth assumed the ironic quirk that all his children had inherited. "If I was to forbid her, Alafair might do as I say, son. For a while, at least. But there are things women know how to do better than we do. They know it, too."

Chapter Seven

How Alafair Moved Into Alice's House and Took Care of Everything

Shaw and Alafair made most of the trip to town in silence. It was dark enough when they left that they had to light the headlamps on the buggy. Alafair sat with her basket of remedies in her lap and her travel case at her feet and stared grimly into the night. They had made it all the way to the turn onto the main street of Boynton before Alafair spoke.

"Thank you for letting me do this."

He shot her glance. "Well, it makes sense. I just wish you hadn't planned it all without talking to me first. I don't much admire getting the run-around from my own family."

"I'm sorry I went behind your back, honey. I wanted to have the plan well in place before I told you so that you could see how well everything works out."

He gave a snort. "I know when I'm outgunned, Alafair. I might have won the gunfight, but I'd have been shot full of holes when it was over."

Alafair tried not to laugh. "Well. You and me are on the front lines, now."

"I will come into town every day and stop by Alice's to see how you're doing."

"Good. It's going to be hard enough to be away from the children. It'll comfort me to be able to lay eyes on you."

Shaw halted the buggy in front of Alice and Walter Kelley's pretty frame house. They were just climbing down when Walter opened the front door and came down the walk to meet them. His usually well-groomed hair was flat on one side and spiky on the other. Even in the dim illumination of the half-moon, they could tell he hadn't shaved in a couple of days.

He relieved Alafair of her basket. "Mr. and Miz Tucker, am I glad to see you. Alice is sick as a poisoned dog, and I don't know what to do for her. I'm right worried."

Alafair pushed past him and strode into the house. His worry worried her, but she was reserving judgment until she could see Alice's condition for herself. She threw her hat onto the settee as she passed and went directly into the bedroom. The Kelley house was electrified, and Alafair viewed electricity with skepticism, but she overcame her trepidation and pulled the chain on the little lamp sitting on the bedside table.

Alice cracked open one rheumy eye to squint at whoever had intruded on her misery. Alafair stifled a gasp.

Alice's blond hair was a mass of tangles and her eyes so red and swollen it was surprising that she could open them at all. Her breathing was raspy and labored, and her nightgown and bedclothes were rank. Alafair caught the lingering smell of vomit and urine, and came very near to rushing out into the parlor to give Walter a clip on the ear. He wasn't expected to know how to nurse the flu, but he should have known enough to help his ill wife stay clean and comfortable.

Alafair put a hand on her daughter's forehead. She was burning up.

"Ma," Alice croaked. "How's Linda?"

Alafair was already hunting through the armoire. "She's fine, honey. Don't you worry about a thing. Mama and Daddy are here." She marched back to the bed with an armload of bedclothes and a clean nightgown. She rolled Alice over onto one side of the bed and began stripping off the sodden sheets. "How are you feeling, darlin'?"

Alice didn't answer right away so Alafair asked again. This time she rallied enough to say, "I'd have to get better to die, Ma."

Alafair stuck her head out the bedroom door and hollered, "Walter, get me a basin of hot water and some cloths." She manhandled Alice's limp body from one side to the other until new sheets were on the bed and the old damp ones piled into the corner. She took the basin of water from Walter without looking at him and placed it on the bedside table, then pulled the patient's gown off over her head. Alice was too sick to protest.

Half an hour after her mother arrived, Alice was clean and dry and wrapped in quilts, with a hot brick at her feet against the chills, and a menthol-scented cloth on her forehead to soothe her pounding headache. She lay on her back with half-open eyes for some minutes, watching Alafair tidying the bedroom. Her fever was down, at least enough for her to make some sense when she spoke.

She groaned. "I feel like I've been trampled and dragged."

"I know you do, honey. The ague gets in your bones and muscles and makes them ache."

"What's that smell?"

"I'm heating up some boneset and mint tea in the kitchen. You'll drink it with some honey and it'll break your fever and help you sleep. I'm also cooking you up some of Miz Carrazal's healing tea for your lungs."

Alice grimaced. She had been the recipient of her mother's herbal teas many times. They worked, but often the taste left a lot to be desired. "What are you doing here, Mama? Is Linda all right? Where's Walter?"

Alafair sat down in the bedside chair. "Ruth rode out and told us you were sick and I come to take care of you, sugar. Linda is just fine. Mary is taking care of all the children until the influenza passes. Walter is in the parlor with your daddy. Hasn't Walter been looking after you?"

"Walter's doing the best he knows how, Ma. He brings me whatever I ask for and helps me when I need to get up. Martha or Ruth usually comes by of a morning, but there are so many sick…" Alice's eyelids fluttered. "Was Martha here this morning, or was it yesterday?"

"You go to sleep, sweetheart. I'm here now. I'll take care of everything."

"You don't have to baby me, Ma," Alice mumbled.

"Yes, I do. You were too hard to raise to take chances."

Alafair went back into the parlor to find Shaw and Walter having a quiet chat at the dining room table. Walter did look worried, and she scolded herself for being uncharitable. When he looked over at her she stopped in her tracks. His cheeks were flushed and his black eyes unnaturally shiny.

Shaw confirmed her impression. "Mama, I think you're going to have two patients directly."

Walter tried to protest. "I'm just tired. I need a rest."

Alafair felt his forehead. "You're on fire. Get yourself to bed right now. I'll bring some of that tonic to both of you in a minute and you'll drink every bit of it. No, don't you dare argue with me."

He gave her an abashed smile. "I wouldn't think of it, Miz Tucker."

Walter pushed himself up and plodded into the bedroom and Alafair sat down next to Shaw. "I shouldn't be so mean to him," she confessed. "I reckon he hasn't had the strength to be much of a nurse today."

"It's good you're here, considering that they're both down now. I wish I could stay. I hate to leave you here alone, honey."

"I wish you could stay, too, but the farm won't run itself. I'll be all right, don't you doubt it."

Shaw put a hand on her shoulder. "You send word right quick if you get to feeling ill yourself."

She smiled at his concern, touched. "Well, we're both good and exposed to the grippe, now, Shaw. Don't you forget to drink lots of hot lemon water, and you'd better double up on the doses of garlic honey. I'll do the same."

"Walter told me that Alice never did take the raw onion or garlic honey that you sent home with her. Said she didn't want to drive all her friends away."

"I'll swan! That girl is too willful for her own good. Well, she's paying for it now. I hope the other girls have more sense."

"Speaking of the other girls, Walter told me that neither Martha nor Ruth has come by since yesterday. I'm going to go by Martha's place and the MacKenzie house and make sure they're both still well. I'll come back before I go home and let you know how they are."

"I'd be beholden."

After Shaw was gone and Walter was settled, Alafair rummaged around in the kitchen, memorizing the locations of all the necessaries—flour, sugar, potatoes, brown paper and string, pots and pans, cutlery and dishtowels. She didn't have to hunt for much. Alice's kitchen was arranged the same way as Alafair's, just as Alafair had arranged her kitchen like her mother's.

Night had well fallen and Alafair's charges were both asleep. Alafair was ladling elderberry tea into a Mason jar when Martha came in to the kitchen through the back door.

"Daddy said you were here, Ma. He told me that before I go home I should stop by and let you know Ruth and I are all right. How're Alice and Walter?"

"Pretty peaked," Alafair said, wiping her hands on her apron and turning from the stove to face her daughter. "Oh, mercy, honey, you look like the dog's dinner!"

Martha sat her carpet bag of supplies on top of Alice's kitchen table and gave Alafair an ironic smile. "Why, thank you, Mother." She lowered herself into a chair. "Actually, it's a wonder I'm still upright. I've never seen anything like this in my life, Ma. There must be fifty families in town where every soul in the house is down with the flu. And the Red Cross nursing committee is getting smaller by the hour since whatever volunteers who didn't turn tail and run are dropping like flies. Since the school is closed, we've been using the kitchen to cook for those who are too sick to do it for themselves. I've shut down the McCoy Land and Title office and sent everybody home until this is over. Besides, our manager, Mr. Rails, is sick, and I don't have the time to oversee the operation myself."

"Are you doing everything you can to keep healthy?" Alafair's question sounded more like a scolding.

Martha snorted a laugh. "Ma, I've eaten so much raw garlic that it's oozing out my pores. My cat won't come near me. Fortunately, most of the folks I've come in contact with lately are too poorly to care if I reek."

"I don't smell anything."

"Of course you don't, Ma. You're as garlicky as I am. I could smell the onion and garlic and chicken soup and boneset tea coming from this house while I was still a block away."

"Sit down, baby, and tell me all about it while I fix you something to eat."

"Thank you. I'm starving." She removed her white Red Cross headdress and smoothed her dark hair back from her forehead while Alafair ladled up a bowl of chicken soup.

"Emmanuel Clover has come down with the flu. Since Emmanuel is the town representative to the Council of Defense, Mr. Ober who runs the brick plant wanted to ask him for permission to close the plant down for a while since he has so many workers out sick. But Emmanuel's temporary replacement on the Council, Joe Chandler, insists that the factory stay open. Can't do anything to slow down war production, you know. Joe came by the school kitchen this morning, looking to give me a tongue-lashing for shuttering the title company. I told him I'd open back up as soon as I learn how to be two places at once." She shook her head. "It's a mistake not to let Mr. Ober suspend production for a spell. The flu will go through the brick plant faster than a scalded cat. I hope Joe Chandler knows how to make bricks all by himself."

"I'm sorry to hear about poor Mr. Clover." Emmanuel Clover was a young widower with a small child. Alafair had known him for years. She had always liked him, at least until the war broke out and he had volunteered to act as one of the members of Boynton's Council of Defense. In her opinion, he was far too enthusiastic about making sure that all his neighbors were doing their patriotic duty. "Who is watching over Forsythia Lily?"

"I'm afraid his little girl is sick, too. But don't worry, they're not alone. Miz Forsythe, the widow who lives next door, is looking after them. It's funny, I went by there earlier and it turns out that the old lady brought a slew of remedies with her. I declare, she had a bushel basket full of herbs and gallons of some liquid I'd just as soon not know about. Mr. Clover and Forsythia Lily will have to get well just so they don't have to drink that vile stuff. "

Alafair laughed and sat down across from Martha. "Well, us folks that grew up back in the coves and hollers didn't often have any doctor but our mamas and grandmas. When I was a little girl, we used to go visit with my Grandma and Grandpa Gunn up around Mountain Home. Way up in the hills they lived, in a deep woods cabin with a stream that run by. Oh, my, that stream was cold! My grandma used to take us into the woods to gather herbs. 'Yarbs', she called them." She smiled at the memory. "Possum grapes, and mushrooms, wild garlic and blackberries. My sister, Ruth Ann, and me, and our cousins, Trudy Johns and Mary Willow Gunn...you remember them, don't you, honey? Mary Willow married that Raider boy, Marcus. We used to go visit with your Aunt Mary Willow and Uncle Marcus some when you were just a sprout. Anyway, Grandma was real careful to teach us the difference between what was good to eat and what would make you sick or even kill you..."

Her voice trailed off when she realized that Martha wasn't listening. She had fallen asleep in her chair.

Alafair spent her first night in Boynton fully dressed and curled up an armchair that she had moved into Walter and Alice's bedroom. She could have slept in the perfectly comfortable bed in the guest bedroom, but then when either of her patients needed something, it would have taken her two precious seconds to get to them. Besides, there was not much sleeping to be done. Both of them tossed and moaned and someone had to be there to help them when the coughing fits came on, or to grab the bucket when one or the other had to throw up, and to gently lave their faces afterwards.

When Alice and Walter both fell into an exhausted sleep early in the morning, Alafair hoisted her weary self out of the chair and stumbled into the kitchen. She lit the fire on the gas stove and made herself a cup of tea so crammed with medicinal herbs that there was hardly room in the cup for the hot water. It would never do for her to come down with the flu now. Then she prepared a broth of shredded chicken meat, laced with onion and whole heads of garlic. She made a pot of coffee strong enough to pry open her bleary eyes and drank it at the kitchen table while eyeing the pile of dirty laundry in the corner.

After one more check on the sleeping invalids, she picked up the laundry basket and lugged it out the back door to the shed where Alice kept her laundry tubs and supplies. It was a crisp and cloudless morning, so pleasant that once she reached the middle of the yard she couldn't make her legs go another step. She stopped to take a deep breath in hopes that a lungful of fresh air would energize her.

She caught sight of a movement in the window of the Gale house that abutted Alice's property in the back, but when she turned to get a better look, whatever had drawn her attention wasn't there anymore.

She shifted the laundry basket to one hip and cocked an ear when she became aware of the sound of a heated argument coming from the Thomasons' house. She recognized Homer Thomason's deep baritone, but the voice of the other man was unfamiliar to her. As she listened, she chided herself that she really needed to get the wash going and not stand here and eavesdrop. Still…

The fight went on for some minutes, getting louder and louder, until finally there was a crashing noise. Then silence.

Alafair stood there for another moment or two, wondering if she should take some sort of action. In the end, she decided she had left Alice and Walter alone too long as it was and hurried to the shed.

Alice owned a washing machine—something that Alafair had never used in her life. It was a big, unwieldy thing, which is why it was housed in a shed in the backyard. A gasoline motor at the bottom turned an agitator that stuck up through the middle of the copper washtub, and a hand-cranked wringer was suspended over the tub. All in all it looked like an interesting idea and it probably did make doing laundry a less backbreaking task.

But there was no way Alafair was going to risk fiery death by an exploding gasoline engine bomb. Besides, it was obvious to her that the little paddle of an agitator was not going to get the dirt out of anything. So she ended up carrying her basket back into the yard, determined to wash the same way she did at home. She would set one of Alice's tubs over a fire in the backyard and boil the sheets until they were as pure and white and infection-free as new-fallen snow.

She intended to go back into the house first to do a quick welfare check, but stopped when she caught sight of Nola Thomason sitting on the steps of her back porch, slumped and red-eyed, looking as though her last friend had died.

"Nola," Alafair called. "Is everything all right? Can I do something for you?"

Nola raised her head, surprised at being caught out. Her cheeks reddened. She stood up and walked over to the fence. "What are you doing here, Alafair?"

"Alice and Walter both have the grippe. I'm here to tend them. I've been here since yesterday. I'm fixing to do a load of their sickbed laundry, so don't get too close."

"Oh, I'm sorry to hear it." Nola's tone was sympathetic, but she did back up a step. She nodded toward her own house. "I suppose you heard."

"Well, yes. It sounded like your husband was none too pleased about something."

Nola heaved a sigh. "Homer was supposed to go out of town on business yesterday, but if he leaves town he ain't supposed to come back until the quarantine is lifted, so he changed his mind. Lewis had supper over at JoNell's place last night and didn't get the word, so he showed up first thing this morning with a mind to spend the next few days here with me. As usual, Lewis couldn't keep his mouth shut and Homer took exception to his disrespect, and it turned into a big blow-up. Homer hauled off and punched Lewis in the eye and told him not to ever come again while Homer is there. I was horrified that it went so far, but after what Lewis said to him I can hardly blame him for seeing red. I don't know what I'm going to do with that boy, Alafair. I figured he'd be better once he moved into his own place, but I think he's even worse. Homer used to be more patient with Lewis, too, but I reckon that he's just finally had enough."

"I wish I could invite you over for a nice talk," Alafair said. "Sometimes all you can do is commiserate with a friend."

Nola smiled at that. "Well, it's a pain and a bother, but if they're never in the same room again, at least I won't have to continually fling myself between them to keep one from killing the other. This endless fighting upsets Dorothy, no end. Me, too. I love them both." She pulled a handkerchief out of her pocket and dabbed her eyes. "I'm not thrilled with that little girl he's seeing, but sometimes I wish Lewis would just get married, move off somewhere far away, and leave us in peace."

The comment shocked Alafair. She could not imagine wanting to be free of one of her children. But the idea of having to choose between a child and her husband was hair-raising, and her shock quickly turned to pity. "I'm so sorry to hear it has gotten so bad. Listen, I have to go back inside and see to my patients, but why don't you and me make a regular appointment to talk over the fence like this every morning after breakfast?"

"That would be a comfort, thank you."

"It'll be a comfort to me, too. I reckon after a day or two I'll be yearning for somebody to talk to who ain't sick."

Nola smiled at that. "I hope that in a day or two we both still qualify as 'not sick'. I'll be looking for you regular at about this time, but you feel free to holler at me any time, or give me a jingle on the telephone."

Chapter Eight

How Doctor Emmett Carney Ended Up in Boynton, Whether He Liked It or Not

All of the practicing physicians in Boynton had been called to duty by the United States early in the war. Even old Doc Addison, who was seventy-five if he was a day, had been invited to Fort Sill down in Lawton to give physicals to prospective flyers and infantrymen. Now that influenza was running rampant through the troops, Doc Addison had been commandeered to care for the thousands of stricken recruits at the Army hospital. The only medic left in Boynton was Doc Addison's wife, Ann, the midwife, who had been in practice almost as long as had her husband. She was an excellent midwife and knew a thing or two about folk medicine. But she couldn't be a hundred places at once.

A week after the epidemic reached Boynton, Scott Tucker, the town sheriff, put in a call to the county health department. The man who took the call, one Mr. Prince, sounded harried.

Scott was feeling pretty harried himself so he didn't spare the man any sympathy. "We need help out here. The government took all our doctors but for one midwife. The nearest doctor is twelve miles away in Haskell and he's got his hands full. Last week y'all at the State Health Office sent this memorandum around saying that all the doctors in the big towns were to hold themselves in readiness in case they had to be sent to needy little towns. Well, we're needy, Mr. Prince. If it weren't for our Red Cross women, who all ought to receive medals, by the way, we'd be in a worse fix than we are."

"Yes, the Health Office has been compiling a list of doctors who may be available for emergency service. I'll tell you, Mr. Tucker, there are a lot of towns that are in a similar fix and there aren't many doctors to spare. But I'll see if I can get the state to rustle somebody up and send him down your way."

"I'd be obliged for sure, Mr. Prince. Will you ring me up and let me know when someone is on the way? We'll try to have everything ready for him. Hell, we'll meet him at the station with a brass band if that's what he wants."

Scott wasn't joking, so Mr. Prince didn't laugh. "I'll do the best I can," he said, and hung up without ceremony.

When Scott arrived at the schoolhouse, he got out of his Paige automobile and followed the smell of soup. The Red Cross ladies had commandeered the school cafeteria and turned it into an emergency kitchen and distribution center, cooking hot meals on top of the big oil-burning stove for sick families who had no one to cook for them. He found Martha and two or three other women in the kitchen, packing baskets and boxes of food to be delivered to the stricken. Martha straightened when she saw him, an expression of alarm in her eyes. Nobody expected to hear anything good these days.

"What is it, Cousin Scott?"

"Don't worry, ladies, it's good news for once. I got a wire a couple of hours ago from the health service in Muskogee. The State Health Office beat the bushes and came up with a doctor to send us. He's a researcher for the medical school in Norman, but they tell me he knows his business. He'll be here tomorrow on the eleven-thirty from Okmulgee."

Martha sagged. "Oh, thank goodness. I hope he'll have some new remedy in hand. Even if he doesn't, it'll be good to have an extra pair of hands to tend the sick."

"I figure to put him up in the American Hotel." Scott's wife, Hattie, ran the American Hotel as well as the Boynton Mercantile, so it was a logical arrangement. "Do you want me to bring him here straight from the station so he can get a feel for the situation?"

"The sooner the better, as far as I'm concerned," Martha said, "but first you'd better ask him what he wants to do. It wouldn't do to discommode the doctor the moment he steps foot in town."

Alafair's first week at her daughter's house was so busy she hardly had time to think. For the first few days she did nothing but nurse Alice and Walter. They both ran high fevers, nearly coughed their lungs out, and shivered with the ague. It was worrisome when Alice grew so ill that she could not take herself to the bathroom without help, nor keep anything down, not even her mother's anti-nausea ginger tea. Walter decided that he didn't want to disturb Alice with his tossing, so he moved into the spare bedroom.

Alafair brewed medicine, boiled soup, cleaned the house top to bottom with hot vinegar or lye water, and hand-washed a load of soiled sheets and nightclothes every morning. Alice only owned four sets of sheets, which was turning out to be inadequate to the task. Alafair figured she hadn't done so much laundry since she had several children in diapers. She had Shaw bring extra sheets from home, and determined that when this was over, she was going to make sure Alice got herself more bedclothes.

Alice and Walter only had two proper bedrooms, but they did have a small sewing room for Alice at the back of the house, just off the screened back porch. There was hardly enough space for Alice's treadle machine and a chair, but Alafair considered squeezing a cot for herself into it. Instead, she had Shaw bring up one of the creaky iron bedsteads and batting-stuffed mattresses from the tool-shed bunkroom where Gee Dub had been sleeping before he left for the Army. She set up the bed in the middle of the parlor, where she would be handy if either of her patients needed her in the night. She didn't expect company and she didn't think Alice was in a condition to object to the arrangement. As it turned out, Alafair still spent most nights in the armchair next to Alice's bed. It was a comfortable, fat chair, but trying to sleep sitting up was unsatisfying, to say the least. She would start awake at every sound, anyway, just as she had done when the children were little and one or the other of them was sick or hurt. When morning came she would struggle to her feet, sore and stiff and unrested, to tend to her chores.

Doctor Emmett Carney disembarked onto the platform at the Boynton station and sighed. The town was as he had anticipated. A tiny little burg surrounded by farms, set in the middle of nowhere. He did not want to be here. He felt some shame about this, but it was true. This influenza pandemic, horrible as it was, had presented him with the research opportunity of a lifetime. He had been following the work of the virologists and bacteriologists Back East as they desperately tried to develop an effective treatment. He had had some success in reproducing their test results, and had even designed an experimental vaccine of his own.

Doctor Carney's right leg had been crushed in a riding accident when he was a teen and had never healed properly, so the armed services wouldn't take him. Even so, he would have thought that in this time of crisis, someone in the United States government would have realized his worth. Even if he did have a bum leg, he was still a fully qualified medical doctor. He was a good researcher. What did it matter that he could not stand for hours in the operating room? He still could do research for his country.

But it was the Oklahoma Department of Health who had ended up drafting him. "We need you more than the Army," the health officer told him, "because they're taking away every able-bodied medic in the state, formally trained or not. We don't care about your gimpy leg. We care about the fact that there is hardly a qualified civilian doctor left in Oklahoma."

Emmett Carney could not fight the Germans, so this epidemic was his war, and he resolved to be a good soldier and fight it to the best of his ability in whatever capacity he was called.

A slender, dark-eyed young woman and an elderly man with a shotgun were the only two people standing on the platform when he disembarked. The woman's hair was caught up in a white scarf, and a white bib apron with a red cross in the middle of the breast covered her blue shirtwaist dress.

Carney doffed his hat. He had slicked back and oiled his fair hair within an inch of its life, which hadn't tamed the cowlick that curled up over his right eye like an upside-down comma.

Martha looked him up and down. He was a surprisingly young man, a small man, not much taller than Martha herself, but he stood ramrod straight. He sported a carefully trimmed, fussy little mustache. Martha wondered if he thought it made him look older. If that was his reasoning, he was mistaken.

She stepped toward him and extended her hand. "Doctor Carney? I am Mrs. McCoy, president of the Red Cross chapter here in Boynton. Sheriff Tucker intended to meet you, but he came down with the grippe last night. He asked me to welcome you to town and show you to the hotel where you will be staying. Or if you would prefer, I can take you first to the influenza headquarters we Red Cross volunteers have set up in the grammar school cafeteria. "

"Yes, I think I would like to see that first, if you do not mind." Carney nodded at the armed man. "Are we expecting an imminent invasion?"

Martha's lip twitched upward when she realized what he was talking about. "This is Mr. Church. The town council has quarantined Boynton. This is the first time the train has stopped for a passenger here in a week. It has been slowing down only long enough for the guard to throw the incoming mail bag onto the platform and hook the outgoing bag as the train rolls by. Mr. Church is here to make sure nobody besides you takes a notion to disembark and look around."

Carney sighed. "You know, Mrs. McCoy, that the incoming mail bag is as likely to be infected as any person stepping off the train."

His tone caused one of Martha's eyebrows to arch. "We realize that, Doctor. But too many people in town have men in the military and are more hungry for news than they are afraid of an infected letter. Home mail delivery has been suspended. Our postmistress is ill, but one of our Red Cross ladies has volunteered to sort the mail into boxes at the post office for anyone who wants to come in and pick it up. If folks are too fearful to handle their mail, they can leave it in the box. But of course now the quarantine is more to keep the flu contained in Boynton than it is to keep it out."

It was common knowledge that most young doctors had been drafted and the only civilian doctors left were either too old or incompetent. But Martha only had to watch Carney take two steps to see why he was not in uniform. His right leg did not bend.

She looked at Mr. Church, who nodded and moved to the baggage car to retrieve the doctor's luggage.

"Doctor Carney, I figured you would have some bags so I came to fetch you in my husband's motorcycle and side car. Now, I can see that you may have some trouble hoisting yourself all the way into the side car...."

Carney shot her a surprised glance. He knew his limp was too obvious to miss. When he had climbed down from the train car, he had had to swing the stiff limb out to the side at each step. Usually, strangers would watch him walk and become very solicitous. But most people never commented on his disability.

Martha, on the other hand, apparently didn't think she needed to spare his feelings. "My brother-in-law has a stiff leg," she was saying. "I can show you how he manages with the side car, if you would like. We can put your cases in the seat."

Carney supposed he should be relieved at how direct she was. No time for the niceties of polite society in time of war. Still, it was rather pleasant when people pretended there was nothing wrong with him.

Mr. Church placed Carney's medical bag and his one suitcase in the seat of Martha's side car, and Martha showed Carney how to perch on the back of the car with his bad leg stretched out over the luggage. Martha drew a pair of goggles on over her scarf, straddled the saddle and kick-started the motorcycle. Her assured competence was so at odds with her delicate appearance that Carney could not help but be amused in spite of his sour mood.

"Are you ready?" Martha raised her voice to be heard over the engine noise. "Hang on, now."

Carney's seat was somewhat precarious, but Martha drove slowly down the unpaved side-streets and he was hardly jolted at all.

Hattie Tucker, the sheriff's wife and Martha's cousin-by-marriage, was the only person on duty at the school kitchen when Martha and Carney arrived. All the other women were out on rounds.

"There are fifteen of us left," Martha said, as she showed the doctor around the makeshift command post. "Eight other volunteers have either come down with the flu themselves or decided they don't want to risk it. We all meet up here at dawn and make our plans for the day. Usually somebody stays here at the school to make soup and deliver messages. We have tried to let folks know that they should telephone here or send a message if they need help. We have access to a telephone in the school office. We divide up house calls. We go to anybody who asks for us, but lately a couple of us will ride or walk up and down the streets looking for a red 'X' on the doors. That is the signal the town council decided that everyone should use to let folks know that there is influenza in the house."

Carney nodded. "A number of other towns have a similar arrangement. What measures are your nurses taking to keep from becoming ill themselves?"

"Masks, of course, and constant washing. Most of the ladies have their own family remedies and preventatives. Many are taking patent medicines."

"I assume you have a pharmacy in town."

Hattie spoke up. "We have two drug stores, Doctor. Owl Drug and Williams' Drug. Both are still open and making deliveries."

"Good. What do your nurses do for their patients when they call on them, Mrs. McCoy?"

"Whatever we can. Try to see that they are clean and fed, that the house is clean and the air in the sick room is not too warm or too stale. I carry aspirin in my kit, and menthol rub, and lemons, when I can get them. My mother and some other ladies in the area make useful tonics and medicines for fever, the cough, nausea, and for diarrhea. Sometimes the best thing we can do is stay with the patients for a while, especially folks who have nobody else to look after them."

Carney lowered himself into a chair and absently rubbed his aching thigh. The women had organized things well. Using the kitchen as a staging area was a good idea. "How many in the vicinity have died?"

Hattie and Martha exchanged a glance. Often when they knocked at houses with the sign, no one would come to the door. Sometimes someone inside would yell at her through the door, or gesture to her from behind a closed window. Go away. We're better. Don't bring more illness to this house.

Other times no one would come to the door because no one could. Martha could tell the difference by the smell. Her nose had become acutely sensitive to the odor of sickness. In that case she would simply open the door and walk in, praying that she would find everyone ill but still alive. She wasn't always so lucky.

On the day that she and Cousin Hattie revved up Scott's touring car and made the circuit of nearby farms, they found that both Fosters and their five children had all succumbed during the night. The women wrapped the bodies in blankets, dragged them into the parlor, and laid them on the floor in a row for the convenience of the gravediggers. Then they filled a washtub with well water, washed themselves with carbolic soap as best as they could, took another dose of garlic honey, and drove to the next farm.

"I don't believe any of us have wanted to take a count. There have been several," Martha said. "It seems to happen real fast. Sometimes they even seem to be on the mend beforehand."

"They get all blue in the face," Hattie said.

"That is called cyanosis," Carney said. "They literally drown in their own fluids. When this influenza strain progresses to the respiratory system, heroic measures must be taken to prevent cyanosis, which is almost always fatal. It is excellent medicine to keep the patient clean and hydrated. Women are best suited for that necessary task, and I have the greatest respect for your gender's capacity for loving care."

He put his hand on the back of his chair as though he was going to stand again, but thought better of it and settled back down before continuing. "This is not ordinary grippe. This particularly virulent strain must be treated aggressively. Trust me, ladies, I have studied the disease thoroughly and am versant in all the latest scientific breakthroughs in the pathology of influenza that have come about in just the last year. So I would like for you to continue tending the sick, and I will make rounds as well so that I can assess each case individually. And if someone under your care takes a turn for the worse, you must try to contact me immediately. Your herbs and spells are all very well and good, but leave it to a doctor to understand the pathology of the disease and treat it effectively."

Carney could tell by the look on the women's faces that they were taken aback and maybe even a little insulted by his tone, and he was torn between regret and a perverse satisfaction at the effect his words were having on them. But he couldn't help himself. His bitter disappointment in his lot had a mind of its own.

Walter Kelley was lying on his stomach with his head resting on one arm, facing the bedroom door. His hair was as unkempt as an abandoned bird's nest and his cheeks sported a good growth of stubble. Alafair leaned over him and put a hand on his forehead. He was still hot, but she could tell the fever was down. He opened one bleary eye and looked up at her. He seemed confused for an instant, then blinked to clear his head.

"Miz Tucker…" he croaked. "How are my girls?"

"Alice is resting now. Linda is staying over with Mary so she won't get sick, remember?"

He shifted. "Oh, yes."

"How do you feel?"

"Better, I think. My head don't ache so much. May I have a glass of water?"

"Sure you can, honey." She poured a glassful from the pitcher on the bedside table and helped him sit up long enough to drink it. "Now, you lie back down and sleep if you can."

Walter settled back into the quilts and muttered something unintelligible. Alafair dabbed his face with a cool cloth, readjusted his covers, then made her way back into the kitchen.

Martha was at the table, trying to do justice to a bowl of beef noodle soup. It had become her routine to report to her mother every evening before going home, both for Alafair's sake and for her own. They exchanged information on who was still ill, who had recently fallen ill, who had died, who was better. How Ruth was faring in that big house north of town, away from the plague, watching over her employer and mentor, Miz Beckie.

Martha looked up from her bowl. "How are Alice and Walter?"

"Alice is still poorly, but she's finally asleep. Walter's ague doesn't seem to be as bad as it was. I think he'll be all right in a few days, if he doesn't try to get up and move about too much."

"Well, that's good news. I'll peek in on them before I leave." Martha blew on her soup and sipped a spoonful before she continued. "The state health department finally found us a doctor. He came in on the train this morning. His name is Carney."

Alafair sawed a piece of bread off the loaf on the counter and handed it Martha. "Oh, that is a relief."

Martha made a non-committal noise.

"You don't like him?"

Martha shrugged, then put her spoon down and leaned back in her chair. "He is not happy to be here, Ma. He's a young man with a hinky leg, so I reckon he couldn't get into the service and resents that he got sent out here to nowhere to take care of us rubes and yokels. Seems he was on track to becoming a great medical researcher before he got shanghaied by the Health Office. He has developed a whole philosophy on human health and hygiene and he is determined that his army of nurses toe the line. I took him on rounds with me this afternoon and he made a point of telling me everything I'm doing that is wrong. He aims to whip us all into shape."

"Do you think he's a bad doctor?"

Martha heaved a sigh. "No. I'm being mean, I know. Actually, he seems to know what he's doing. It's just that he's so insufferable about it."

"Maybe he doesn't mean to be. Sometimes folks behave badly when they're unhappy."

An ironic smile appeared on Martha's face. "Leave it to you to ascribe the best of motives to the worst behavior, Ma. But you're likely right about him. He can't join up like all his medical school classmates did. He didn't want to serve out the war in little old Boynton, Oklahoma."

Chapter Nine

Remembering Raven Mocker

The Thomason family was having supper around the dining table when Lewis came in the front door, bearing the cloth bag he carried when he intended to spend the night at his mother's house. The shiner that Homer had given him a few days earlier was beginning to fade to a mottled yellow-purple.

Nola jumped up from the table when she saw him, and Dorothy cringed. Homer drew a breath to fling a hot comment at his stepson, but Lewis held up a hand.

"Now, Homer, I know I'm about as welcome as a wet shoe, so I won't stay long. But before you bite my head off, I'm just here to say I'm sorry about the last time we seen one another. I know you and me have never been on good terms, but after the last blow-up, I'd like to try and make peace for Mama's sake."

Nola gasped. Lewis' statement was met with a surprised silence from Homer. Lewis Hulce and Homer Thomason had been butting heads for nearly fifteen years, and this was the first time Lewis had offered any sort of olive branch. Homer looked at his wife, who was gazing at him with hopeful tears in her eyes.

He looked back at Lewis. "I'd like that, too. For your mother's sake."

A tiny smile curled Lewis' lips and he lowered himself into a chair at the end of the table.

"Good."

"You want some supper, Lewis?" Nola attempted to control the quaver in her voice.

"No, thanks, Ma. I have a splitting headache. Got to go. Wanted to fix it up with Homer, though."

Dorothy piped up. "Lewis don't look so good, Ma. His face is red."

"It's hard for me to admit I'm wrong," Lewis said. "Makes me red in the face."

Nola rounded the table and lay the back of her hand on Lewis' forehead, alarmed. "Son, you're burning up…"

"Now, Ma," Lewis said, just before he slid sideways out of the chair and onto the floor.

Dorothy shrieked and Homer leaped to his feet. "Dang! He's got the grippe, Nola. He's brought the grippe to this house!"

Nola fell to her knees next to her retching, feverish son. "Dorothy, you get out of here. Go to your room right now. Homer, help me get him up."

Homer backed up a couple of steps. "Nola, this is the end. I can't take no more. That boy has brought me nothing but grief from the moment I set eyes on him, and now he'll be the end of us."

◇◇◇

Alafair had been through influenza season many times, but there hadn't been an epidemic like this since the Russian flu tore through Arkansas the year she married Shaw. It seemed like every other person in town was down with it, and not just down, but violently ill.

Every morning she and Nola Thomason exchanged news about the health of their families over the backyard fence—at a discreet distance. The Thomasons managed to escape the illness for a long time, but one cloudy morning Alafair saw the quarantine sign on their front door before she heard the news from

Nola. She went into the parlor and stood before the telephone table for a few moments, finally overcoming her resistance and picking up the telephone receiver. She clicked the drop hook on the column a couple of times like she had seen Alice do, and heard a tinny voice on the other end say, "Number, please." She held the receiver close to her ear, but she was not quite ready to touch it to her head.

"Kate," she yelled, "is that you?"

"Sure is. What can I do for you, Alice?"

"Kate, this is Alafair Tucker. Alice and Walter are both ailing and I'm watching over them for a spell."

"I declare! I think pretty soon the whole town will be down with this Spanish plague! How are they?"

"They're poorly right now, I'm afraid, but better than they were. How are y'all?"

"Staying out of public places, so nobody at my house is sick yet. Scott asked me to keep the lines open, else I'd be home, too. At least I don't have to wait on folks in person."

"Well, listen, Kate, can you connect me with the Thomason house next door to Alice? I don't know the number, I'm sorry."

"Sure I can, honey. By the way, you don't have to holler into the phone. I can hear you just fine. Hold on one second."

There was a click, then silence, then ringing on the other end before Nola Thomason's voice said, "Who is there, please?"

"Nola, it's Alafair over to next door. I seen your quarantine sign."

She heard her friend sigh. "Yes, Lewis was visiting last evening and come down sick while he was here. Fever and headache so bad that he don't make sense when he talks. I don't think he knows where he is. He can't keep anything down. I hope it don't spread to the rest of us. Homer can't afford to be getting sick, so as soon as I put Lewis to bed, Homer went on ahead to Muskogee like he first planned. I think he'll stay there at least until Lewis is well. Homer is scared to death of the flu. Both his own folks died of it when he was a lad. He didn't take to the idea of leaving me alone, but he said he'd have Burrows' Café bring meals here to the house so I don't have to shop or do much cooking. How are your patients doing today?"

"Still pretty sick. I'm keeping a close eye on them, but up to now it looks like just an ordinary bad case of the grippe. Is there anything I can do for you? Do you have plenty of medicines? I have a batch of tea that's like a miracle for bad lungs."

"I was about to ask if I could do anything for you. What with Lewis working at the pharmacy, we're always well set for medicine, so you just feel free to holler over the fence whenever you want to borrow something."

"I'll do it, and I expect you to do that, too. Now, you take care of yourself and so will I, you hear? It wouldn't do for you or me to go down until somebody in town gets well enough to look after us!"

"Well, I'm off to make chicken soup."

"And I'm off to brew tea," Alafair said, and they rang off.

◇◇◇

When the telephone rang, it woke Alafair from a troubled half-sleep. She had been awkwardly curled up on the armchair in Alice's room with her knees practically under her chin. She was on her feet before she quite realized what that irritating noise was. She ran into the parlor and snatched the earpiece off its hook before the din roused everyone in the house.

"Who is calling?" She meant to be pleasant but the words came out in a growl.

"Alafair, is that you?" Mrs. Smith sounded tentative.

"It's me, Kate. Sorry to bark at you. I jumped up from a sleep. What time is it?"

"It's close to eight in the morning. I'm sorry to wake you, honey. I've got Martha on the line. You take care, you hear?"

"Thank you, Kate. And you take care of yourself, too. Martha, where are you, sugar? Are you all right?"

"I'm at home, Ma. I stopped by the MacKenzie place on my rounds an hour or so ago. Ruth is fine, but Miz Beckie came down with the ague last night. She's not too sick yet, but you know how Miz Beckie is. Ruth has her hands full."

"Oh, my goodness. Is nobody to be spared?"

"Sorry I didn't drop by and deliver the news in person, but I had to come home to change clothes and have a bath and feed the cat. I'm just leaving to see how Mr. Clover and his daughter are doing."

"Thank you for letting me know, honey. You take care of yourself and tell Ruth to do the same."

"I'll be by later today, Ma."

Martha rang off and Alafair crept into the guest bedroom to find Walter sitting up on the side of his bed, trying to get dressed. He had managed the trousers, but only one arm had found its way into a sleeve before Walter had had to have a rest. He gave her a rueful glance. His color was better. No more hectic red of fever. She put a hand on his forehead. The fever was down.

Alafair crossed her arms. "You think you're in good enough shape to get out of bed?"

"I think I'd feel better if I could sit up for a while, Miz Tucker."

"Come on, then, I'll help you." She briskly guided home his unsleeved arm and buttoned his shirt. "You can sit in the armchair by Alice for a spell. She's been pining for you."

Alafair steadied him when he stood, but Walter walked to the front bedroom on his own. Alice was awake and propped up on pillows. She had heard them talking and was waiting anxiously for her beloved, looking pale and watery-eyed, but alert. Alafair almost clapped her hands for joy.

Alice smiled at the look of naked relief on her mother's face. "I do think I'll live, Ma."

Alafair was checking Alice's temperature as she talked. "You're still warm, but your fever is down, too."

Walter's visit lifted both his and Alice's spirits considerably, and his watchful presence in the room freed Alafair to head to the kitchen to make something for the invalids to eat. "Walter, sit down in that chair before you fall down. Pour yourself and Alice a glass of water from that pitcher by the bed and drink it.

I'm going to make y'all some broth and some bread soaked in milk, and you're going to try and eat it."

Alafair was encouraged that Walter ate all his broth and most of the bread and milk. Alice did the best she could with the broth and picked a little at the bread, but she drank her tea thirstily and asked for more.

Alafair was so happy that her charges were on the mend that she practically floated out of the bedroom. She was halfway across the parlor when she saw through the window that Martha was sitting on the front steps with her head slumped forward on her chest, the picture of defeat. Alafair stopped in her tracks, dismayed at the thought that her new-found good mood was about to be spoiled.

She sighed and stepped out the front door. Putting it off wouldn't help anything.

Alafair didn't want to ask Martha what was wrong. She looked away from the wilted figure and gazed for a moment at the array of bronze and yellow asters that lined the sidewalk in front of Alice's house. A honey bee hovered over one lemon-colored bloom. The morning was well along and the fall air was golden and still. Funny, Alafair thought. The world goes on being beautiful no matter what. She took a breath.

"Martha, darlin'."

Martha opened her eyes.

Alafair walked across the porch, sat down on the steps. and put an arm around her daughter's shoulders.

"Emmanuel Clover died," Martha said. Her tone was matter-of-fact. "He turned blue. He turned almost black. It was a very hard death. Dr. Carney tried everything but nothing worked. Mr. Clover's little girl is an orphan now. She is about over the flu, but Miz Forsythe has gotten sick and can't take of her any-more. Dr. Carney is still there, but I've got to get back directly."

"Oh, sweetheart! That poor baby. Bring her over here. Alice and Walter are better, too, so she won't be a bit more trouble for me to take care of until her grandma can come fetch her."

"Thank you, Ma. I'll confess I was hoping for just that. I don't know what else to do with the child. You think it'll be all right with Alice?"

"I'm sure it will, but I don't see what other choice you have right now. How are you going to get her over here? Can you drive Walter's automobile?"

"Oh, that's not necessary. The Clover house is not even two blocks from here, and Forsythia Lily is no bigger than a minute. I'll just carry her over."

Martha leaned forward and placed her elbows on her knees before giving her mother a sidelong glance. Her eyes were ringed with exhaustion. "You know what worries me the most? Not that I'll probably come down with the flu myself, by and by. It's that I'm not particularly bothered anymore by all the awful things I've seen."

"That's God's mercy," Alafair assured her. "Believe me, it'll hit you good when this is all over."

Martha's expression was doubtful. "I think my heart has gone dead, Ma."

A lump rose in Alafair's throat. She swallowed it down. "Now, I hope you know that it ain't your fault if Jesus decides to take someone to his bosom. The Lord don't care if we succeed. He cares that we try as hard as we can, and I know you and Dr. Carney did everything that any human person could do."

Martha smiled. "Now, where in the Bible does it say that, Ma? Never mind. No need to quote me chapter and verse. I know you're right. Sometimes it doesn't matter what you do." She placed her hands on the small of her back and stretched. "Mercy. Well, I better get going."

Instead, she leaned back against the step and sighed. "It's just that Mr. Clover died so bad. Most folks I've tended get real sick, but then they get over it. The ones who die, they die so hard. It's terrible to see. You know what it made me think of, Mama? How your Granny Gunn used to tell us about the Raven Mocker."

Raven Mocker. Alafair had not heard that name in decades, and for Martha to utter it so unexpectedly turned her blood to ice. "Don't even say it."

Martha blinked at her. "It's just a story, Ma." Her mother's reaction surprised her. She didn't think of Alafair as particularly superstitious.

Alafair shook her head. "How do you even remember that, honey? I declare, you were only a tyke when my grandma told you those Cherokee tales."

"How could I not remember when you and Daddy took us to see your grandma over in Arkansas? She lived in that raggedy one-room cabin all by herself. It seemed to me that we hiked up the mountain and through the woods about a hundred miles to get there from your folks' house. I thought your grandma looked like one of those dried-apple dolls you used to make for us. She was so sweet. She told us all those stories about how the Earth came to be, and how the plants decided to give us medicine, and about the Little People. But she told us about the Raven Mocker, too, and how he searches out people who are old or sick or injured and torments them until they die. Then he eats their hearts. Of course I remember. Your grandma died not long after that. I couldn't sleep for a month. Anyway, I suppose it came to mind because the other day you reminded me about how Granny Gunn used to gather the herbs for medicine. I hadn't thought of her Raven Mocker story in years, until poor Mr. Clover suffered so before he passed."

Alafair's heart picked up its pace as she listened to Martha talk. Alafair was a down-to-earth, practical woman. She lived in modern times, a new century of science and understanding. But she had seen things in the course of her life. She knew better than to believe that anyone really understood anything.

"Well, try not to think on such an awful thing. Think of the Twenty-third Psalm instead, and how his goodness and mercy shall follow you all the days of your life."

Martha stood up and rolled her shoulders. It was time to go. She wasn't feeling bathed in goodness and mercy right now and was not in the mood to pretend she did. She did feel better, though. Finding a safe place for a sick child and spending time in her mother's soothing presence had done that for her. "I'll be back with Forsythia Lily in a little while."

After Martha left, Alafair kept her seat on the porch step longer than she should have. She needed to prepare a place for the orphan to sleep. She also needed to tend to her patients and start on more laundry. She wished that Martha hadn't reminded her of Raven Mocker. When she was growing up in the Ozarks, the shriek of a raven always made her skin crawl. Everyone back in the hills knew of the evil being, the witch who may even have lived among them during the day. Perhaps a neighbor, or the tinker passing through. But at night the witch sailed over the trees on black wings, calling like a raven and searching for victims to torture and hearts to devour. It could take the shape of someone old or young, man or woman, but the evil inside would eventually desiccate the body of the being it inhabited. Her preacher father had told her to think of Jesus and to put the tales of evil beings out of her mind, for to dwell on a thing was to conjure it.

But her father's own mother had taught Alafair that Jesus may save your soul, but it took the right medicine and the proper actions to keep an evil being like Raven Mocker at bay. Alafair stood up. She was a modern woman. She believed in logic and practicality.

Alafair went into Alice's kitchen, retrieved a broom from the corner, and laid it across the threshold of the back door.

She found another broom for the front door and grabbed a blue box of table salt so she could lay a salt line under each window in the house. A practical woman took no chances.

Alice and Walter both gave Alafair a questioning look when she returned to the bedroom. "Did I hear you talking to Martha, Mama?" Alice said. "I hope it wasn't bad news."

Alafair thrust her hands into her apron pockets. "Listen, children, Martha told me that Emmanuel Clover passed away a while ago, and poor little Forsythia Lily has nobody to look after her right now. I told Martha to bring her over here until her grandma can get into town to fetch her. I hope that's all right. I'll fix up Linda's cot for her."

Walter and Alice glanced at one another, but there was no hesitation. "Miz Tucker, bring that child here," Walter said.

"Is Forsythia Lily sick?" Alice said.

"Martha tells me that she has been down, but that she's on the mend."

Alice reached for Walter's hand and he supported her as she struggled to sit up against the headboard. "You don't need to put her in Linda's bed right away, Ma. You put her here in the bed with me tonight. I'll take care of her."

Alice was smart, strong, and willful, but she had never been particularly angelic. Still, she looked like an angel in her white nightgown, Alafair thought, her light blond hair afloat around her face, pale and ethereal after her illness. When Martha showed up with Forsythia Lily, the seven-year-old didn't have to be invited twice into the comforting arms of the beautiful lady. By the time Alafair left to finally make supper, Alice was sitting up against the headboard with her husband holding her hand and a little orphan snuggled up to her side.

Chapter Ten

How Everything Suddenly Got Worse

Forsythia Lily Clover was a sweet, affectionate creature who rewarded everything her new caretakers did for her with a hug. The worst of her influenza was over, but she was still weak and tired, with little appetite and not much to say. She asked about her father only once. She seemed to accept it quietly when Alafair told her that he had gone to Jesus, and settled down to wait for her grandmother without complaint. Alafair suspected that when Forsythia Lily felt better physically, she would have more energy to mourn her lost father.

After a light luncheon late the next morning, Walter went back to the guest room to lie down, while Alice and Forsythia Lily napped and Alafair nodded in the armchair next to the bed. Alafair knew she should clear away the soup bowls that were sitting empty on the bedside table, but it felt so good to sit there that she couldn't make herself move. Just a few more minutes, and then another load of laundry, she told herself. She did not think she slept, but she must have napped a little, for she dreamed that she could hear sleigh bells.

A wild shriek jolted her awake and she leaped to her feet. Alice raised up on an elbow.

"What?" Alice said. "Is that an animal?"

"That's coming from next door. Just stay where you are and I'll see what is going on."

Lewis Hulce's lady friend, JoNell Reed, was in the Thomasons' front yard, rolling around on the ground in a frenzy, screaming and clawing at her face. Alafair ran down the steps and scrambled over the fence that separated the yards. A couple of the neighbors had come outside to see what the commotion was, but no one was brave enough to venture over to help.

JoNell was flailing around on the grass like a crazy woman. Alafair dropped to her knees and tried to get a grip on her. She kept repeating JoNell's name, louder and louder, unable to grasp clothing or a limb firmly enough to restrain her. Finally Alafair sat back on her heels, eyes wide, unable to do anything but watch the hysterical girl fling herself about.

Alafair was in awe. She had seen wild outpourings of grief before, but this was beyond words. Most of the noises JoNell made were meaningless, but occasionally Alafair heard something that sounded like "Lewis." By the time JoNell had exhausted herself and collapsed into a sobbing heap, Alafair had decided that Lewis was dead and that fact had driven his beloved out of her mind.

She lay a hand on JoNell's head. When the younger women didn't fling herself away, Alafair grasped her by the shoulders, hauled her to her feet and guided her back toward the front door. JoNell submitted, numb.

No one came to the door. Alafair's brow knit and she opened the screen with one hand and steered JoNell into the house. "Nola?" she called, but there was no answer.

She sat the girl down on the sofa, and grasped her chin to force her to look at her. "What happened, JoNell? Did Miz Thomason go to town and leave you to nurse Lewis? Did Lewis die?"

JoNell's lip began to tremble and her eyes filled. She pointed toward the dining room. "He's dead."

"Where's Miz Thomason? Where is Dorothy?"

"Dead. They're all dead."

Alafair straightened, shocked. "All dead?" She asked the question but she didn't stay around for an answer. Her first thought was for Sophronia's friend, Dorothy.

The Thomason house was laid out in a similar fashion to the Kelley house next door—an open parlor with French doors at the back leading to a dining room, and a kitchen at the rear. There were two bedroom doors on the right side of the parlor. There would be a third, smaller room off the kitchen at the back of the house. Alice used hers as a sewing room, but Alafair figured that here it was used as a child's bedroom.

Alafair found Lewis halfway between the kitchen and the dining room. She was surprised to find him on the floor, but after JoNell's hysterics, Alafair knew that he was dead, so the sight of the body didn't cause her much distress. Like Martha, I'm becoming numb to horror, she thought. That did distress her. She studied Lewis' mortal shell for a long moment.

He lay on his back, his eyes and mouth open, his arms outflung. His skin was the color of clay and his lips were blue, almost indigo. The whole house smelled of medicine and herbs, rancid sweat and sickness, plus the messy odor of bodily fluids. She closed Lewis' eyes. Before she closed his mouth, she noticed that he had bitten his tongue. Convulsions, probably.

She covered her mouth with her hand to keep from crying out when she saw Nola on the kitchen floor, one arm extended up the side of the cabinet. She had been trying to brace herself before she fell. Her body was convulsed and her face was livid. She had vomited and there was a pinkish froth around her lips. Alafair swallowed a great lump that rose in her throat. She squatted down next to her friend's body and gently closed Nola's half-open eyes. The body was cold.

What a way to die, Alafair thought. So quickly that she couldn't even find a place to lie down. If Nola knew she was getting ill, why hadn't she telephoned Alafair, or the Red Cross, or somebody? The grippe didn't overtake its victims without any warning at all. Not the kind of grippe that Alafair knew about.

She hurried through the door off of the kitchen, into a small, frilly room that didn't have space for much more than a child-sized bed with a white carved headboard. Dorothy was lying in the bed on her stomach with her face turned toward the door. The flowered coverlet had been kicked off onto the floor. The gray eyes were open. Alafair's heart leaped when she realized that they were looking at her. Dorothy was still alive.

Alafair pushed the dark hair back from the girl's face and rolled her over onto her back. She was horrified to see that the front of Dorothy's gown was covered with blood and vomit. "Dorothy, honey, talk to me, baby." Dorothy didn't respond but her gaze followed Alafair's movements. The child was deathly pale and covered in a sheen of sweat, her breathing shallow. Alafair felt her forehead and behind her ears. No fever. This was not influenza.

She leaned close to whisper in Dorothy's ear. "It'll be all right, sugar. Now, listen, Dorothy. I think you may have eaten something bad or taken some bad medicine. I don't want you to get even sicker, so we're going to make you throw it up. Does your mama have any ipecac?"

Dorothy's eyes widened, so Alafair knew she had understood, but she said nothing. She began to pant and her eyes rolled back.

Alafair was not happy to add to Dorothy's misery. "I'm sorry, honey, but it has to be done." She hurried into the kitchen and retrieved a mop bucket from the pantry. She sat down on the side of the bed, lifted Dorothy into her lap, and without hesitation stuck a finger down the girl's throat. Dorothy struggled and gagged and even bit her, but Alafair did not relent until the gagging became retching. Alafair grabbed up the bucket and held Dorothy's hair back while she vomited. There wasn't very much to throw up, but afterwards the girl seemed eased. She flopped back onto her pillow and took a breath. She was drenched in sweat. Alafair took the bucket into the bathroom and left it under the sink. She poured a glass of milk to soothe and coat Dorothy's stomach, wet a washcloth, and returned to the girl's side to clean her up.

"I know you're scared, punkin, but I'm going to try to take care of everything. I want you to just rest here while I see to your mama and your brother and telephone the doctor."

It was the first time that Alalfair had said anything to Dorothy about her family, and she paused. "Dorothy, what happened, can you tell me? Do you know? Did you all eat something that made you real sick?"

But Dorothy just looked at her out of enormous, sunken eyes and said nothing.

Alafair lifted a curly-haired rag doll off the floor and tucked it into the blanket at Dorothy's side. "Here's your baby, honey. I'll be back directly. I'll take you over to Alice's house and make you some nice ginger tea with lots of cream and sugar."

When she rose to leave, Dorothy was staring at her with an expression that suggested she had just found herself on another planet and had no idea how she had gotten there.

Alafair found a couple of quilts in a chest in Nola's bedroom. She returned to the kitchen to cover her friend's body before heading back into the parlor. She cleaned up and tidied poor Lewis as best she could, then arranged his hands over his heart and covered his body as well. The stupefied JoNell, still on the settee, had toppled over onto her side like a felled tree. Alafair decided that JoNell would keep. She picked up the telephone on the parlor table and asked Kate to ring the sheriff's office. Slim Tucker, Scott's eldest son and temporary deputy, answered.

"Slim, this is Alafair. I need to talk to Scott."

"Dad is still down with the flu, Cousin Alafair, and so is Mama. I'm trying to hold down the fort on my lonesome."

"Oh, laws-a-mercy! Is there somebody over to their house who can take care of them?"

"My wife is there now. They're both pretty sick, but I think Helen has matters in hand. She's banished me until further notice. What can I do for you?"

"Slim, I just found Nola Thomason and her son, Lewis, dead." She kept talking over Slim's groan. "I didn't even know she was sick. Listen, there's something not right about this. I'm not sure they died of the flu. I think you'd better get over here, or send that doctor, if you can locate him. And somebody needs to find Homer Thomason and tell him what has happened."

"I can't leave the office for long, Alafair. I'll have Kate at the telephone exchange see if she can locate the doc, and I'll head over to Thomason's office across the street."

"Nola told me that he's in Muskogee. You might be able to get hold of him at the Tool and Die headquarters.

"All right, I'll send a wire. I'll leave a message at the undertaker's, too. He's out to the Baker farm collecting their dead right now."

Alafair hung up the telephone and was about to retrieve Dorothy when Shaw called through the front screen and came in without waiting for an invitation. He halted when he caught sight of Alafair standing in the middle of the parlor floor.

"Alafair…" He paused, cast a glance at JoNell sprawled across the settee, then looked back at his wife. "Alice told me you heard screaming. What in blazes is going on?"

"Shaw, everybody in this house has died but for Fronie's friend, Dorothy. JoNell there came in unexpected and found them. I ran over when I heard her carrying on."

JoNell emitted a sob when she heard her name mentioned, and covered her eyes with her hand, as though that would alter what she had seen. Shaw couldn't think of anything to say that wasn't blasphemous, so he bit his lip.

Alafair crossed the room and took his arm. "Honey, there's something strange about this. It looks to me that Nola passed real quick and at the same time as Lewis. They are both on the floor, like they dropped where they stood. Only Lewis took long enough to turn blue before he went. Dorothy is white and limp and sick, but she doesn't even have a fever. I suspect that Nola and her children ate or drank something that poisoned them. I telephoned the jailhouse and talked to Slim. I told him I thought that the doctor ought to have a look before Mr. Lee carts the dead away, but he said it'll take a while to find him. I aim to take Dorothy back to Alice's house until Slim can find her daddy."

Shaw nodded toward JoNell. "What about her?"

JoNell finally hoisted herself into a sitting position. Her face was swollen from weeping. "I hear y'all. You don't need to talk like I'm not here. I don't intend to leave Lewis. Y'all take Dorothy. I'll stay here and wait for the undertaker."

Shaw took the pale and shaky child in his arms and followed Alafair back to Alice's house. They left JoNell in a chair in the dining room, keeping vigil over Lewis' body. Alafair had heard that it was sometimes taking a day or two for the undertaker's wagon to retrieve the bodies of those who had died in this epidemic. She didn't like the idea of JoNell sitting for hours or, God forbid, for days, beside the place where Lewis had died, tending a soul who didn't need tending anymore.

They returned to the Kelley house to find Walter on the settee in his parlor. "Mr. Tucker," he said, "take Dorothy into the back bedroom. I've put Linda's cot in there, too, for Forsythia Lily. That way both girls will be together. I'll move back in with Alice."

Alice was waiting for them. She was clad in her nightgown and a robe, her hair hanging down her back in a long braid. But she was on her feet.

Dorothy cooperated limply as the women stripped off her ruined gown and got her into an old but fresh flannel shirt of Walter's. The only move she made was to push Alafair's hand away when she tried to remove a tiny turquoise bird on a chain around her neck. Alafair left the necklace alone. She tried again to ask Dorothy if she knew what had happened to make her sick, if she knew what had happened to her family. Dorothy only looked away, and Alafair didn't press the matter. Forsythia Lily lay propped up on pillows in Linda's little cot, watching the action with interest.

It took a while to bring Shaw up to speed on the events of the morning. His original plan for the day was to make his daily visit to bring his wife the news from home. After he and his son-in-law John Lee Day had finished their morning chores, Shaw had ridden into town, stopping by Mary's farm, his parents' house and his sister's place on the way, going by the post office, and doing a little business with Mr. Turner at the livery. He then rode the quarter-mile north of town to check on Ruth and Miz Beckie so he could deliver to Alafair a full and complete report on the condition of all the kinfolks.

So much for the plan. When he had finally gotten to Alice's house, the bottom had dropped out of the world and it took him some time to get reacquainted with the new reality. Alice and Walter were out of bed, and a strange child had taken up residence. Alafair was not to be found.

Alice had filled him in with enough information that he was able to deal with the situation as it happened. But he didn't get the full story until after he and Alafair returned from the Thomason house with Dorothy in tow and they had made sure the children were settled. Then he sat down at the dining table with Alafair, who told him everything that had occurred since he had left town the night before.

"Well, this just knocks everything into a cocked hat, Alafair. Now you have even more folks to tend. You're running a regular hospital. You're going to get run ragged. What can I do to help? Do you suppose Phoebe would want to come help you out?"

"There's no room for Phoebe, Shaw, unless she wants to sleep on the floor. My preventives have worked up to now on me and Martha. Neither of us has got sick yet. Alice and Water are both on the mend, it seems. I expect I can manage."

"I'll take your word for it, sugar, if you're sure. Are you sure you're all right here?"

"Of course. Martha comes by every day and now Alice is up. I still have plenty of medicinals. I think it'll be all right."

"Only I saw the broom across the threshold, and I can see the salt under the window from here. Are you feeling scared?"

Alafair looked away. Of course Shaw would know exactly what those things meant. His mother did the same thing when she thought evil was stirring. "I will be scared until this epidemic passes and all our kin are well. But I got overtook by superstition, I reckon. Last time Martha was by she was remembering to me about how Granny Gunn told her the story of the Raven Mocker. Maybe it's a silly thing…"

Or maybe not. Shaw paled a little. "I had forgot about Raven Mocker." He was sorry to be reminded. "Well, honey, you do anything that'll make you feel better."

Shaw didn't leave right away. He told Alafair he would stay until someone showed up to take care of the situation at the Thomason house. It took a long time for anyone to show up. Alafair wasn't surprised that the undertaker's crew or the doctor were delayed, but Alafair was distressed at the thought of the family's mortal remains lying where they fell for so long. She tried to keep watch, but never saw JoNell Reed leave the house next door. She took some comfort in the thought that at least the dead were not unattended, even though sitting alone among the departed couldn't be good for the poor girl.

Even though she had hardly regained her strength, Alice took care of the orphans with great tenderness, laving their faces with a cool cloth, trying to cajole one or the other into sipping tea or water. At first Alafair was worried that Alice was overdoing, but she was beginning to think that having someone to nurse was actually helping her.

Alafair made two late dinners that afternoon; broth for her patients and a proper meal of chicken and dumplings for Shaw and herself.

Neither of the bereft girls showed the slightest interest in food. Forsythia Lily's fever had abated but she was still weak and pale, and Alafair was not sure she even knew where she was. Dorothy only wanted to curl up in a ball facing the wall, traumatized.

Alafair passed Shaw at the dining table as she took the invalids' empty bowls back into the kitchen. Shaw was doing proper justice to his meal. Alafair smiled and Shaw looked up at her with a raised eyebrow.

"It cheers me to cook for a man with an appetite. If you're all right for a minute," she said, "I'm going to pop over next door and see if I can get JoNell to come back here to wait for the undertaker."

Shaw made a move to stand. "I'll come with you."

"No, I'd rather you stay here with them. I'll just be a tick. I don't aim to linger and argue the point with her."

Chapter Eleven

How Alafair Decided Not All Was As It Seemed

Alafair walked into the Thomason house without knocking. She paused when she saw Homer Thomason standing in the middle of the parlor, hat in hand. He turned to see who had entered. He looked stunned.

"Mr. Thomason, I didn't know you were here."

"I just got here. I've been in Muskogee."

"How did you get around the quarantine?"

He looked abashed. "Took the truck around a side road. There's a roadblock on the Muskogee highway outside of Boynton. I went on to Muskogee after Lewis got sick because I just can't be getting the flu, but it's as bad there as it is here. I been trying to stay away from everybody. Sleeping at the hotel and staying put at the Tool and Die main office, doing business by telephone and letter. But when I got Deputy Tucker's wire I drove back as fast as I could. The doctor and a nurse are in the back right now with Nola."

"I'm sorry you lost your wife and stepson," Alafair said.

Thomason straightened. "Tucker told me that you have Dorothy next door. Is she sick? Is she all right?"

"She doesn't seem to have a fever. I tried to find out what happened but she won't talk to me. I don't know what she heard or if she saw what happened to her mother and brother, but JoNell made such a fuss when she found them that I'm sure Dorothy knows they're gone." There was no use to pussyfoot around. "Is JoNell still in there with Lewis?"

He glanced toward the dining room. "She's sitting there with her head on the table next to Lewis' body. She hasn't said anything to me."

"You haven't talked to her?"

"The doctor did, but I have not. I doubt we would be much of a comfort to one another."

"Did you see Nola?"

The color drained from his face. His eyes flooded and he blinked hard a couple of times before he answered. "Someone covered her up. I didn't look. When did she pass? Do you know?"

"I don't know for sure. I ran over here when I heard JoNell screaming. That was about noon. I don't know how long either of them had been gone. I telephoned Deputy Tucker right away. I couldn't get JoNell to leave. I think she's half out of her mind with grief and shock."

"Dorothy is all right?"

"Well, like I said, I don't think she has the flu. No fever that I can tell."

Thomason did not follow her as she headed for the dining room. JoNell was in a chair next to Lewis' body, slumped forward with her head and forearms on the dining table.

Lewis' body was still supine on the floor, but someone had turned back the quilt to expose his face. He didn't look too bad, for a dead man, Alafair thought. Though his skin was mottled and gray, his lips were not nearly as blue as they had been earlier. His mouth had flopped open again, but his eyes were still closed. The face had relaxed. He looked like he was having a good sleep.

Alafair put a hand on the young woman's shoulder. "JoNell, JoNell, come on now, come with me and Mr. Thomason. We'll go wait next door until the undertaker's wagon comes."

JoNell didn't sit up, but she turned her head so that one cheek rested on her arms and looked up at Thomason, who was standing at the open French doors. Alafair couldn't see her expression, but she heard the young woman's tone when she said, "You hated him."

Bitter.

Thomason dropped his hand to his side. "We weren't friends, but I didn't hate him and I'm sorry that he died, and that his mother died."

JoNell pushed Alafair's hand off her shoulder and glared at Thomason. "You hated him. He told me so." She placed her forehead back down on her arms.

Thomason gave Alafair a pleading look. She gestured to him and he followed her back into the parlor.

"It's my fault. It's all my fault. I shouldn't ever have left Nola to take care of them all alone. The last words I said to her were harsh…" He choked back a sob, then took a moment to compose himself before he resumed. "I let that boy get to me. He made me do things I shouldn't do. But I loved her. How can me and Dorothy go on without her? What shall I do?"

Alafair studied his face before answering. "Mr. Thomason, there isn't anything you can do. Come back with me over to my daughter's house. Dorothy needs you."

"No, thank you, ma'am. I'd be so obliged if you'd keep an eye on Dorothy for a while longer. I'll fetch her directly. But I think I'd better stay here now. Stay with my wife."

They stood for a moment, neither quite knowing what to do next. Alafair could hear people talking and moving around at the back of the house. She recognized Martha's voice.

"You know," Thomason said, "I do blame Lewis for this. He's the one brought the flu to the house."

Before Alafair could swallow her surprise and think of an appropriate response, Martha came into the parlor, followed by a slight young man with a limp who was clutching a leather case. Both were gloved and aproned and masked.

"Mama," Martha said. "I thought I heard your voice." Alafair moved to give her daughter a hug, but Martha motioned for her to keep her distance. "Not until I've scrubbed and changed, Mama." She stepped aside for the young man behind her. "Ma, this here is Doctor Carney who the State Health Department sent out to help us with this epidemic. Doctor Carney, this is my mother, Miz Shaw Tucker. She's been looking after my sister and her husband, next door."

Carney stepped forward and nodded a greeting. "Mrs. Tucker. Forgive me if I do not shake hands. I swear I do believe this town is largely made up of Tuckers and their kin. Mrs. McCoy and her brigade of nurses have been of incalculable help to me." His duty done to propriety, he turned his attention to Thomason.

"Mr. Thomason, if you would like, Mrs. McCoy will take you back so you may pay your respects to your wife. Please do not touch her, though."

Thomason's shoulders tensed. "I don't think I could stand to see her."

"You want me to go back there with you?" Alafair said.

His face crumpled. He shook his head and sat down heavily in an armchair. Alafair glanced at Martha but didn't try to persuade Thomason to change his mind. She didn't want to unman him. "It's all right. I can bring you a bowl of chicken and dumplings if you've a mind to eat a bite. You need to keep up your strength for Dorothy's sake."

Thomason didn't move from the chair when Alafair gestured for Martha and the doctor to follow her back into the kitchen, past Lewis' shrouded form and his vigilant paramour at the table.

Nola was still on the floor and still covered with the quilt that Alafair had thrown over her, but the body had been decently laid out and Alafair could see the outline of Nola's arms crossed over her heart.

Alafair drew the little group together in the corner of the kitchen, far as possible from Nola's body, as though their discussion might disturb her. "Doctor Carney," she said, "what do you make of this?"

Carney's brown eyes widened. "What do you mean, Mrs. Tucker?"

"Don't you think this looks odd, they way these folks died? I mean, they died so fast. Right where they stood, it looks like. And Miz Thomason didn't have even the beginnings of flu when I last spoke to her."

"When was that?" Carney said.

"Last night."

Martha took it upon herself to answer. "It sometimes happens fast like that, Ma."

But Alafair was looking at Carney's eyes, the only feature she could see above his mask. When she had said the word "odd," Carney's eyes had narrowed and now he was gazing off to his right. Something didn't sit well with him, either.

"Doctor Carney?"

He looked at her. "I have seen this influenza kill people all kinds of ways, Mrs. Tucker. Not everyone who dies quickly exhibits cyanosis. That is, they do not all turn blue like Emmanuel Clover did."

"Lewis has been sick with the grippe for days, Mama," Martha said. "When his flu turned virulent, it may easily have infected his mother."

"Not Dorothy. Not yet, at least. When I found her, she was out of her mind with shock but she doesn't have a lick of fever. Nola and Lewis…" She took breath. "Doctor, it looks to me like they may have died of something other than the flu."

Martha looked at Doctor Carney, and Doctor Carney looked at Martha, who then looked back at her mother. The lower portion of her face may have been covered with a mask, but Alafair could plainly see the skepticism in her dark eyes. Alafair wished that Shaw had come with her. She had a reputation in the family for having "feelings" about things when no one else did. At least Shaw usually gave her the benefit of the doubt.

"I seriously doubt it, ma'am," Carney said. She had expected Carney to dismiss her out of hand, even laugh at her, but his tone was not as condescending as she had feared.

"Mother—" Martha began, but Alafair cut her off.

"Doctor, I've nursed just about every disease there is. I've set bones and sewed wounds and dug out bullets and nails and thorns. I've doctored animal bites and stings and burns. And I've seen what poison looks like in both man and animal."

"You think Miz Thomason and her children were poisoned?" Martha was shocked at the idea.

"It is not an impossibility," Carney said. "Since I have been here in Boynton I have seen more ridiculous and useless home remedies than I ever imagined could exist. If Mrs. Thomason tried to stave off the grippe by giving her children handfuls of aspirin or some mixture containing turpentine she could very well have poisoned herself and her family."

Alafair didn't like the implication. "You think Nola may have poisoned herself and her own children?"

"Not on purpose, of course. Mrs. Tucker, did you say the Thomason girl was showing no flulike symptoms?"

"No fever, but she won't answer when you talk to her. I saw Nola's body. It just doesn't look right. I was already thinking poison by the time I found Dorothy, all pale and panting and bloody, so I made her throw up."

"I need to see the girl. Did she tell you that her mother had been making her take anything unusual?" Carney threw the question at her over his shoulder as he strode toward the front door as fast as his stiff leg would allow him.

Alafair followed close on his heels. "She hasn't said boo, Doctor."

Homer Thomason jumped up when Carney and his entourage swept through the parlor but no one spared him a glance. He did not follow.

◇◇◇

Carney tried to shoo everyone but Martha out of the bedroom while he examined Dorothy, but Alafair wouldn't hear of it, not after all the child had been through. Alice wanted to stay, as well, but Forsythia Lily would not be deprived of her presence so the two of them removed themselves to the parlor. Alafair held Dorothy's hand while the strange man in a mask poked on her and asked her questions.

"Has you mother been giving you aspirin? Have you been taking lots of medicine? Hot tea? What was the last thing you had to eat? When? Does your tummy hurt? Mrs. Tucker said there was blood on your gown. Have you been bleeding?"

Carney fired off his questions while he listened to Dorothy's chest, took her temperature, prodded her belly, and looked into her eyes and ears and down her throat. He hardly seemed to notice that Dorothy never said a word in response, simply allowed him to manipulate her like a rag doll.

Carney folded his stethoscope and dropped it into his bag. "Well, you are right, Mrs. Tucker. She does not have a fever and she does not exhibit symptoms of the grippe." He spoke to Alafair as though Dorothy wasn't there. "I expect that if the problem is something that the family ingested, the child did not partake of enough to cause permanent harm."

Alafair was aware that Dorothy was listening. "Let's talk about this outside."

◇◇◇

Martha stayed in the bedroom with her patient, but Shaw, Walter, and Alice gathered around as soon as Carney and Alafair came into the parlor.

Shaw waited until Carney was seated before he said, "You do think that the Thomasons were poisoned, Doc?"

Carney turned in his chair to address the older man, and Alafair suddenly found herself peripheral to the conversation.

"I do not know, Mr. Tucker. As I was telling your wife, this strain of the influenza manifests differently in different people. But it could be that Mrs. Thomason dosed her family and herself with something lethal. I do have to leave now, since there are still many ill people in town who need my attention. But I did take some samples from the bodies before I left the Thomason house and Mrs. Tucker has given me Dorothy's soiled gown to test. Perhaps if I have time and Mr. Thomason approves, I will be able to do a more thorough examination of the deceased. I brought a microscope with me from Norman, but I need certain chemicals before I can test for poison. Do you suppose that any of the doctors who normally practice in town would have such a thing in their surgeries?"

"Doctor Addison keeps a small laboratory," Shaw told him.

"Good. I will ask Mrs. Addison if I may have access. Now, I must be off, but I will be back to check on the children this evening, unless an emergency arises."

"Is there anything in particular we should do for Dorothy?" Alafair asked.

"At this point she only needs good care, and that I believe you can well provide. Please ask Mrs. McCoy to stop in next door to see if Mr. Thomason or Miss Reed needs anything. Tell her I will meet her back at the schoolhouse tonight. Mrs. Tucker, will you show me out?"

Alafair walked Carney to the front door, where he paused and removed his surgical mask. Alafair blinked at him. She had grown so accustomed to the mask that she had practically forgotten that there was more to his face than eyes. He was a nice-looking young man, or he would have been without the stern expression. "Mrs. Tucker, you should not make someone vomit before you know what he has swallowed. What if Dorothy had swallowed lye or gasoline? You could have made things worse."

Alafair drew back, affronted. "Doctor Carney, I didn't have time to study on it. I had no desire to watch the young'un die right then and there. I figured I'd take my chances."

"Well, luckily, whatever killed her family spared her, whether it was poisoning or influenza. Believe me, madam, scrupulous cleanliness will be much more efficacious and helpful to your patients than these the herbal remedies you learned at your old granny's knee. They may make you feel less helpless in the face of suffering, but most of the time, potions and teas made out of leaves and branch water do more harm than good. You seem to have things in hand. Since Mrs. McCoy is coming by here every day, I will ask her to keep me apprised of your situation.

If you need me, if anyone else becomes ill or takes a turn for the worse, please telephone the Red Cross nurses at the school and I will come as soon as I can." Carney placed his fedora on his head. "By the way, if you do not mind, please remove the broom that has fallen across the threshold. I almost tripped over it when I entered the house."

Don't get your tail up, Alafair warned herself. She said, "Thank you for coming by, Doctor." She closed the door behind him and turned to see Shaw standing behind her, his arms folded across his chest, watching her with an irritatingly amused look on his face.

Chapter Twelve

How Alafair Gave Doctor Carney the Benefit of the Doubt

As soon as Shaw was satisfied that he could do no more, he left for home. Walter and Alice had both exhausted their strength and gone back to bed. Martha helped Alafair scrub down the house with lye water and carbolic soap, then Alafair persuaded her to sit down for a cup of ginger tea before she left to finish rounds.

Martha closed her eyes and breathed in the fragrant aroma of tea. "I'm glad to see Alice and Walter were able to get out of bed for a while."

"They're both doing better. Especially since the girls are here. It makes Alice feel better to have somebody to fuss over who is sicker than she is. She's pining for Linda, and I'm pining for Grace and Blanche and Fronie and all the rest of them. I can't wait to go home."

"Doctor Carney says if folks don't want to relapse, they should rest for three weeks even after they feel well. Sometimes after a week or so they feel so much better that they think they're over it, then the grippe comes roaring back with a vengeance and they die of pneumonia."

"I think that the worst is over for Alice and Walter. Though after what you just told me I'm going to make sure they stay in bed a while longer."

"I hope the worst is over, too, Ma. I only have five Red Cross volunteers left. All the others either took sick themselves or are tending their own folks or are too scared to show up. What about you, Mama? Are you still feeling all right? Are you taking care of yourself?"

"Yes, honey, I'm taking care of myself and I hope you are too. Are you…?"

Martha anticipated the question. "Yes, Mother, I am. I've scrubbed so much that I hardly have any skin left. And never mind garlic honey. I have taken to eating garlic and onion raw. Everything I eat or drink tastes like garlic. I wear a mask all the time, but nowadays it's to more protect my patients from my breath than to keep me from getting the flu."

Alafair chuckled. "You're joshing, sweetheart, but I hope you really are doing that."

Martha's teasing tone faded. "I really am. Doctor Carney says the garlic is useless, but after what I've seen, I'm doing everything in the world to keep that plague away from me."

"Doctor Carney doesn't know everything." Or much of anything, she thought. "You listen to your mother and trust the old ways as well as the modern scientific learning. These old treatments wouldn't have been passed down all these years if they didn't work."

"I agree with you, Ma, but unless I'm hankering for a lecture I keep my opinions to myself when Doctor Carney is around. Still, don't be too hard on him. He really can help folks with the coughing fits and body aches. And I swear I saw him bring a woman back from the edge of death with a shot of a heart stimulant. He has some good treatments in that bag of his." She stood up. "I have to go."

After Martha left, Alafair ate a bowl of leftover chicken and dumplings, standing up over the kitchen sink for fear that if she sat down at the table she would fall asleep.

◇◇◇

It was well after dark when Carney knocked on the door and woke Alafair from her doze on the cot in the parlor. She had fallen onto the bed fully dressed, so she only had to stagger up, turn on a table lamp, pick up the broom, and lean it against the wall before she let him in.

"I have just come by before going back to the hotel to ask if there have been any changes in anyone's condition here. How is young Dorothy?"

"I looked in on everyone about an hour ago and they were all sleeping well."

"How about the other child? Does she still have any fever?"

"Not since yesterday. Nor my daughter or son-in-law, either."

"Would you like for me to look at them?"

"I think it's better they sleep, Doctor."

Carney put his hat back on. "You are probably right. Well, I will say good night then."

"Doctor, have you come to any conclusion about what happened to Miz Thomason and her son?"

"I have not had a moment to look into it, Mrs. Tucker. I know that Mr. Lee has removed the bodies from next door and taken them to his mortuary at my request."

Alafair was surprised. She hadn't noticed when the undertaker's wagon had come to fetch them. Why had Thomason not come by to fetch Dorothy?

Carney said, "I have been thinking about the scene this morning, though. From the condition of the bodies, I am fairly confident that Lewis Hulce died from complications of influenza. As for Mrs. Thomason, I cannot say. I spoke to Mr. Thomason and he will not allow me to do a postmortem examination on his wife, but he told me I could do one on his stepson." Homer Thomason had actually told Carney not to touch his wife, but he didn't care if the doctor cut up Lewis into little pieces. Carney kept that to himself. "Mr. Thomason gave me permission to do some tests on Mrs. Thomason's bodily fluids, though. With so many fatalities in the community, Mr. Lee the undertaker has resorted to taking the deceased directly to the graveyard and interring the bodies immediately. Because of the circumstances surrounded these deaths, Mr. Lee has agreed not to remove the body of Mrs. Thomason's son for another day or so. I hope to do the examination at the funeral home first thing tomorrow, if I have the time."

"Then you will be able to tell what killed him?"

"Possibly. However it may take several days before I can tell from the tests if they died of disease or poisoning or some other cause."

Alafair made a quick decision. "Have you had supper, Doctor Carney?" Martha's comments about the young doctor had softened her initial impression of him.

"Not yet. I am hoping the café downtown is still open."

"I think Miz Burrows will have closed up by now. I have soup on the warmer. Come into the kitchen and I'll fix you up a bowl with a hunk of cornbread and butter. Maybe a cup of tea."

Carney hesitated before answering. His mildly surprised expression betrayed the fact that he was not used to being invited to stay around. Alafair figured that most of his patients were glad to see him leave. "If it is not too much trouble," he said.

"None at all." She escorted him through the darkened dining room and into the kitchen, where she seated him at the table and ladled up a bowlful of chicken vegetable soup. "Tell me, Doctor, are you not worried about getting sick yourself? I worry about Martha a lot."

He sniffed at the simmering concoction in his bowl with interest. "It is a possibility," he admitted. "We try to maintain the best hygiene we can. I am reasonably confident about myself, though. I have been vaccinated."

Alafair turned away from the stove to look at him. "Have they finally come up with a vaccination for this horrible disease?"

"No, this is my own vaccine. I inoculated myself with it before I left Norman. It has not been tested in a laboratory or approved by the U.S. Health Services, however, so I cannot in good conscious offer it to my patients. Unless there is no other hope for them." He sipped a spoonful of broth. "What kind of soup is this, may I ask?"

"Potatoes and carrots in chicken broth."

"I think there is more to this broth than chicken."

It was an innocuous statement, but his accusatory manner didn't help her resolve to be polite. "I simmered onion and some herbs and garlic cloves in the broth." She tried to keep her tone pleasant.

"Garlic. I thought I recognized the odor. Mrs. McCoy told me you swear by it. The Italians in Brooklyn use a lot of garlic in their cooking, and in their folk medicine, too. But I do not come across much of that out here in the West. That is a lot of garlic! Is this some sort of kitchen medicine?"

"I raise the garlic myself. One of my sisters lives in Arizona and I learned about using garlic to stave off colds and such when I was visiting there a couple of years ago."

Carney made a non-committal noise and took another spoonful. "Mrs. McCoy told me that you have a good supply of carbolic soap. Lye soap, too? That is good. Disinfectants are infinitely more helpful to the nurse in dealing with illness and its attendant distasteful tasks than herbs and roots."

Distasteful? Did he not understand the feeling of compassion that wells up when someone needs your help, or of what an honor it is to be of service, to help someone maintain his dignity, to show by action just how much you care for her? Alafair was insulted. She was not used to having her skills denigrated. She was glad that he had not asked about the enormous ceramic jug on the counter. It contained the herbal remedy for lung ailments that Mrs. Carrizal had taught her to make. It looked and tasted a bit like pond scum, but as far as she was concerned, it was a miracle cure and she was not going to hear any differently from some snot-nosed child. You had better hope you never get sick, she thought, and chastised herself at her own lack of charity. She should pity Carney for not knowing what is really important.

Alafair was not in the mood to explain herself. She said nothing to him. It did no good to annoy someone who could possibly be of help to you. Besides, she had enough experience to tell that he would not take it well if contradicted. She would take care of her charges in her own way and let him think whatever he wanted.

Chapter Thirteen

How Sophronia Made Her Escape

Mary Lucas' haven for quarantined children was a happy, noisy madhouse. Plump, cheerful, easy-going Mary was hardly the taskmaster that Alafair was. But she managed to keep everyone clean and fed, and enjoyed herself mightily while doing it. Of course, trying to keep an eye on four whirlwinds under the age of four required a concentrated team effort. Blanche and Sophronia, at thirteen and twelve, were Mary's designated lieutenants, but eight-year-old Chase Kemp and six-year-old Grace Tucker had been drafted into the toddler-wrangling army as well. Blanche and Grace were wonderful with the three little granddaughters. Grace loved to read to Zeltha and the babies, and Blanche was a talented gardener, a practiced diaper-changer, and competent in the kitchen as well. Chase took charge of Tucker Day, since they were the only boys in this gaggle of females. Chase was a willing caretaker, but he had carved out quite a task for himself. Tuck had more energy than a puppy and a wickedly impish sense of humor for a two-year-old.

That left Sophronia. Alafair had trained her girls in all the housewifely tasks from the time they were old enough to hold a spoon and a broom, so Sophronia was as able a cook, maid, gardener, and farmhand as any girl her age. That didn't mean she liked it. The little children were fun, up to a point. But the frenetic pace and the constant noise wore thin after a while. Sophronia wanted to be outside. She wanted to spend her time with animals, and in the fields and the woods. To pick apples from the trees, not peel them. She wanted to read a good book while propped against a tree next to a stream.

She volunteered to feed and care for the dogs and the chickens and Mary's one sweet milk cow. The children were confined to the large yard around Mary's house, so the horses' stables and the sties that housed Kurt's pigs were off-limits. Sophronia didn't mind about the pigs so much, though it was fun to slop them as long as you didn't fall into the pen while you were doing it. You could end up as pig dinner that way. No, Sophronia didn't mind about the pigs, but it broke her heart when she was told to stay away from the horses.

She could hardly make it through the day without her Sweet Honey Baby. "Can't I take him with me to Mary's, Daddy?" she had begged.

"No, darlin'," he had replied. "He'd be lonesome without his herd."

Sophronia knew that wasn't the reason. Sweet Honey Baby was a handsome gelding with a white mane and tail and a bad reputation. With Sophronia he had never been anything but gentle and calm, but if he took against you, he could do some serious damage. Sweet Honey Baby had a long rap sheet and Shaw was unwilling to leave him in close proximity to the youngsters for any length of time.

She would be glad when the war and this disgusting epidemic were over and everything could get back to normal. She missed her brothers. She missed going to school and visiting her friends. She wanted to be able to roam, like a normal person. She missed her animals. She missed her mother.

Sophronia had been the youngest child in her family for six and a half years before Grace came along. Grace was an easy-going child and a good playmate. Grace's advent into Sophronia's life had not torn a hole in the fabric of existence like the vortex of infant energy she was now enduring. The nieces and nephew may have been amusing in small doses, but this continual mayhem was liable to drive her mad.

Judy Lucas got into the bag of dried apples and shared them with her cousins Linda and Tuck. All three stuffed themselves and ended up with a rollicking case of diarrhea, which necessitated a couple of extra of loads of wash, three much-resented doses of blackberry syrup and nettle leaf tea, and a squirmy, stinky, bath that took all of the Tucker sisters to administer. Mary and Blanche thought it was all so funny. Sophronia would have found it more enjoyable to try and wash cats.

Mary and her helpers had just wrestled the little ones into bed when they heard Shaw yelling at the house. It had become routine for him to walk over from the farm before supper to check up on them and to report on what was going on in town. He stood outside the fence while Mary and the older children came out to talk to him across the gate.

There was bad news to report tonight. Shaw put it off as long as he could. He found it hard to concentrate as the children related the tale of the dried apples with a combination of delight and disgust and much laughter.

Had Blanche aged a year in only three days? She looked serious and purposeful, disturbingly like a grown woman, graceful and willowy. Grace was growing leggy, her eyes so dark that it was hard for an observer to tell where iris ended and pupil began. Chase jumped up and down while he told his uncle a particularly hilarious piece of the story. As he listened, Shaw's arms began to ache with the desire to hug his happy, healthy crew.

Mary finally asked, "How is Mama doing?"

Shaw straightened. "She's all right. So are Martha and Ruth. Alice and Walter are better. Children, y'all go on into the house now while I talk business with Mary for a spell."

This was not an unusual occurrence. Shaw and Phoebe's husband, John Lee, were overseeing the Lucas farm while Mary maintained quarantine. But it was still her farm and she insisted on a business briefing every evening.

"Did any mail come today?" Blanche asked.

"Not today. Now, go on in, Blanche. Sophronia. Chase, be good, now. Good night, Grace, baby." The children had already disappeared inside when it occurred to Shaw that his freckle-faced, dimpled Sophronia had not said a word the entire time he had been here.

As soon as they closed the front door behind them, Sophronia pulled the other youngsters into a circle. "Something's up," she whispered. "Something has happened that Daddy don't want us to know."

Blanche gave her a look of disdain mixed with curiosity. "What makes you think that?"

"I can tell that something's eating on him. Question is, what's wrong with you that you didn't notice? Besides, he looked at me extra long. He called me Sophronia. Daddy never calls me by my whole name."

Blanche was affronted by the insult, but she had to admit that the name thing was unusual. "Surely Mary will tell us what it is when she comes in."

"Oh, pfft! Not if Daddy don't want her to. It must be something bad if he doesn't want us to hear it. Now, how are we going to find out what it is?"

Blanche bit her lip and pondered for a moment. "It's likely nothing." She said it with conviction, then turned to Chase. "You think you can go out the back door and sneak around the side of the house close enough to hear what Daddy and Mary are saying?"

Chase didn't have to be asked twice. While the boy crept around the house to spy on his elders, the girls created a distraction by standing side by side with their noses pressed against the front window, blatantly watching Mary and Shaw talk. Mary had her back to them, but they could see Shaw glance up at them every once in a while, none too pleased to have an audience. The adults spoke over the gate for a minute, as quietly as they could while keeping a distance from one another, then Mary's hands went to her cheeks in a gesture of distress. Sophronia poked Blanche in the ribs. "See, I told you."

Sophronia scraped the leftovers into the day's scrap bucket and took it outside to dump into an old washpan for the dogs. She sat down on the back porch step and watched the two hounds dig in, feeling as tired as if she had spent the entire day fence-mending or chopping cotton or wrangling mules.

She had been right about Mary's reluctance to tell them everything that Shaw had told her. She would only say that a lot of people in town were sick and it was a bad situation.

Fortunately, Chase Kemp turned out to be a talented spy. He barely made it back into the house before Mary could catch him, so Sophronia and her sisters had had to wait until Mary was occupied in another room before he was able to relate what he had overheard.

Dorothy Thomason's mother and brother were dead.

Maybe it was influenza that had killed them, but it might have been poison. Only Dorothy and her dad were still alive. Alafair had gone over and found them all, and now Dorothy was staying at Alice's house until her dad could figure out what to do next.

Poor Dorothy, my poor friend, Sophronia thought. If only I could help her somehow.

She looked up at the sky. It was seven o'clock and the sun was barely down. She sniffed. Ever since Congress had passed the daylight savings bill back in April it seemed like the day never ended.

Sophronia stood up from the step and walked to the wire gate in the fence that surrounded the yard, the border beyond which the children were not to cross. She hesitated, but only long enough to glance back toward the house. Bacon and Big

Fella were too engrossed in their supper to pay attention to her. She lifted the latch and walked out of the yard toward freedom.

She didn't know how long it would be before someone noticed her absence, but she knew she had no time to waste.

Sophronia ran the quarter of a mile from Mary's house to her own. Since the path was well trodden and there was still enough light in the sky to see where she was going, she reached the clearing around the barnyard in about ten minutes. She stopped at the edge of the woods and squatted down to survey the perimeter before advancing on her objective. Smoke was rising from the stovepipe on the roof of the house, and the kitchen window was aglow with lamplight. Shaw, John Lee, and Phoebe were either still at supper, or nearly done. Shaw and John Lee would sit around the table for a bit after supper, then one or the other of them would make his way out to the barn before bedtime to see that the animals and all the outbuildings were secure for the night.

Sophronia ran across the barnyard in a crouch and slipped into the barn by the side door. She stood still for a few moments, dismayed. It was still twilight outdoors, but since the barn was already closed up, it was dark as the insides of a cow in there. She didn't want to fumble around in the gloom and risk knocking something over or falling down and making enough noise to alert Shaw's dogs. She left the outside door open, but she had no choice but to waste precious moments standing in quivering anticipation of discovery until she got her night vision.

When she began to make out shapes, she took a breath and began to feel her way forward. Shaw Tucker raised horses and mules for a living, but most of his animals were either kept in the fields, corralled, or housed in the long stable up the hill north of the house. The barn was mostly for storing feed and equipment, but Shaw did keep the milk cow and a few of the family's riding horses in the half-dozen stalls at the back of the barn.

Since he was somewhat antisocial toward his own kind, Sweet Honey Baby's place was at the far end, next to a stall that was being used for storage. The animals moved restlessly when they became aware of a human presence. Sophronia began to make low, soothing noises. They recognized her voice and quieted. She could tell who was who by the way each blew a breath or gave a snort. Marigold the cow, then Shaw's saddle horse, Hannah, and John Lee's Nugget. Gee Dub's horse, Penny, was there, too, even though she didn't need to be. Sophronia guessed that Shaw was just sentimental about her. The gentle nag that all the children had learned to ride on, Pork Chop, was next, and then the empty stall where Mama's Missy usually resided.

She crept up to the end stall to find Sweet Honey Baby waiting for her, his big head hanging over the gate. He blew a greeting and she blew one back before laying her forehead on his, so glad to see him that she had to hold back tears. She could have stood there for hours, but time was wasting. She led the horse out of the stall and fumbled her way to the saddle rack. Getting him bridled up was easy enough, but the saddle was a problem for her. She knew how to saddle a horse, but she was a small girl and the saddle was almost too heavy for her to heft onto a tall mount like Sweet Honey Baby. She usually had her father or one of her taller siblings help her. She lugged the saddle over and pulled a stepstool up to the horse's side. Fear of getting caught gave her a rush of adrenaline, and it only took her a couple of tries before the saddle landed squarely on the horse's back. She cinched it tight around his belly and shortened the stirrups before climbing up a couple of slats in the stall gate and hoisting herself onto his back.

She guided the horse toward the open side door of the barn and slipped out into the yard. Sweet Honey Baby was eager to stretch his legs, but Sophronia kept a tight hold on the reins until they were well away from the house. She didn't try to head directly toward the section line road. She would have to pass the house that way. Instead she headed across the fallow field to the east, past the temporarily abandoned Day farmhouse, and set out for Boynton.

Sophronia had ridden Sweet Honey Baby all the way to town and was just turning onto Second Street toward Alice's house before it dawned on her what she had done. Her parents had expressly forbidden her from leaving the safety of Mary's farm for fear that she would fall ill with a horrible, life-threatening disease. She wasn't overly concerned about catching the flu. She was twelve years old and immortal. But she was very concerned about how her mother was going to react when she rode up to Alice's front door.

Her mama seldom had cause to punish her children for any but minor infractions, but what Sophronia had done was hardly minor. And what about her daddy? By now someone would have gone out to secure the barn and discovered that Sweet Honey Baby was gone. Her daddy would immediately know who had taken the horse, so he would ride over to Mary's and find out that Sophronia was missing as well. He was going to be madder than a wet hen. She had seen her father's anger before. It was not a sight she wished to see again, especially if it was directed at her.

She reined in the middle of Second Street, a few doors down from Alice and Walter's house, and sat there on Sweet Honey Baby's back for a few minutes, pondering her options.

She briefly considered turning around and going back to the Lucas farm. She probably had not yet been exposed to anything harmful. She'd get an earful from Mary, and would more than likely have to clean the outhouse for a month, but nothing more serious than that.

On the other hand, Dorothy had lost her mother and her only sibling. Sophronia's best friend needed her. It didn't matter that there was nothing she could do to make it better. She could be present. Besides, maybe Mama would be glad to see her. She could be a great help to Mama, running errands and bringing in supplies and doing yard work.

But she knew Mama was not going to be glad to see her. Mama was going to be angry that she had disobeyed, but mostly she would be scared that Sophronia had put herself in danger.

The idea of two or three more weeks imprisoned in that house and narrow yard with a bunch of poopy, screaming little monkeys, of being unable to lie on the grass in the meadow while Sweet Honey Baby grazed beside her… unable to run into the woods with Bacon or old Charlie Dog and look for black walnuts and swing on wild grapevines.

The idea that Dorothy would have to cry all alone…

No, it was not to be borne.

She would take her licking, if that's what it came to. She dug her heels into Sweet Honey Baby's flank and crossed her own river of no return.

Chapter Fourteen

How Sophronia Threw a Wrench in Alafair's Carefully Laid Plans

Martha pushed her empty soup bowl away. "Have you seen the *Index* today, Mama?"

"No, Alice's paperboy hasn't come by for days. He's likely sick. Why? Is the war going badly?"

"No, just the opposite. It looks like the Hindenburg line is crumbling. Mr. Kirby thinks Germany can't last much longer."

"Oh, that's the best news I've heard in a while!"

"The paper also said that the suffrage amendment failed to pass the Senate by two votes."

Alafair knew the Constitutional amendment granting the vote to women was a cause dear to Martha's heart. "I'm sorry, honey. But they knew it was going to be close, didn't they?"

"Yes. But I was hoping against hope. The reasons they come up with to not pass it are so stupid. Some Suffragette in Montana spit on the flag so all Suffragettes are anti-American?"

"Martha, I doubt if anybody really believes that. I think they'll get back to it and it'll pass when the war is over."

"It'll be something else after the war. Just wait and see. Ma, why do men think they need to control women? What do they think we're going to do? Sneak out of bed in the middle of the night and murder them all? It's men who are dangerous, to my observation. Look at this horrible war. If women ran the world there wouldn't be any war."

Alafair gave Martha a speculative glance before she replied. Martha had been asking some version of this same question since she was a little girl. Alafair was beginning to wonder what sort of answer Martha wanted from her. It didn't satisfy her when her mother told her to go about her business and ignore any slights and insults that some misguided member of the male race inflicted on her. Even though Martha was happily married to a man who, as far as Alafair knew, treated her as an equal, she had been growing increasingly discontent with her lot over the past few years. The fact that the suffrage movement had stalled seemed to have added a layer of cynicism to Martha's view of the world. "Not all men are like that, sugar."

Martha sighed. "Oh, I know it. Don't listen to me. I'm just in a horn-tossing mood." Her eyes welled and a tear spilled down her cheek. "I miss Streeter. He's always on my side."

Alafair stood to give her a hug. There was not much else she could do. "You need to go home and get some sleep, sugar. Things will look better in the…" She paused and cocked an ear toward the parlor. "Did you hear that?"

"Hear what?"

"Somebody is on the front porch. Law, I hope one of the girls hasn't taken a notion to get up and take a stroll." She hurried into the parlor with Martha on her heels. A quick check found both the Kelleys and the orphan girls in their beds. Alafair was heading for the front door when it opened and Sophronia stepped in.

The three of them stopped in their tracks and spent a long moment gaping at one another. The sight of her second-youngest appearing in Alice's parlor was so unexpected that at first Alafair could not believe the evidence of her own eyes. Not until Martha cried, "Fronie, what in the world?"

Alafair's heart leaped and she raised a hand to her throat. "What's wrong? Who died?"

Sophronia's eyes widened. It had not occurred to her that her mama would think she had come to deliver bad news. "Nobody, Ma. I snuck off and rode into town because I heard what happened to Dorothy. I want to help my friend. I want to stay with you."

Relief weakened Alafair's knees, but her relief was immediately overwhelmed by anger. She rushed forward and grabbed Sophronia's arm hard enough to leave a bruise. "Sophronia Tucker, what do you mean by scaring the dickens out of me? Mary's probably beside herself wondering where you've got to. And on top of it you've likely exposed yourself to the grippe. I declare! I ought to snatch you bald-headed."

Sophronia had been expecting a cold welcome, but her mother's reaction was over-the-top. She emitted an alarmed squeak as Alafair shook her.

Martha came to the rescue by squeezing herself between her furious mother and her terrified sister. "Now, Ma, now, Ma, calm down. It's not that bad."

"Not that bad? What if she gets sick? Fronie, what if you take the flu back to the children?"

"Don't make me go back," Sophronia wailed. "I want to help Dorothy!"

Martha extricated Sophronia from Alafair's grasp. "Ma, maybe she doesn't have to go back to Mary's. I'll bet you that Daddy will be here looking for her pretty quick. Maybe she can go back with him and stay at the house with Phoebe. Nobody is sick there yet."

Alafair drew a breath to deliver a stinging response, but she was interrupted by Alice's feeble call from the bedroom, wondering what was going on. Alalfair stuck a forefinger in Sophronia's face. "I'll deal with you directly."

Once Alafair had stomped off, Martha plopped down in an armchair and gave an incredulous laugh. She hadn't seen her mother in such a state in…well, she couldn't remember when. "Fronie, you are dumb as a bag of hair."

"Thanks for saving my life." Sophronia sounded shaky.

"Don't thank me yet, Fronie. I think you've just had a brief stay of execution."

Sophronia was already regretting her decision to make a break for it. Martha was right in guessing that Shaw would show up that evening. Sophronia had thought her mother's reaction was frightening, but her father's display of fury was truly spectacular. He railed at her so long and so colorfully that even Alafair began to feel sorry for her. They wouldn't let her see Dorothy. Instead she was sent off to Alice's sewing room to reflect on her sins while her parents decided her fate.

She didn't stay there long. She crept back into the dark kitchen and pressed her ear against the swinging door so she could overhear the deliberations. Fortunately for her, Martha was still there and was attempting to mitigate her sentence.

At first it sounded like Shaw intended to take her back out to the farm with him. This was not Sophronia's first choice, but she figured it was better than being forced to go back to Mary's. At least if she were at home, she would be able to have some space to roam and would not be separated from her horse and the other animals. But her parents' thoughts on what to do with their disobedient child changed as they considered their options.

Alafair's tone was mild when she said, "I've been thinking on it, Shaw. If Fronie was going to get exposed to the flu, it's done already. All my patients are on the mend, it seems. I can't feel fever in any of them, so I'm thinking they are not infectious anymore. And besides, after the shock that poor Dorothy has had, having Fronie around might just help her get through the next few days, at least until her daddy shows up to take her away. Maybe Fronie ought to stay here for a bit and help me out. My preventives have worked up to now on me and Martha. Neither of us has got sick yet. I expect they will keep Fronie healthy, too."

"Well, now, you do surprise me, honey. After what she did, running off like that, we can't let her think she can get away with disobeying us."

"I don't intend to let her get away with anything, Shaw. There will be plenty of time to punish her. And it won't be no picnic around here. Besides, I halfway blame that horse for her running off. Sweet Honey Baby brings out the barbarian in our young'uns."

Shaw snorted. "It ain't the horse. Seems like our younger children are less saddle-broke than the older ones were."

Martha took the opportunity to chime in. "Y'all are just easier-going than you used to be."

"To hear you tell it, we are," Alafair said with a laugh. "But you've just got a rosy memory. You older ones weren't exactly angels."

"Maybe." Shaw sounded skeptical. "Still, I'd think Fronie would be more trouble than help to you."

Alafair's eyebrows lifted. "Why, that ain't so. All my girls are a big help to me."

Shaw reached across the table and took Alafair's hand, amused, but mostly touched by her maternal loyalty. "If you want her to stay, it's all right with me. But I'm going to put the fear of God into her before I go."

When the talking stopped, Sophronia bolted back into her cell. Her parents' foul temper had ebbed by the time they made their way back to inform her of their decision. Instead, they were both solemn and sad, which made Sophronia feel worse than the anger had. Alafair stood in the door, and Shaw sat down and drew Sophronia to his side.

She was twelve, and in her opinion was far too old to be spoken to like she was a little girl. Under the circumstances she knew better than to protest.

He told her that she could stay because it might be good for Dorothy to have a friend right now, and maybe she could cheer up Forsythia Lily, as well. But Shaw was taking Sweet Honey Baby back to the farm with him tonight. Her behavior would determine whether she was to be allowed to continue taking care of the horse hereafter. If she stayed here, she would be required to do any chore her mother required—mopping, washing, scrubbing, digging, chicken-plucking, or any other tedious task that presented itself. She was not to step foot off the property, nor speak a contrary word to her mother. In fact, after this rash act, it would be a long time before she managed to regain her parents' trust.

It could have been much worse. Sophronia was sorry that she was being deprived of Sweet Honey Baby, but she was reasonably certain that she could worm her way back into the folks' good graces before losing permanent custody of him. She didn't mind working hard, and she was overjoyed that she was to be allowed to see Dorothy. And she did not have to go back to the claustrophobic zoo that Mary's house had become. She promised on a ten-foot stack of Bibles that she would behave like an angel and never again cause her beleaguered mother and father another instant of worry.

Thus assured, Shaw and Martha both left for home. Alafair retrieved newly washed blankets and sheets from the laundry cupboard and made a pallet for Sophronia in the corner opposite the sewing machine. She brought in a basin of hot water and made Sophronia scrub herself all over with carbolic soap. Then she took the girl's clothes and gave her one of Walter's clean shirts to sleep in before forcing her to drink a cup of the strongest, most tongue-curling herbal tonic Sophronia had ever choked down.

After feeding her the rest of the beef noodle soup, Alafair tucked her wayward child into the makeshift bed. "Now, if Dorothy feels like it, maybe you can see her in the morning. Till then I don't want you to come out of this room. If you have to pee, use the night jar I brought you. Do not go into the bathroom. You cannot go into the front part of the house unless you get permission from me. You hear me?"

"Yes, ma'am."

Alafair brushed back Sophronia's hair, and Sophronia caught her mother's hand and pressed it to her heart. "Mama, I'm sorry I added to y'all's trouble and worry. I'm sorry to be such a bother."

Alafair pressed her lips together to keep from smiling. "You are an awful bother." Her tone was as stern as she could manage.

"Ma, do you still love me?"

"Oh, Fronie." Alafair had never quite known what to make of Sophronia. She was sunny and outgoing, with many friends of all ages and types, and yet she loved to find a hidden corner somewhere and lose herself in a book. She was athletic and free-spirited, loved animals and could communicate with them in a way that was downright spooky. She loved baseball and poetry, drawing and target shooting, wrestling and fishing, singing and quilting. Teaching and storytelling and foot-racing. Pretty clothes and overalls and bare feet. Alafair had never known anyone who was more eclectic in her tastes and habits. Jack of all trades and master of none, Shaw had called her. But Sophronia didn't care if she was master of none. As long as it was interesting and fun, she'd try anything, and was both a good loser and gracious winner.

The truth was that after spending several days tending to and worrying about Alice and Walter, and after the horrible events that had befallen the two little girls, seeing Sophronia, so energetic and lively, fresh and healthy, had cheered Alafair up considerably. Yes, even though she'd die a thousand deaths if that would keep any of her children from harm, she had to admit that Sophronia, her fey child with the unruly curls and the big dimple in her freckled cheek, could just possibly be her favorite.

"There is nothing you could do that would make me not love you, Fronie." She grasped Sophronia's face between her hands. "But don't you ever do anything so foolish again or I will have to give you back to the fairies."

Chapter Fifteen

How Sophronia Slid Around the Rules

The pallet bed was soft and fragrant and comfortable, but Sophronia couldn't fall asleep. She was in worse trouble than she had ever been in her life or was ever likely to be again. It was possible that Mama and Daddy would make her pay for it until doomsday, but all things considered, she was glad she had done it. Her daring escape had been exciting and not knowing what was going to happen next was an adventure.

She lay on her back and stared at the ceiling for a long time, planning what she would say to Dorothy. She didn't know Forsythia Lily, but she had heard that the little girl was about the same age as Grace, and she knew what Grace liked to do. Her reverie was interrupted by a noise. Sophronia sat up, listening. The sound had come from outside. For a long moment there was only silence, then she heard it again. It was a hollow, rhythmic sound, like a baby's rattle.

Sophronia rolled out of her blankets and looked out the little window into the backyard. She could see the hulking shape of the outbuilding that housed the garage and laundry room, and the smaller garden shed off to the left. She couldn't see the moon so she had no idea of the time. Nothing was moving about in the yard. She cracked open the door that led into the kitchen and peeked out. The house was totally dark. Her mother was probably asleep on the cot in the parlor.

There was the noise again. It did sound like someone shaking a rattle, or wooden sleigh bells like the ones her father put on the draft horses in the winter. Sophronia wondered if she should call out and wake her mother. She told herself that she didn't want to disturb Alafair's rest, but the truth was that she didn't want to call attention to herself. She knew she shouldn't leave the sewing room, no matter how curious she was to find out what the sound was.

Mama had told her not to go into the front part of the house, but the sewing room and kitchen were at the back of the house. The back door was right there. Besides, how much more trouble could she be in?

She considered putting on her shoes since the October night was chilly, but decided that stocking feet were quieter and stealth was more important that warm toes. She crept through the kitchen and slipped out the back door into the yard.

Sophronia could finally see that the moon was down. It was late. She walked into the middle of the yard and listened to the silence. The crisp air smelled of damp leaves. She took a deep breath and felt her shoulders relax.

Whatever the noise was, it was gone now. She knew she was pushing her luck, but before going back inside, she crept around to the side of the house and stood looking for a moment at the window into the back bedroom.

Her mother hadn't told her where Dorothy was sleeping, but she was reasonably certain that she would be in that room. Was the other little girl there, too? The window was too high for her to see into from the ground, but Sophronia was familiar enough with her sister's property to know that there was a small step ladder in the shed.

She still had to hoist herself up on the sill to be able to peer though the glass. At first she couldn't see anything in the darkened room, but she refused to admit defeat and pressed her nose to the window pane. Something weird and shapeless rose from the small cot in the corner.

Sophronia was only frightened for an instant before she recognized that the ghostly white figure was a child, wrapped in a quilt.

She tapped lightly on the window. "Dorothy, is that you?"

The ghost stood up and glided over to raise the window. A piping little voice from out of the dark said, "Who are you?"

Sophronia heaved herself up over the sill and dropped into the room. "I'm Dorothy's friend, Fronie, Forsythia Lily. I heard what happened to y'all and I want to come help y'all feel better." Sophronia could barely make out the still figure on the double bed next to the wall.

"Miz Tucker says we'll feel better by and by." Forsythia Lily sounded unconvinced. "Dorothy never says nothing or moves. I have to wait here until my grandma comes to get me."

Sophronia led the child by the hand back to her cot. "It's late now and I'm tired." Her voice was barely above a whisper. "I'm just going to sleep here in the bed with Dorothy. We can talk in the morning. Now go back to sleep." She waited until the little figure snuggled back down into the cot, then slid the window closed. She climbed into bed next to Dorothy without a word and reached out to grasp her hand. It was like grasping something inanimate, limp and cold. Dorothy was awake, Sophronia could see that. The big, dark eyes in the white face were looking right at her.

"I know I can't do anything to help," Sophronia murmured. "I can be here with you, Dorothy, so you're not alone. That's all."

Dorothy did not respond. She withdrew her hand and turned her face to the wall. Sophronia threw an arm over her shoulders.

It was barely light when Alafair was startled by the knocking at the front door. She was already awake and sitting on the side of the cot in the parlor, mostly dressed except for her shoes. Before anyone else in the house was disturbed, she hurried to open the door and found herself looking up at a man in his mid-thirties with cheerful blue eyes and a receding hairline. Slim Tucker, Scott's son and deputy, was as tall and lanky as his nickname suggested. "Slim, come on in. You're out and about early. Do you have some news about the Thomasons?"

Since she was speaking in a half-whisper, Slim answered in kind. "Not yet. I've just come from Dad's house. He's better, but he's still peaky. He wants to know everything that's going on. You know how he is."

"I do know. And how's your mother?"

Slim gave a "so-so" gesture. "How is little Dorothy doing?"

"She's still asleep. Last I looked on her, she still wasn't sick with the flu, if that's what you're asking."

"That's not what I'm asking."

No, Alafair hadn't thought so. "She's in bad shape, Slim. What do you expect? The poor child has lost her mother. Has lost almost all of her family. She doesn't talk to me at all, not even to say yes or no when I ask her a question. She's limp as a rag. She doesn't even cry." Alafair teared up. "It's just so sad, poor baby."

"Has Thomason come by?"

"No, he has not. I'm riled about that, too. Do you know where he is?"

"He's holed up in his office downtown. That's where he told me to let him know what the doc finds out about his wife's death. He's a wreck, Alafair. Probably just as well that Dorothy don't see him like that."

"I know he's grieving, but that child needs her daddy." She impatiently wiped her eyes with her fingers. "Don't just stand there, Slim. Sit down. You want a cup of coffee?"

Slim took a chair but passed on the coffee. "Does Dorothy know what happened?"

"I don't know. She knows her folks are dead."

Slim leaned back. "You know I'm going to have to question her, Cousin Alafair. She's the only one who was present when her family died. Dad says she's the only one who might be able to tell us what happened."

"I wish you didn't have to, Slim. Not right now, at least. Can't you wait until she speaks of her own accord?"

"I've got to try, Alafair."

Alafair spent a moment twisting her long braid into a lopsided bun at the back of her head before she said, "Well, come on, then. You can try, I reckon."

She led the deputy to the back bedroom and cracked open the door. Since Walter had moved back into his own bed and Forsythia Lily was occupying Linda's cot, Dorothy had the big bed to herself.

She wasn't alone now.

Alafair wasn't particularly surprised to see Dorothy and Sophronia snuggled up together in the bed. She did wonder how Sophronia had gotten past her, though. Alafair had spent a quarter-century listening for her children's movements in the night.

Banished again. Sophronia sat down cross-legged on her pallet and stewed for a few minutes. Something horrible had happened to her best friend and they wouldn't even let her hang around long enough to help. She was mad at herself for getting caught in Dorothy's room, but she was grateful that her mother didn't seem to be much disturbed by it. She had just woken the girls up and told Sophronia to go back into the sewing room and wait there while Cousin Slim talked to Dorothy. Once again it crossed her mind that she might have been better off to tough it out at Mary's house, but the thought didn't last long. If she were at Mary's, she'd still have to swallow the same potions a hundred times a day, and at least it was quiet here and she would be able to read and think. Besides, Sophronia figured she had a real purpose now that Dorothy was here and she could help take care of her.

Sophronia stood up and stretched. She could hear the adults talking in the parlor. It sounded like Alice and Walter were up. It would be a while yet before she would be allowed to go back into Dorothy's room. She cracked open the sewing room door and slipped out through the kitchen and into the backyard for a breath of fresh air.

It was a cool day, slightly overcast with a nippy breeze that made her wish she had a sweater or wrap. She didn't want to go back inside, so for a few minutes she ran around the yard, skipping and flapping her arms to get the blood circulating. Alice had a tiny chicken coop in the back corner, and Sophronia's gyrations caused the five hens to flap their wings in alarm. The noise amused her, but she really didn't want to torment the chickens, or worse, alert her mother that she was outside, so she took herself to the opposite corner of the yard and jumped up and down in place, chanting to the rhythm of her bouncing.

Miss Sally had a baby. She named him Tiny Tim.
She put him in the bathtub to see if he could swim.
He drank up all the water, he ate up all the soap.
He tried to eat the bathtub but it wouldn't go down his throat.
Miss Sally called the doctor, Miss Sally called the nurse,
Miss Sally called the lady with the alligator purse.
Mumps said the doctor. Measles said the nurse.
Influenza, said the lady with the alligator purse.
Miss Sally socked the doctor, Miss Sally kicked the nurse,
Miss Sally thanked the lady with the alligator purse.

The exercise did the trick. By the time Sophronia was out of breath, she was also warm enough not to notice the chill in the air. She wandered around the yard, wishing she knew what was going on with Dorothy. It was nice to be outside, but it wasn't nearly as amusing to play in Alice's yard without her friend.

She briefly considered climbing over the fence into the Thomasons' yard and creeping into the house to see what had happened, but dismissed the idea. She knew that people had died in that house and she had no desire to catch whatever they had died of. She didn't really believe that she was going to come down with the flu, but she was smart enough not to push her luck.

She followed the fence and made a circuit of the small yard. Sophronia circled around to peer into the yard of Alice's neighbor to the back. There was a narrow alley between the yards, just wide enough to drive an auto or buggy through. The property behind Alice's house was offset, stretching from the middle of the Kelley property to the middle of the Thomasons'. Curious, Sophronia stopped walking so she could get a good look. As many times as she had been to Alice's house, she had hardly ever cast a glance at this yard. She knew that someone named Mrs. Gale lived here, but she couldn't remember ever seeing the woman. Were there children? Was there sickness at that house, too? She wished she could see if Mrs. Gale's front door sported a red "X."

Mrs. Gale's yard was smaller than Alice's, without even room for a five-chicken coop. In fact, there was nothing to speak of in the yard at all. Just one scrawny, leafless, apple tree in the back corner.

Sophronia was about to turn away when a movement at a back window caught her eye. A face. An old man was looking out the window at her. He had probably been watching her gambol about like an idiot. The thought caused her to smile, and the old man smiled back.

The old fellow looked to be about a hundred years old. His face was pale and sunken, and his grin was toothless, but he looked friendly enough. She waved at him and a skeletal hand waved back. Her curiosity was aroused when after a brief struggle he managed to lift the window sash about six inches. She expected him to speak to her. Instead, he gestured for her to wait there. He disappeared for an instant, then reappeared with a half-grown yellow cat in his arms.

It looked to Sophronia like the old man whispered something in the cat's twitching ear before he tossed it out the window. The move startled her and she said, "Oh!" But the kitten landed on its feet and strolled across the yard toward her with its tail in the air, as though being heaved out of a window was nothing to get excited about. It crossed the alley and cleared the chain-link fence in a couple of bounds and dropped to the ground. To her delight, it began winding itself around her legs, purring loudly. She picked it up. She looked back up at the window, intending to say thank you. The window was still slightly open, but the old man had disappeared.

Alafair was impressed with the way Slim handled himself as he tried to question Dorothy. Slim had daughters of his own, so he was not inexperienced in the art of dealing with young girls.

Alafair had removed Forsythia Lily to the parlor and sat down on the side of the bed next to Dorothy while Slim spoke to her. Dorothy had given the strange man a curious once-over, but as soon as Slim broached the subject of her family, Dorothy turned away and wouldn't look at him. Slim persisted, gentle and cajoling, patient, and even funny, but it was no use. Dorothy buried her face in Alafair's side, and Slim sat back with a sigh. He gave Alafair a questioning look. She shook her head.

Slim leaned forward in his chair and propped his elbows on his knees. "Well, never you mind, Dorothy. You don't have to talk to me right now. I'll tell you what. As soon as you feel like it, you can tell Miz Tucker here about what happened, or Miz Kelley, or whoever you want. You just take your time."

After assuring Dorothy that she'd be back soon, Alafair followed Slim into the parlor.

"Thank you for not scaring her, Slim."

"I don't think there's any hurry, Alafair, things being as they are. If the doc finds out that her folks were poisoned by some remedy instead of died from the flu, there isn't much we can do about it now."

◇◇◇

As soon as Slim was out the door, Alafair went to the telephone table and lifted the receiver. No one else was on the line, so she clicked the cradle a few times and Kate Smith answered.

"Kate, can you ring the local Muskogee Tool and Die office? I need to speak to Homer Thomason, and Slim tells me he's camping out there."

"Sure enough, Alafair. Hang on."

There was a click and a pause, followed by tinny ringing. The ringing went on for a long time, and Alafair was about to give up when Thomason answered.

"This is the office of Muskogee Tool and Die." Thomason sounded tentative, as though he didn't quite believe it.

"Mr. Thomason, this is Alafair Tucker. Deputy Tucker told me where you are. Are you aiming to come be with your daughter any time soon? The child is hurting and could use her daddy."

There was a moment of silence on the other end. Alafair knew that her scolding tone was probably not diplomatic, but she couldn't make herself feel sorry about it.

"How is Dorothy?" Thomason said.

"Like I said, she's mighty sad…"

"Is she sick?"

"No, she doesn't have the flu."

"But there are other people in the house who are sick?"

The question gave Alafair pause. "Yes, but I reckon they're all over the worst by now."

"Miz Tucker, I know it's an imposition, but would you please watch over Dorothy for a little while longer? Maybe another week? I can't be coming down with the flu."

Alafair could hardly believe her ears. A rush of fury overcame her. What kind of unnatural father was this man?

Before she could deliver her scorching response, Thomason said, "Please, ma'am, I'm all she has now. I can't die."

She bit off her invective. "Mr. Thomason, Nola told me a while back that your folks died in the epidemic of '90 and you're scared. But…"

Thomason cut her off. "I can't take care of her right now, Miz Tucker. It's my fault Nola died." His voice caught, but he mastered himself. "I had a plan for the future. But I didn't know I'd feel like this. I didn't know I could feel like this. What if it had been Dorothy? I shouldn't have left, but that Lewis. He always messes things up."

Alafair listened to him babble on for another minute. She was thinking that Thomason was right about not yet being fit to care for his daughter. "Mr. Thomason, Mr. Thomason, listen. Dorothy is just fine where she is right now. We love her and we'll take good care of her until you're feeling better. I know you're grieving, but hurry and take yourself in hand, Mr. Thomason. You've got to step up, now, for Dorothy's sake."

Alafair had not forgotten about Sophronia, banished to solitary confinement. She knocked on the sewing room door and called Sophronia's name. When there was no answer, she cracked the door open to have a look. The room was empty.

Sophronia was in the backyard, playing with a yellow kitten and singing.

"Say, oh playmate, I cannot play with you. My dolly has the flu, Boohoo, boohoo, hoo, hoo…"

Alafair didn't call her right away. She stood in the back door for several minutes, watching as Sophronia teased the cat with a piece of string, singing to herself, unaware she was being watched.

Well, Alafair thought, I suppose she's as safe alone in the backyard as she is in the sewing room.

Alafair had nearly had a fit when Sophronia decided to break quarantine and come into town, but she had to admit that her daughter's vivacious little self was probably the best medicine for Dorothy right now. Still, she wondered if what Martha had said was true. Were they more permissive with the younger children than they had been with the older ones? Was she doing Sophronia any favors by letting her slide around the rules? Maybe Alafair was just more relaxed now than she had been. She had had a lot of time to learn what was really important.

"Fronie," she called. "You can go back into Dorothy's room now."

Chapter Sixteen

How Doctor Carney Did Not Find
What He Expected to Find

The undertaker, Mr. Lee, and his assistants were as fearful of infection as anyone else. Mr. Lee refused to embalm the bodies of anyone who had died of influenza. In fact, he would only consent to transport the bodies of flu victims for burial if there was no other recourse. Most of those who died in the epidemic were carted to the graveyard or buried in the family plot on the back forty acres by whichever of their relatives were still able to do it. If there was no one else, the undertaker's men, gloved, coated, and masked, would put the body into a hearse if it was coffined, or into the back of a wagon if it was not, and take it directly to the cemetery, where it was dropped into a grave with as much alacrity and guilty respect as the workmen could manage. The Madsen brothers, Ollie and Otis, gravediggers, were kept busy trying to keep ahead of the need for open graves.

Once he received permission from Homer Thomason to do an autopsy on the earthly remains of Lewis Hulce, Carney had to work fast. Autopsies were a rarity in Boynton, Oklahoma, in 1918, since people usually did their dying without fuss and were sent to their final resting place in an efficient and timely manner.

Besides, the religious sensibilities of most of the population were such that cutting on a body, which after all was destined to be raised whole from the grave on Judgment Day, was highly disapproved of. Therefore, there was no suitable place in town besides the mortuary to do a postmortem examination. Mr. Lee refused to allow Carney the use of his embalming table until Scott stepped in and insisted. Mr. Lee was not happy about it, but he was too tired to resist.

Carney had not performed an autopsy since medical school. But the hospital in Norman, where the University was located, did allow researchers to observe postmortems, and Carney had done so a few times over the past couple of years. Lewis had been suffering from influenza, so when he opened Lewis' chest, Carney expected to find wet, foamy, bloody lungs, congested, blackened. But he was surprised to see that the lungs were relatively clear. There was evidence of bronchitis, but otherwise it looked as though Lewis had been on the mend.

Whatever killed him, it was not pneumonia.

Confused, Carney examined the stomach. If, as Mrs. Tucker suspected, Lewis had been poisoned, the stomach lining would likely be inflamed. It was not. This fact did not rule out some sort of toxin, so Carney took samples of the stomach contents, tissue, and blood to test when he could get around to it.

Carney examined Lewis' heart almost an afterthought. He had not expected to find heart damage in such a young man, but there it was. Not the scar tissue that would indicate heart trouble in the past, but unhealed, brownish, shriveled strips of heart muscle from a recent cardiac event. Something had stopped Lewis Hulce's heart.

Carney knocked on the door at the Addison house before the sun was quite up. He had worked all night to finish the autopsy and clean up the room so Mr. Lee and his minions could remove Lewis Hulce's body to its final resting place the moment they arrived in the morning.

Carney was not worried about waking Mrs. Addison at such an ungodly hour. It seemed that the woman never slept. This morning was no exception. She opened the door for him at once. "Doctor Carney, I've told you repeatedly that you do not need to knock. Just come on in whenever you've a hankering."

Mrs. Addison stood aside and he sidled past her. "And I have told you repeatedly that I have no intention of imposing myself upon your privacy, madam, though I do thank you for your hospitality and thoughtfulness." Carney's opinion of traditional midwifery was not much higher than his opinion of folk doctoring, but it was hard not to respect Ann Addison. She was a tall Cherokee woman whose whole bearing, dignified and self-assured, elicited respect. Besides, she was old enough to be his grandmother, and Carney had been taught to respect the elderly.

When Carney had first asked her permission to use the small laboratory her absent husband had set up in one of the downstairs rooms of their sprawling house, Mrs. Addison had not hesitated to say yes. She had left Carney to his own devices in the lab. She was as busy caring for flu victims as anyone and sometimes was away for two days at a time, making rounds of outlying farms in her buggy. But when he needed some chemical or piece of equipment for a test, Mrs. Addison knew exactly where in the lab it was located or where it could be procured.

She relieved him of his bag while he removed his jacket and hung it on the hall tree. "How many new cases did you tend yesterday?" he asked her.

A look of resignation passed over her face. "Too many." She recited the names of the farm families she had tended the day before. "And yourself?"

"Also too many. Ma'am, I would like to avail myself of your husband's laboratory over the next few days. I intend to run tests on these samples, as well as the other samples from the Thomason house, as soon as I can manage it."

"You have concluded the autopsy on Lewis Hulce?"

"I have. There was no fluid in the lungs, to speak of, and the alveoli were clear so, despite his physical appearance, he did not die of pneumonia. His stomach lining was not irritated. I was surprised to see that there was recent damage to his heart. It looked to me as though he suffered cardiac arrest. He may have overdosed on some home remedy that his mother concocted that contained cocaine, or digitalis, or belladonna. Did Mr. Hulce have a history of heart problems?"

"Not that I am aware of. Lewis was a pharmacist, however. It would have been easy enough for him to put his hands on any of those." She reached for her bonnet. "I'll leave you to your work now. And whenever you wish, you are welcome to sleep in the guest bedroom next to my husband's office and save yourself the trip back to the hotel."

"Thank you, but right now I only intend to refrigerate these tissue samples before I leave for the schoolhouse to coordinate with whomever is left of the Red Cross. I cannot say when I will have the time to work in the laboratory."

Mrs. Addison ran a hatpin through her bonnet and picked up her own medical bag from the table by the door. "I will be interested to learn your results, Doctor Carney."

"So will I, ma'am."

Chapter Seventeen

How Alafair Made a Frightening Discovery

Once Alafair overcame her reluctance to use a telephone, she found it very convenient for keeping tabs on those of her relatives who were on the exchange. Her in-laws were well, no surprise. Shaw's parents, Sally and Peter, didn't get to be so old without knowing how to take care of themselves. Besides, Sally knew more about country doctoring than any wet-behind-the-ears graduate of University of Oklahoma Medical College. Shaw's sister Josie Cecil came down with the flu early on, and endured a long, bad, illness, as had her husband, Jack. They had been nursed by a succession of their daughters and daughters-in-law, one taking over for another when she dropped. Josie was up now, but Jack was still weak. The daughters and daughters-in-law were hanging on.

Thus far the only members of Alafair's immediate family to come down with the grippe were Alice and Walter. Alafair was cautiously grateful, but knew better than to credit anything but luck and the fact that most of them were in strict quarantine.

Walter and Alice were finally on the mend, and Sophronia was turning out to be a good nurse's aide and companion for the convalescent girls. Dorothy was not ill, but she was pale and silent and only wanted to sleep, in spite of Sophronia's attempts to engage her. Several days had passed but Doctor Carney had not yet come up with definite results from his laboratory tests on the fluid samples from Dorothy's mother and brother. No matter what had killed her mother and brother, Dorothy was still in shock and it was going to be a while before she could begin to cope with her loss. After the doctor released Lewis' body, he had been buried quickly and without a funeral, as had many of the flu victims in town. It might have comforted Dorothy to be able to see her father, but Mr. Thomason was still holed-up in his office and had not come to visit his daughter once. Alafair blamed him very much for that.

Forsythia Lily was well enough now that she wanted to get out of bed, but other than the nightgown she had on when Martha brought her over, she had no clothes of her own to wear. Alafair had been making do for Forsythia Lily with a couple of Grace's gowns and dresses that Shaw had brought from the farm. Grace was a year younger, but far taller than Forsythia Lily, and her clothes were already too big. So on the day Alice was able to dress herself and eat a proper meal, Alafair stole an hour to run errands and retrieve some of the girl's own clothing from the Clover house. First, she saddled Missy and rode the half-mile north of town to Beckie MacKenzie's Victorian meringue of a house to see with her own eyes how Ruth was faring.

Miz Beckie was an elderly woman, but hardly delicate, so her mild case of the flu had not caused Ruth much alarm. After close inspection, Alafair approved Ruth's nursing and disinfecting skills, then replenished her daughter's supply of herbs and lye soap.

She rode back into town at a trot and dismounted at the post office. The door was open, but as usual, no one was there. Patrons had simply been helping themselves to the mail in their own cubbyholes if the desk was unmanned. If there was any mail to be had, that is. Since the quarantine, mail delivery had been sporadic.

Today the mailboxes were filled, and Alafair gasped with pleasure when she saw the stack of letters in the box marked "Tucker, Shaw."

She had enough self discipline to walk around the counter instead of scrambling over the top to get to the treasures in the cubbyhole. She hefted the stack in her hand to check the weight. Delighted, she figured she must be holding twenty pieces of mail. She spread them out on the countertop so she could take the entire collection in at a glance. There was the usual weekly letter from her sister Elizabeth in Arizona and one from her mother in Arkansas. The rest were from her boys. Six postcards from Charlie, all from England. That made her laugh. He tried his best, but he just didn't have the patience to write an entire letter. Thank God he was still in England, though. Four letters for Shaw, one from the Grange and three from the United States Army Procurement Office. More orders for mules. She began to arrange the correspondence in piles by sender and date.

She had told herself before she came into the post office that if she had mail, she'd take all the letters back to Alice's and read them aloud to her, one by one, in order of date. There were ten envelopes from France. The oldest was dated two months back, the latest sent only three weeks ago.

She ripped it open.

It was one page, front and back, written in Gee Dub's hand, neat, but cramped as he had tried to get as much as he could onto the single sheet.

Dear Folks,

I'm all right. Nobody has shot me yet. I'm still in ██████████. The weather is miserable, raining all the time. The brass is telling us that the war looks to be over pretty soon. The Bosch is on the run. Not that I've seen much ██████████. The other day Sgt. Hamilton showed the men how to make hard apple cider with a bunch of old dried up apples a couple of the boys gathered up off the ground outside what was left of an orchard when they were coming back from leave in ██████████. I don't even want to tell you how. It was disgusting. But it sure did make me miss Grandpapa's sweet pressed cider. I got a field promotion last week. I'm a first Lt. now. I was hoping it'd make me smarter, but I haven't noticed that my brain works any better yet. That fact doesn't give me confidence in the brain power of the generals running things over here. I'm about to be rotated over to a British unit for a special assignment in a few days. They haven't told me where. I can't tell you what I'll be up to, but don't worry, it isn't that dangerous. I've been in charge of this unit since we got over here, so I'll be sorry to leave these boys. It's a lucky unit. We've only lost ████████████ up to now, and that was to ████████ ███. I talked to an old boy who just got here from █████████████ and he told me he thinks he saw Charlie in ████████████. Or at least he saw some youngster on a motorcycle who matched Charlie's particulars. If it was him, he's still ███████████ on his ████████████ over at ████████████ for ███████ ███. Maybe once this assignment is done they'll let me take leave over there and I can look him up. I know he's still champing at the bit to get sent ████████████, but until he adds a birthday or two, I wouldn't put money on his chances of getting sent ████████████ before the war ends. Some of these English and French boys still have their milk teeth, but up to now the Americans are waiting until you get old enough to sprout a whisker before they put you in a trench. You all try not to worry. I'm looking after myself as best as I can. I'll write when I can. Tell the sisters that I'm thinking of them. Sure do miss you all.

Sincerely, your son Lt. George W. Tucker.

p.s. Mama, I'm pining for a mess of your collards and fatback and a big hunk of cornbread with butter and sorghum. I'd go to wash it down with a gallon bucket of red eye gravy. But I'm dreaming. Right now I'd be happy with a cup of coffee that didn't taste like it was scooped up off the bottom of the trench. GW

Alafair had trouble reading the last bit through the tears that filmed her eyes. She folded the letter, inwardly scolding herself for not being able to hold off reading it until she got back to Alice's. Now she was going to have to stand here for a few moments and get herself in hand before she could leave. She pulled her dishtowel-sized linen handkerchief out of her skirt pocket and wiped her eyes and nose, then checked the mail cubbies to see if any of her other children had mail that she could deliver. Both Martha's and Mary's boxes held letters from their husbands, Streeter and Kurt, who, it seemed, wrote their wives from Washington every day. Beckie MacKenzie's box yielded one Eiffel tower postcard from her grandson, Wallace, and one letter for Ruth from her intended, Trenton Calder. Alafair brazenly read Wallace's postcard, which didn't say much more than don't worry, I'm fine and enjoying Paris. She examined Ruth's letter closely. The postmark was over a month old. At last word, Trent was on a battleship in the North Sea, and his mail was sporadic at best. Still, Alafair worried about her red-haired son-in-law-to-be almost as much as Ruth did, and any word from him was a relief. She was tempted to rip it open right then and there, but she mastered herself and slipped it into her bag.

Emmanuel Clover had been an agent for the W.E. Clare Insurance Agency. Alafair remembered how terrified Emmanuel had been that Boynton was about to be invaded by the ravening Hun, so much so that soon after the war began he had volunteered to be one of the local representatives of the Oklahoma Council of Defense. He had taken his job very seriously. His fear had transformed a gentle, lovely man into someone who looked under every rock for trouble and suspected people he had known for years of treason and sedition. It made Alafair sad. He may have gone too far in his zealous prosecution of those he considered insufficiently patriotic, but he had been sincere in his beliefs and never accused anyone out of personal animus.

But it hadn't been the Hun who got him in the end, nor traitors or saboteurs or spies. It had been a simple force of nature, a disease that didn't care a whit for Emmanuel Clover's age, gender, occupation, or political views.

She rode the two blocks from the post office to Mr. Clover's little bungalow on Buckner Street to retrieve Forsythia Lily's clothing and perhaps find a doll or toy to comfort her. It was a small frame house with a familiar four-room arrangement, a parlor in front, a kitchen in back, and two small bedrooms to the side. The front door was not locked so she walked right in.

Since Forsythia Lily's mother had passed away nearly two years earlier and no one lived at the house but the little girl and her father, Alafair wasn't expecting much in the way of housekeeping. But the place was in perfect order, and she was touched to see that Mr. Clover had turned his daughter's bedroom into a child's haven. The tiny room was painted white, with a bright-blue rag rug on the floor beside a child-sized bed with a lacy white coverlet. Most of the back wall of the little room was taken up by a huge doll house, fully furnished with handmade furniture.

Alafair was almost brought to tears by the thought of fussy Mr. Clover lovingly carving little tables and chairs for his motherless babe.

The house had been left just as it was the day Mr. Clover joined the choir invisible. There was a secretary's desk in the parlor. Cubbyholes full of papers. Papers and an ink pen lay on the writing surface as though Mr. Clover had been working on them when he fell ill. Alafair had forgotten that he had been an insurance agent. The policy he had been writing on was for Harriet Tucker—Scott's wife, Hattie. Since the document in question concerned her own relative, she felt no guilt whatsoever as she made herself comfortable in the desk chair and began to read.

It was a life insurance policy. Hattie was taking out a five hundred dollar policy on herself and naming her newest grandson as beneficiary. That made Alafair smile. Hattie took out a policy on herself every time one of her boys produced another child. She could afford to do that. She only had four children and four grandchildren. With ten children and who knew how many potential grandchildren, Alafair and Shaw had thought it prudent to name only each other as life insurance beneficiaries, with their children as secondary heirs if the parents should both meet their maker at the same time.

After reading Hattie's policy, she fingered through the rest of the pile. Mr. Clover must have been preparing newly purchased insurance policies for filing at the company headquarters in Oklahoma City. She wondered if she should mention her discovery to Scott. These people had probably paid already and thought their coverage was duly in effect. Would Great Western Insurance honor them if something happened before the policies were officially filed? Mr. Ross had taken out a policy on a new delivery truck for his dairy. The Buckhorns had extended their fire insurance to include their new barn. She'd have to tell Shaw about that one. Next in the pile was another whole life policy. Alafair was scanning for the beneficiary's name when it dawned on her who had bought the policy in the first place.

Homer Thomason had recently purchased twenty-five thousand dollars' worth of insurance on his wife's life.

Alafair stood up so quickly that she nearly knocked over her chair. She removed the paper from the pile and brought it up to her face, as though if she peered at it closely enough, it would say something other than it did.

She read the words and re-read them. Twenty-five thousand dollars, to be paid to her husband, Homer E. Thomason, upon her death. She could barely conceive of such a sum. Homer himself had said that he had a plan of some sort. Nola had told her that Homer wanted to start his own farm implement business. Twenty-five thousand dollars would certainly do the trick.

She sank back down into the chair. What kind of monster would poison his own wife for money? And not just his wife, but her children. He had told her himself that he had a plan for the future.

It cannot be, it cannot be. Besides, how could he have managed it? He wasn't even in town when they died.

And yet Alafair already suspected that something had poisoned Homer's family, and here she held in her hand a motive for murder. She pulled papers willy-nilly out of the cubbyholes in the desk, looking for policies on Dorothy or on Lewis Hulce, but none appeared. Maybe he had only meant to murder his wife but somehow the poison had been distributed to the children as well. Of course, it was no secret that Lewis and Homer had no love for one another. Perhaps there had been more than one intended victim after all.

Chapter Eighteen

How Alafair and Carney Both Determined That Murder Had Been Done

The only thing good that Scott Tucker could say about the flu epidemic was that while it was going on, the crime rate in Boynton and environs had dropped to nothing. One great blessing was that the night riders had disappeared. For nearly a month there had been no instances of vandalism or bullying of people whose only offense was that they had a foreign-sounding name or an unaccustomed accent. Scott didn't believe that a Christian person should go around wishing for woe to befall evildoers. But he had to admit that if all the members of the Knights of Liberty were too desperately ill to bedevil their neighbors, there was a certain justice in it.

He had been sick himself, and though he was never close to dying, a couple of times during the course of his illness he had felt like death would be a relief. He knew he had been much luckier than some. He had had his devoted wife, Hattie, to tend to him, and his son, Slim, to keep the door of the town sheriff's office open. Then as he was recovering, Hattie took ill and he tended to her as best he could, with the help of his saintly daughter-in-law, who had sick children of her own to nurse. The worst was past now, and more people were beginning to venture out of their self-imposed quarantine and go back to work. Scott had been back at his desk for two days, still feeling peaky, but at least able to enjoy his feed again and stay upright and awake for hours at a time.

He was going through wanted bulletins and Slim was catching up on paperwork at the other desk when he saw Alafair ride up on her gray mare and dismount in front of the jailhouse. Scott leaned back in his chair and hooked his thumbs in his belt, wary. He loved his cousins, but Alafair, in particular, had a nose for trouble, and Scott wasn't sure he was up for dealing with any mischief more serious than blocking the sidewalk. He caught Slim's attention and nodded at the figure outside the window. "Looks like the day is about to get interesting."

Alafair made herself comfortable in a hardback chair under the window, and for a couple of minutes, they exchanged family news—who was still poorly, who was on the mend, who had never become ill at all.

Then Alafair said, "Scott, I don't know for sure if there is anything to my suspicions...."

She hesitated at Scott's resigned smile, then plowed on. "...but I don't think Nola Thomason and her son died of bad medicine or from the influenza, either. I'm afraid they were murdered."

"What makes you think...?" Before Scott could finish his sentence, Doctor Carney hurried though the door and planted himself in front of the desk.

"Sheriff Tucker, the test results on the Thomason woman's effluents show that she died of arsenic poisoning. I tested for every medicinal substance I could think of before it occurred to me that her symptoms could have indicated arsenic...." He caught sight of Alafair and did a double take. "Mrs. Tucker, you were right when you suspected poison, but I doubt if it was an accident. There was enough arsenic in her bodily fluids to kill two people."

Scott shot an incredulous glance at Alafair before he stood up. "Lewis and Dorothy, too?"

"I have not tested the samples I took from Lewis. I did do a postmortem examination on him the day after the died, and I was surprised to find that his lungs were relatively clear. He did exhibit all the outward signs of suffocation, as though he had died of pneumonia. I was misguided by his symptoms. I'll test the samples when I get a moment. I may discover that he was poisoned, as well."

"And Dorothy?"

"I did not find any traces of poison in her effluvia. I believe the blood on her gown was her mother's. Dorothy's apparent illness was more than likely shock at the horrifying deaths of her mother and brother."

"Why would anyone do such a thing?" Scott was wondering aloud more than asking for the name of a suspect.

But Alafair was ready to supply one. "Scott, I just stumbled across something you should know about."

After Alafair related what she had found at Emmanuel Clover's house, no one spoke for a long moment.

"I'll have to get permission to use those papers as evidence," Scott said.

"I want to search the Thomason house for the source of arsenic that poisoned Mrs. Thomason," Carney said.

Slim looked uncomfortable. "Couldn't you tell from the tests what she had been eating?"

Carney cast a glance at Alafair, considering whether or not to offend her delicate sensibilities by speaking of such a repellant subject. He decided that any farm wife with a passel of children was not that delicate. He turned back to Scott. "I did not have enough…bodily materials to be able to tell. Without being able to do an autopsy and with the tools I have available, I can only guess at what she had been eating and drinking. I can test samples of the food and medicines in her house for arsenic contamination, however."

Slim leaned back in his chair. "Dad, don't druggists have to keep a record of anybody who buys poisons?"

"Anybody can buy arsenic for poisoning critters and pests, Slim, but they have to sign their names in the druggist's poison book when they do."

"Well, if somebody bought arsenic from one of them, wouldn't his name be in their book?"

Scott thoughtfully raised a brow. "If I was aiming to poison somebody, I wouldn't purchase the goods to do it with in my own backyard, especially if I had to sign my name to it. Still, it's worth a gander, I reckon. Son, when you get a chance, go and talk to the druggists and ask if either one of them remembers if Homer Thomason or anybody connected to that family bought arsenic within the past year. Ask to see their poison ledgers, too."

Scott had the doctor take a chair while he telephoned the district judge for a warrant to search the Thomason house. It took some minutes for Scott to be connected through, then explain the situation to the judge, and then to make arrangements to receive the warrant. Carney thrummed with impatience. Alafair remained seated quietly in the corner, hoping not to be noticed and sent away.

Scott replaced the earpiece on its hook and sat back. "All right. He'll wire over the warrant, but it is in effect as of this minute so go ahead and collect your samples, Doc. Slim, you go along to represent the law and to cast an eye around the place. Remember, a crime likely took place in that house, so look for anything out of place or suspicious."

Slim had worked in the office of the Pure Oil refinery before the war started and Scott lost his long-time deputy to the Navy. "Dad, don't you think that you're better suited to have a look around for clues than I am?"

"You'll do fine, son. Just don't disturb the scene too much. I'll come by as soon as I can. Right now I'm headed out to talk to Homer Thomason before this news gets around. I want to see what he has to say for himself. Doc, be sure that you inventory anything you remove from the house."

Slim grabbed his hat and coat and followed Carney out of the office. Alafair stood up slowly, trying not to catch Scott's eye, but the attempt was futile. Scott locked eyes with her, and they gazed at one another for half a minute. Alafair said nothing, and neither did Scott. Eventually, Scott's lip twitched and he turned away to retrieve his coat. Alafair walked out the door.

Alafair rode back to Alice's house but only stayed long enough to unsaddle her horse and check on her patients before making her way next door. She hadn't asked permission to tag along with Carney and Slim on their foray into the Thomason house, so she hesitated for a moment before she walked up the porch steps. The red quarantine sign was still tacked up beside the half-open front door. The front of the house was quiet and dim, but she could hear the men moving around in the kitchen. Before making her way to the back, Alafair paused to look at the floor where Lewis' body had lain. Thomason had left everything exactly as it was after the undertaker had gathered the mortal remains of his wife and stepson. The quilt had been flung aside, dried blood and excrement caked the floor. Alafair's gorge rose. She had to ask Scott or maybe Homer Thomason if they couldn't have the place cleaned up before the maggots started.

She went back into the kitchen to find Carney poking around in the Hoosier cabinet. He hadn't bothered with a mask, but he had donned cotton gloves.* Slim was standing over the place where Nola had fallen. Bodily fluids were encrusted on the floor there, as well, and a bowl and spoon that Alafair had not noticed when she discovered Nola's remains. Nola had probably swept them off the cabinet with her arm when she went down.

Slim cast a glance around. "What are we looking for?"

"Food, drink, anything that can be ingested. Mrs. Tucker, please hand me the container with the small glass sample jars from my bag on the table, there." Alafair was surprised that he was aware of her presence, since he hadn't looked away from the cabinet. He continued as though he had been waiting for her to show up. "The deceased ate or drank something that may still be here, so I want to run tests on anything that they may have put into their mouths. The victims may have ingested the poison up to half an hour before they felt the effects, so Mrs. Thomason may have had time to put away or even dispose of whatever it was. Deputy, look in the icebox. Mrs. Tucker, please see if you can locate the slop bucket."

Alafair moved to do the doctor's bidding. "But they looked to have died so quickly," she said, as she checked for the slop bucket next to the washbasin, which is where she kept her own.

Carney didn't turn around. "It probably did not seem quick to them, Mrs. Tucker. They more than likely suffered greatly for several minutes, even hours, before they were granted release."

Alafair swallowed a lump in her throat. "Why didn't she call for help? I wish she had called for me. I might have been able to help her."

"Once it hit her, I doubt she was able to do much more than writhe around in agony." He turned abruptly and handed Alafair several stoppered glass vials, each containing a tiny sample of something from the cabinet. She recognized flour and sugar. At least she hoped that they were flour and sugar and not rat poison. "Please put these in that little box and write 'cabinet' on it. You can write, can you not? Good. I am going to sample the grease jar and the slop bucket. Deputy, please go into the bathroom and check the shelf for medicines—pills, tonics, and the like. Do not bring them to me. If there are some things I need to sample, I will do it there. Mrs. Tucker, when you finish that, please do the same in the bedrooms. Look on the bedside tables and in the closets, too."

Carney was in his element. Thank goodness someone who knew how to test for poisons was available right here in town. Otherwise, Alafair didn't know what would have happened, not with Doc Addison and Doc Perry both pressed into service for the Army. If Nola and her son had been murdered, Carney apparently had the skills to determine how it was done and how the poison had been delivered. It was just too bad that he was such a tyrannical, rude little pisser, she thought, as she labeled the box of samples. *Can I write, indeed.*

Chapter Nineteen

Dorothy Speaks

Alice owned a fair collection of books, including some of Sophronia's favorites, like *Shepherd of the Hills* and *Pollyanna.* Sophronia had taken to reading aloud beside the invalids' bedsides while they rested. Alice didn't own her favorite book, *Tarzan of the Apes,* so Sophronia had done her best to act it out for her audience. Forsythia Lily had loved the show, and so had Alice and Walter, judging by their laughter and clapping. Dorothy did watch the performance with half-closed eyes, but Sophronia couldn't tell whether she liked it or not.

Once the quarantine on the town was eased, Forsythia Lily's grandmother came in from Mangum to fetch the little orphan home with her. Alafair was pleased at their loving reunion and glad that Forsythia Lily was eager to go with her grandmother. After the little girl left, Alice sat down on the settee next to Walter and wept. Walter put an arm around her and held her until her tears abated. Alice wiped her nose and looked up at Alafair, who was still standing by the front door with Sophronia after seeing Forsythia Lily and her grandmother off.

"Ma, nobody in this house has the grippe anymore. Can't Linda come home now? I need my baby."

Alafair considered it for a moment. She was as anxious for life to get back to normal as Alice was. She missed her own youngsters, and her own house, and her own bed with Shaw in it. And she imagined that even good-natured Mary was ready for some relief. Alafair knew from experience that several toddlers in a confined space for a considerable length of time would try the patience of a saint. "Sugar, I want to go home, too. I think the epidemic has eased, around here, anyway. But there are still people getting sick, and neither you or Walter is quite well yet. I can't see my way to leaving you here alone to take care of Linda as well as Dorothy for who knows how long. You need to get your strength back. Besides, you know what Martha said about this flu. Folks think they're well and try to get back to business, and end up with a relapse worse than before. Let me take care of you for another couple of days. Y'all don't want to overdo and end up with pneumonia."

"I think we should listen to your mother, darlin'," Walter said. "It's just for a little while longer. We'll both feel better. Then Linda can come home and I'll go back to work."

Alice apparently saw the sense of the argument because she burst into a fresh spate of tears.

Walter stood. He was still pale and his dark eyes were sunken, and he was definitely skinnier than he had been before he had gotten sick. But his hair was combed and his face shaven, and he had been trying as best he could to be helpful. He was an unskilled nurse at best, and could only stand up for an hour or so before he had to take a nap, but Alafair appreciated the effort. "Miz Tucker," he said, "you've done so much, leaving your home for so long to take care of us. How can we ever thank you?"

Alafair was astonished that he would ask. "You're my children." And that answered everything.

Sophronia tugged at her mother's sleeve. "Ma, can I go sit with Dorothy in her room now?" She hardly waited for a nod of assent before flying off.

Sophronia spent as much time at Dorothy's side as her mother would allow, trying to talk to her about ordinary things—school and the weather and such. If anyone can provide comfort when you are hurting, Sophronia thought, surely it is your very best chum. She had been encouraged that Dorothy seemed interested in her chatter, and even managed a wan smile every once in a while. She didn't have anything to say afterwards, though. Just wanted to sleep. Still, a little engagement was better than nothing.

Sophronia ran into the back bedroom to find her friend. Alafair had been insisting that Dorothy get up and dressed in the morning, so she was lying fully clothed on her back on top of the covers with her hands folded over her chest, staring at the ceiling. She turned her head as Sophronia climbed up onto the bed beside her. "Is Forsythia Lily gone?"

Sophronia was so surprised to hear Dorothy speak that it took her a moment to answer. "Her grandma and her left just a few minutes ago."

"Good. She cried too much."

Sophronia wanted to say that of course the little girl cried a lot. Her daddy died. But Dorothy had lost practically her whole family so pointing it out seemed cruel. Instead she said, "Well, she's only seven. You want me to read some more *Pollyanna* to you?"

"Naw. Pollyanna is too durn cheerful."

The comment struck Sophronia as funny and she laughed. "Listen, why don't we go out in the backyard? It's a nice day. Nippy, but you can borrow my jacket. We can play penny toss, or just sit in the sun for a spell."

Dorothy's gaze returned to the ceiling. She didn't respond.

Sophronia was undaunted. "Say, who's that old fellow who lives behind Alice's, here?"

Dorothy looked at her again. "Mr. Escoe? You saw him?"

"The other day. I was in the backyard and he waved at me from his window. He chucked a little yellow cat out the window for me to play with. Maybe the cat is still around. It was real playful."

Dorothy sat up. "Well, maybe we can go outside for a minute, if your mama says it's all right."

Alafair thought it was more than all right. While she bundled the girls up in sweaters and caps, she tried to engage Dorothy in small talk. Dorothy may have been out of bed and showing interest in something other than the ceiling in her room, but she still had nothing to say to Alafair.

"Now, Fronie, don't let Dorothy get too tired." Alafair shot her daughter a warning glare before sending the girls out into the sunshine.

Dorothy sat on the porch steps while Sophronia spent some time looking around the house and over the fence, making high-pitched squeaky noises as she searched. If the yellow kitten was still around she failed to rouse its interest. Dorothy got up and walked over to Sophronia's side, and the girls stood for a few minutes at the fence, staring at the back window of Mrs. Gale's house.

"It was funny how it happened," Sophronia said. "The old man showed up at that window and flung the kitten out at me just like he knew I was needing a pal right then."

For a long moment they stared at the dark window in companionable silence, then Dorothy said, "Miz Gale used to let him sit in her backyard sometimes. He liked to holler at me whenever I'd go out to play. Wanted to talk. He liked to tell stories. I'd climb over the fence and talk to him whenever I thought I wouldn't get caught. Every single time he'd pull something out of his pocket and give it to me."

"Like what?"

Dorothy shrugged. "Nothing much. A buckeye or a feather. A cookie or a piece of bread. Sometimes a little animal that he'd carved out of a sliver of wood. I've got a whole collection of googaws that he's give me." She hesitated, considering. "I don't talk to him anymore. He got too old. Mama told me that his mind is gone." She lifted the little turquoise bird necklace out of her collar. "It was him gave me this when I was ten."

Sophronia shot a glance along her shoulder at her friend. "I'd like to see your collection of goo-gaws someday." She considered asking Dorothy if she wanted to sneak back into her own house and retrieve something that would comfort her, but decided it was a bad idea. If it was me, she thought, I'd never be able to go back in that house again. She leaned down and picked up a couple of pebbles. "Let's see if we can get his attention," she said, and heaved the pebbles at the window. They fell short and landed in the middle of Mrs. Gale's backyard.

Dorothy gasped at the daring move.

"Here, let's try again." Sophronia grabbed another pebble and shot it underhanded across the fence with all her might. It ricocheted off the glass with a loud ping.

Dorothy laughed. "Fronie, you are a caution."

The window flew up and a thin, dark-visaged woman leaned out. "What are you little vandals up to?" she screeched. "Now, git, before I tell your mama on you." By the time she slammed down the sash the girls were already on the opposite side of the yard.

"That didn't go well." Sophronia's tone was ironic.

"Well, Miz Gale is kind of mean."

"You don't say. Let's just sit down and maybe the kitten will decide to drop by for a visit directly."

The two girls made themselves comfortable, side by side on the back steps. It was still chilly, but the wind was calm and the sun was warm as it shone down on their upturned faces. Sophronia glanced over to see that Dorothy's eyes were closed. She looked more relaxed than she had in days.

"What did Cousin Slim want to talk to you about?"

Dorothy didn't open her eyes, but her face tightened. "He was asking me questions about what happened to my mother and brother."

"What did you tell him?"

"Nothing."

"How come?"

"I don't want to think about it."

"No wonder. It's too awful." Sophronia let that hang in the air for a moment before she continued. "What did happen?"

Dorothy shrugged. Her eyes were still closed as she basked in the sun. "I don't know for sure. Besides, what good would it do to go over it all again? Nothing's going to bring them back."

"They ain't going to leave you alone, you know." She didn't have to explain that "they" were the adults—those beings who controlled every aspect of their twelve-year-old lives. "Pretty soon some lawman is going to come around and you'll have to talk to him, whether you like or not, and he may not be somebody as nice as Cousin Slim."

"I don't care." Dorothy's voice was flat. "I don't want to talk about it."

Sophronia sighed. "Can't say I blame you."

The girls fell silent for several minutes. Sophronia hadn't persuaded Dorothy to tell her what had happened, but she was glad that her probing had not unduly upset her. She was mulling over her options and had decided to drop the matter when Dorothy spoke.

"I heard them dying."

Sophronia caught her breath and froze, afraid that any sound or movement would break Dorothy's resolve.

Dorothy's eyes were still closed as she continued. "I was asleep, but I woke up because Lewis was yelling. He had been doing that. He was terrible sick with the flu. Mama told me that sometimes he saw things that weren't there, apparitions and phantasms that he made up because he had the brain fever, and they scared him so he'd yell at them to go away. He had been a lot better, but when I heard him yelling I thought he was having another spell. I lay there a long time waiting for Mama to shush him and tell him it wasn't real and give him medicine, like she always did before. But he kept on yelling. And it was odd. It sounded like he was in the kitchen, next to my bedroom, and not in his own room.

"I got scared, and got up to see why Mama wasn't helping Lewis. I called out to him. I don't know if he ever heard me. There was a shadow." She paused.

"What kind of shadow?" Sophronia prompted.

"A shadow that passed by my door. I thought it was Lewis at first, but it wasn't. He screamed. Then he started coughing and gasping, I heard that. But then it got real quiet. It was so quiet. It felt like forever until JoNell came in and made a terrible kerfuffle. She was screaming that Lewis and my mother were dead and it didn't seem like there was any reason to ever get up again after that."

Dorothy stopped talking, and Sophronia let the silence stretch for another minute before she ventured, "Why did they die? Was it the flu? Could your Mama and Lewis have eat or drink something that poisoned them?"

One of Dorothy's eyes cracked open and she peered at Sophronia. She was oddly calm. "Who knows? Mama had made some ginger tea that morning. For dinner we had leftovers from Burrows' Café. Some chicken and rice and gravy. I had some oatmeal cookies, and Mama ate the little cake with berries in it that was sitting on the cabinet. Daddy has been having Miz Burrows send dinner to us for a while."

Dorothy related the story without emotion, but Sophronia couldn't help but weep a little. The idea of losing one's mother was too horrifying to bear. At least Sophronia had a huge family to support her and take care of her if, God forbid, the worst thing happened. She wondered what would happen to Dorothy now. Could she and her father still live in that house of death? Where was Dorothy's father, anyway? Did she have a grandma, aunts and uncles? Sophronia wiped her nose on her sleeve. She was about to apologize for bringing up such a painful subject when Dorothy pointed to a bush beside the porch. A flash of yellow appeared between the leaves and was gone, then the kitten bounded out of the bush and leaped up into Dorothy's lap. It had been eavesdropping all along.

Alafair was standing at the kitchen table, sprinkling laundry, when she heard the girls laugh. It was such an unexpected and welcome sound that she stood up and went to the back door to see what they were doing. She smiled when she saw the kitten, glad there was something that could distract Dorothy from her gloom for a moment. She was even happier to see that Dorothy and Sophronia were talking.

She let them play while she finished rolling the dampened clothes and packing them into the laundry basket, ready to be ironed. She wished that she didn't have to intrude on the children's peaceful moment, but Dorothy was still weak and she didn't want to let her overdo. She called the girls in and escorted Dorothy back to the bedroom for a dose of elderberry syrup and a nap.

Dorothy's newfound interest in life disappeared as soon as she stepped back into the house. She did as she was told and allowed Alafair to manipulate her, limp and without will. Alafair tried again to engage her with questions about the kitten, but Dorothy refused to answer her or even look her in the eye.

So, not time yet, Alafair thought. Why was Dorothy so unwilling to talk to adults? And yet she felt comfortable speaking to Sophronia. Alafair returned to the kitchen, where she had put Sophronia to work cleaning vegetables for soup, and sat down at the table. "Fronie, I heard y'all talking out there on the porch."

She was going to ask what Dorothy had said, but when Sophronia looked up from the carrot she was scraping, Alafair could tell from her expression that she was already bursting with news.

Chapter Twenty

How Scott Thought He Had It All Figured Out

Burrows' Café was located right on Main Street, in the same building as Kelley's Barber Shop and Clark's Hardware, and next to the lot with the covered bandstand where local musicians played and the town held bond rallies every Saturday. The café was a small but pleasant joint with a long counter and bar stools on one side, three wooden booths on the other, and one table at the back for anyone who was feeling particularly fancy that day. The food was plain but plentiful and tasty, and the place was usually busy. Anita Burrows had always been willing to package up the daily blue plate special and deliver it right to your door for a small charge. Since the influenza epidemic hit, she found there was more call for take-away than in-house business. She didn't mind. She couldn't afford to get sick herself, so she shut down the dining room and concentrated on hiring boys to deliver food to the homes of people who were either stricken with the flu or too terrified of getting sick to venture into public. She had warned her delivery crew about getting too close to the customers, even ran tabs so they wouldn't have to handle money, but thus far she had been through four delivery boys.

She and Jill, her sister and cook, were in the kitchen at the back when she heard someone knocking on the locked front door of the café. Irritated at whoever wouldn't or couldn't read the "closed" sign she had posted, Anita wiped her hands on her apron and stalked into the dining room. She paused and frowned when she recognized Scott Tucker peering through the front window.

"Afraid we're closed, Scott," she hollered. "Just doing deliveries till next month."

He waved at her and gestured toward the door. A wary look passed over her face.

"Don't worry, Anita." Scott yelled loud enough for her to hear him through the glass. "I'm not catching anymore. I need to ask you about something."

Anita opened the door and ushered him back to the table. She poured a couple of cups of coffee and sat down across the table from him, still careful not to get too close.

After a quick briefing on the health of their respective families, Scott got to the point. "I understand that Homer Thomason has been having you send dinner to his family every evening."

"Well, yes, until they passed on to glory, he did. I was awful sorry to hear about that. Miz Thomason was a nice lady."

"Did you send an order to their house on the night before they succumbed?"

Anita's eyebrows lifted. "What night was that? I don't remember exactly. A few other of my delivery customers have gone on to their reward, as well."

"A week ago. That would be Monday evening."

"Well, I can't call to mind just when it was, but that sounds about right."

"Do you remember what you sent over?"

"I don't recall that Homer asked for anything special, so I'm sure I sent the same meal to his family that I did everybody else that night. I been making pretty bland specials these days, easy to digest, you know. Wait a minute." She stood up and disappeared into the kitchen for a moment. She returned with a piece of paper in her hand. "This here is my menu plan for last week. On Monday I sent boiled chicken and rice with cream gravy and biscuits to them who still have the flu. I did butter beans with ham and cornbread for them who were well enough to eat it."

Scott pulled a scrap out of his pocket and gave it a once-over. "Did you send the Thomasons cookies or a cake?"

"A cake? No. If Homer had ordered cake or cookies, I'd have sent some along, but nobody has asked for dessert lately and I wouldn't send such a thing as a matter of course. What's this about, Scott?"

"Probably nothing, Anita. The new doc is trying to cover his bases, is all. Thanks for the coffee. Say 'hey' to Jill for me, and try to stay healthy, now. Take it from me, this grippe ain't no fun at all."

Scott left a message for Carney at the school, but Carney was out on rounds and it took a long time to track him down. It was nearly dusk when Scott found the doctor trudging down a residential street with his bag in his hand, looking decidedly wilted.

"Doc, have you finished the tests on the food you found at the Thomason house?"

Carney snorted. "Mr. Tucker, I haven't had time to think, much less test all the food and drink and medicine we took out of that house."

"I can help you there, Doc. Start with the cookies, and the cake with berries."

Arsenic is tasteless and odorless, so it would have been easy for Thomason to put it in food. Carney tested the single cookie he had saved from the kitchen and found it untainted. At first, Carney did not remember finding cake of any description in the house, but as he went through his sample bottles he found one labeled "cake from icebox." He had taken the food samples from the kitchen himself, and he had to stare at the bottle for a minute in order to conjure a vision of where he had found it in the icebox. The cake had been in the back, just a sliver, sitting demurely on a small plate. It was the frosting, he remembered, that had caught his attention. You didn't see frosted cake much these days, not since the war-time sugar restrictions. But this tiny leftover slice had consisted of almost as much fluffy frosting as cake. He had sliced off one bite-sized morsel and put it in the small stoppered glass bottle.

He had been keeping his samples in the small icebox in Doctor Addison's lab, but it had been several days since they had been collected, and the cake was looking worse for wear. He plopped the sample out onto a glass pane, separated the frosting from the cake, and put each in its own vial for testing.

An hour later he was standing in parlor of Scott Tucker's home, holding out a test tube for the constable's inspection.

Scott peered at the yellow material at the bottom of the vial. "What am I looking at, Doc?"

"Arsenic, Mr. Tucker. Pure unadulterated arsenic, tasteless and lethal. It was in the cake, just as you suspected." Carney's brow furrowed. "Well, not in the cake. It was in the frosting."

Scott had run in innumerable drunks in his time, busted up many a fight, and arrested more people for mayhem and murder than he liked to think about. He had been socked, stabbed, slashed, and shot at during the execution of his official duty, so he took appropriate precautions when he set out to arrest a suspected killer.

He unlocked the drawer in his desk, removed his gun belt and strapped it on, summoned Slim to act as backup, then walked across the street to the offices of the Muskogee Tool and Die Company, where Homer Thomason had been holed up since his wife's burial.

Scott pounded on the locked front door for a couple of minutes before Thomason peeked out from a room in back to see who was making such an infernal racket.

When he recognized Scott, his annoyed expression changed to one of curiosity. He strode across the darkened office and opened the door. His eyes were red and swollen, and Scott's first thought was that he was ill. A closer look revealed that Thomason had been weeping. "Do you have some information for me, Sheriff?"

Scott looked stern. "We need to come in, Mr. Thomason."

Homer's eyes widened. "I heard you were sick."

"I'm over it. Now let us in."

Thomason stepped aside to let the two lawmen enter. "Come on back." He led them into a storeroom behind the office.

The office had not reopened since the end of the quarantine, so Homer hadn't had to worry about customers intruding on his solitude. He had set up a hideaway in the back room, where he normally kept most of his samples and sales records. He was using a long leather couch as a bed, and there was an outhouse just behind the building for his convenience. Thomason had been having food delivered; the fly-blown remains on the long table under the window attested to that. There was a basin and ewer for washing and shaving on the table, as well, though Homer had not availed himself of either for a while, judging from his stubbly face and the ripe odor of his rumpled shirt.

"I apologize for the state of the place. I haven't had the will to do much of anything lately." Thomason sat down on the couch. "Is Dorothy all right? Do you know what killed Nola?"

Scott took a breath. "Homer Thomason, I'm here to arrest you for the murder of your wife and your stepson. Get your coat, now, and come with me."

Homer's brow wrinkled. He didn't move, just sat there looking up at Scott without comprehension.

Scott bent down and took Homer's arm. "Come on, get up. We're going to the jailhouse."

Homer did not stand, but he turned so pale that Scott feared he might faint. "You cannot be serious."

Scott beckoned to Slim, and between the two of them they hauled Thomason to his feet. He was so shaky and loose-jointed that the two lawmen had to half-drag him through the office and into the street. "You cannot be serious," he repeated. "You cannot be serious."

They made it the entire three blocks to the jailhouse and Scott was locking a cell door behind him before it sunk in on Thomason that this was really happening. "But why would I kill Nola?" His question came out in a wail. "I loved her. I'd never, I'd never, I'd never…"

Scott had heard it all before. He had no sympathy for poisoners and even less for wife-killers. Pity was wasted on a murderer who would say anything to weasel out of the rap.

Tears were coursing down Thomason's face. Scott wavered for just an instant before he hardened his heart and gave the man a skeptical glare. "Don't say anything, because anything you say can be used against you in court. Do you have a lawyer?"

Thomason jerked back like he had been struck. He didn't reply.

"I'll contact Abner Meriwether. He'll explain everything to you, what the charges are and what happens next. Now, sit down and be quiet." Scott turned to go, but Thomason called him back.

"Sheriff, my daughter. She is still at the Kelley house? Is she well?"

"Last I heard, she don't have the grippe, but her mama's death has about rendered her mute with distress." His tone was accusatory. If the man was so concerned about his daughter, why had he not enquired about her welfare in over a week?

"Sheriff, please, would you send a wire to my sister, Mrs. Wilbur Cook, in Sallisaw? Ask her to come get Dorothy as soon as she can."

"I will." This would make the fourth time in a month that Scott had sent a wire to a relative on behalf of a child who had been orphaned by the flu.

Scott went back into the front office, removed his gun belt, and locked it in the desk drawer. He sat down and quietly regarded Slim, who was standing in the middle of the floor with his hands on his hips, staring into space.

"You look troubled, son."

Slim's eyes rotated to look at his father. "He don't act like a man who just poisoned his wife."

Scott leaned back in his chair. "They never do."

◇◇◇

After Scott arrested Homer Thomason for the murder of his wife and stepson, Alafair decided she was glad that Dorothy hadn't had to rely on her father for emotional support over the previous few days. She discussed the matter with Alice and Walter, and with Shaw when he came by that afternoon, and they all determined that Dorothy deserved to know what was happening. At least she should be told before she heard it from an unkind source.

Alafair stood in the door of the bedroom where Dorothy and Sophronia were playing jacks on the floor. Both girls looked up at her when she appeared, and both shrank a little when they saw the look on her face.

"Dorothy, I want to talk to you for a minute."

Dorothy paled and turned away from Alafair to face the wall. Alafair gestured at Sophronia to leave the room. Sophronia did not argue.

Dorothy was still sitting on the floor, facing the wall, and said nothing when Alafair knelt down and repeated her name.

Alafair reached out and took hold of Dorothy's arm. The girl made a half-hearted attempt to pull away, but Alafair did not let go. Dorothy looked up at last, taken aback. Thus far, no one had compelled her to respond. Her show of unwillingness had been sufficient to cause the adults to leave her alone.

Her heart sank at the expression of determination on Alafair's face. Dorothy's avoidance tactics weren't going to work this time.

Still…she looked away again and went limp. Alafair stood up and seized her by the upper arms, gentle but firm, and lifted the girl to her feet. She sat down on the edge of the bed and pulled Dorothy into her lap.

Dorothy was a long-legged girl, at twelve almost as tall as Alafair, and nearly as heavy as a grown woman, but Alafair cradled Dorothy in her lap like the grieving child she was. For some minutes she held Dorothy close, rocked and crooned a nameless lullaby in the girl's ear.

Alafair was warm and soft and smelled like soap and herbs, fresh bread and soup, overlaid with the tang of garlic and lemons. It felt so good to sit there, Dorothy thought, so right, like all the times she had sat in her own mother's lap and let all the evils of the world drain away. But her mother was gone, and would never comfort her like this again. In spite of herself, Dorothy placed her head on Alafair's breast and closed her eyes.

Dorothy did not want to cry, but a tear trickled down her cheek anyway, and then another and another, until she was wracked with sobs and the front of Alafair's bib apron was soaked.

Alafair kept rocking. "It's all right, honey. You just cry, now. It's all right."

"Do you know where my papa is?"

Dorothy had not spoken directly to an adult since her mother's death, so her snuffling question was so unexpected that it took an instant for Alafair to understand what she had said. Alafair had tried to be sensitive and had not allowed anyone to talk about Nola's death in too much lurid detail within Dorothy's hearing. But Alafair was not going to keep the circumstances of her father's arrest a secret from her, either. She expected Dorothy deserved to hear the whole truth.

"That's what I want to talk to you about, sugar. Dorothy, your daddy has been sent to Muskogee. Honey, he's in jail. Doctor Carney found out that the little strawberry cake that your ma ate was full of poison, and that's why she died. The police think that your daddy is the one who gave your mama the poisoned cake. There's going to be a trial to find out what really happened."

Dorothy did not react with either surprise or indignation. For some moments, she did not react at all.

"Papa didn't give Mama the cake," she said at length. Her voice was calm and matter-of-fact. "He was in Muskogee when Mama got sick."

"I know he was, sugar. The police think that your daddy may have paid somebody to deliver the cake to your house. Is that what happened? Do you know who brought the little cake to your house?"

Dorothy's head was still pillowed on Alafair's soggy breast. She sighed. "I don't know. It was just there for days, sitting on the cabinet along with all the other food that Miz Burrows sent."

"But Miz Burrows says she didn't send any cake with the rest of the food she sent to your house. Who else could have sent that cake besides your dad, honey?"

"I just don't know."

"Did you ever eat any of it, baby?"

"No, it had strawberries in it. I can't eat strawberries and neither can Lewis. They give us both the hives. Mama was going to save it for Daddy. He loves strawberries. But Daddy was gone so long that she was afeared the cake was going to go bad."

Alafair emitted an enlightened, "ahh…" So Nola finally ate it herself before it went bad. And having the cake contain strawberries was how Thomason made sure his daughter would avoid the poison.

"What is going to happen to me now? Will I have to stay here from now on?"

"Sweetheart, Sheriff Tucker sent a wire to your aunt, Miz Cook, in Sallisaw. As soon as she can get things arranged, she's going to come and get you and take you home with her. She'll take care of you for as long as your daddy can't do it."

Dorothy thought about this for a moment. She liked that particular aunt and uncle all right, and the cousins were not too bad. Besides, it was better than an orphanage.

"Miz Tucker, are they going to hang my father?"

"I hope not, darlin'. Maybe the jury will decide it wasn't him who poisoned your mother and brother. And even if they do decide that he's guilty, they might just send him to prison. How do you feel about that?"

If Dorothy felt anything, she declined to say what it was. "May I see my father before the trial?"

"I'll ask, baby. We'll see if we can arrange something."

"Can I visit him if he goes to prison?"

"I'm sure you can."

Dorothy fell back into her private silence then, and Alafair let her. She was deep in her own reverie, anyway. Dorothy was allergic to strawberries. Homer Thomason would have known that the only person in the house who would eat that poisoned cake was his wife.

When Martha came by that evening, she brought Doctor Carney with her. The influenza epidemic was still running rampant in parts of Oklahoma and the rest of the country, but the worst had passed in Boynton, and for the first time in a month, Martha and Carney finished their rounds just after dark.

Supper was long over and the children were already in bed. But Alafair had saved most of a pot of buttered noodles, and she and the Kelleys sat around the kitchen table and discussed the state of the world with the late night visitors while they ate.

It seemed that things were generally getting better, and not just with the flu epidemic in Boynton. It appeared there would be justice for Nola Thomason; Dorothy would soon have a place to go and a family to love her; and the war was winding down.

Carney and Martha didn't stay long after they were fed. Morning came early and there were still many suffering people to tend.

Alafair left Walter and Alice in the kitchen and ushered the visitors to the front door. "Well, I hope y'all can get some rest tonight. You're both likely done in. Martha, I don't like the look of you, honey."

Martha sputtered a laugh. "Ma, you say that to me every time you see me. I'm just tired."

"I don't know, your eyes are awful red. Look at her, Doctor."

Carney shifted his bag so he could put a hand on Martha's forehead. "You do not seem feverish Mrs. McCoy, but your eyes do look swollen. Perhaps you had better go straight to bed and take a day off to rest tomorrow. I will escort you home."

Martha drew away from his touch. "Oh, not you, too, Doctor. My mother gives me enough grief that you don't need to start in on me as well. A good night's sleep will set me right. I'm just tired down to my bones."

Before they stepped outside, Alafair said, "Doctor Carney, I don't cotton to many doctors. And I reckon your bedside manner leaves a lot to be desired. But I've been mighty impressed with how you've been taking care of folks around here. Martha tells me you've done a lot of good."

Carney's eyes widened at her unexpected compliment. He was not accustomed to housewives passing judgment on his skills. "Thank you, I think."

Alafair suppressed a smile. "Besides, if you hadn't have paid attention to me when I suspected the Thomasons were poisoned, if you hadn't been here to run them tests and find out it wasn't no accident, a murderer may have got clean away with it. Those poor folks might have gone to their graves without ever having justice."

"But that is what a good scientist does, Mrs. Tucker. I only followed where the evidence led me."

"Still, I'm glad you knew what you were doing. I may have to revise my opinion of scientific methods a mite."

"I am very glad to hear that, madam."

A moment of awkward silence descended between them. Carney could tell by her expression that Alafair didn't intend to revise her opinion all that much.

"I just wanted you to know that," Alafair said. She turned to Martha. "Honey, you go home and go right to bed, now. I swear you look like you're about to fall down."

Martha adjusted her pace to match the doctor's as they made their way toward downtown. The air had taken on a distinct chill. The sidewalks and streets were deserted, as they had been since before the quarantine was instituted and still were after the quarantine had been lifted. Neither of them spoke until they turned off Bruckner and onto Main Street.

"Your mother is a woman of strong opinions," Carney said.

Martha snorted. "You could say so, yes."

"Why does she dislike doctors so?"

Martha gave him a sidelong glance. He had never expressed an interest in a layperson's opinion before. Not within earshot of her, anyway. "She doesn't dislike all doctors. She likes Doc

Addison fine. She just doesn't like ones who are…" She hesitated as she decided how diplomatic she wanted to be. "…corrupted by all the newfangled ideas you modern doctors are taught."

"Corrupted?" Carney's tone was incredulous.

Martha shrugged. "I had a brother once, name of Bobby. He died when he was two…oh, my, that's near to a dozen years ago, now. It's a long story how it came about, but I'll just say he got hold of a jar of kerosene and managed to suck some into his lungs. Mama ran with him to a fancy doctor from Houston who had just set up a practice in town, but that Houston doctor told her there was nothing to be done and she should go home and start planning a funeral. I'm guessing that Bobby was probably long gone by the time she got to town, but to this day Mama faults the Houston doctor for not even trying. That's the thing she finds most blameworthy in the world, to not try, even if you know you'll likely fail."

Carney faulted the fainthearted Houston doctor, as well. But he said. "Well, it is not fair to blame all doctors for the failure of one. I would rather have someone treat me who was in possession of the latest scientific knowledge before a country doctor who has not opened a medical book in fifty years."

"Doc Addison teaches a practical medicine course at Arkansas University every few years, did you know that? Seems the college thinks more of his long experience than you do. Besides, he treats my mother's practical knowledge with respect. Respect goes a long way to getting someone to like you, you know."

Carney's cheeks reddened. He had escorted her to the door of the McCoy Land and Title Company and they had stopped on the sidewalk. Martha's apartment was on the second floor. "All right. I am chastened, Mrs. McCoy. There is great value in experience."

Martha's eyebrows peaked. "Do I detect a hint of humility, Doctor?"

Carney made a noise that conveyed both amusement and irritation. "Having dealt with your mother, I now see that you come by your plainspoken ways honestly."

Chapter Twenty-one

How Alafair Finally Set Eyes on Home

As October progressed, the day finally came when Alafair's charges were all free of fever and capable of looking after themselves for awhile. Would it be all right, she wondered, if she saddled her mare and made the trip home to see the family for a few hours? Alafair waited until Shaw came by for his daily visit in the early afternoon and sought his guidance as they sat at the kitchen table with Alice and Walter, working their way through a pan of nutmeggy egg custard which Alafair had just removed front the oven. Dorothy and Sophronia were in the backyard together, Dorothy bundled up and sitting in a chair, silently watching as Sophronia cleaned Alice's small chicken coop.

Alice weighed in before Shaw could offer an opinion. "I think that's a wonderful idea, Mama. You've been housebound for so long it'll be good for you to go home for a day."

Alafair shot a questioning look at Shaw, who said, "Do you think Alice is up to taking care of Walter and Dorothy on her own?"

"I expect I'd only be away for a few hours. But I am longing to set eyes on the young'uns, and to make sure that Mary and Phoebe haven't lost their minds trying to take care of all of y'all.

I'd like to see how Ruth is holding up with nobody but Miz Beckie for company, too."

Alice leaned forward in her chair. "Bring Linda back with you, Ma. Surely we're all past getting her sick."

"Oh, baby, are you sure? The epidemic isn't done with, and surely you don't have the energy to run after a two-year-old yet. Much less a two-year-old as well as a girl who is so sad she can hardly get out of bed." She didn't say it aloud, but Alafair was as concerned about her own flagging energy level as she was about Alice's.

Walter jumped in. "We'll both stay home and see that Linda is not exposed to the flu, Miz Tucker. I'm as eager to hold my girl as Alice is."

"I thought you were going to go back to work directly, Walter." Alafair was trying to keep an accusatory tone out of her voice. "There is no telling what flu-ridden fellow will come into the shop for a haircut so you can bring his infection home on your clothes."

"Oh, Darnell Grimes, one of the barbers who works for me, has already asked me if he can start cutting hair again. I'll let him open the shop and I'll stay home until there hasn't been a new case of flu in town for a week."

"Alafair will be glad to fetch her home," Shaw said, and gave his wife a cautionary look. Alafair sniffed, but she knew that returning Linda to her parents wasn't her decision to make. If Alice and Walter wanted their child to come home, then that's the way it would be.

The back door was open, and Alafair could hear Sophronia talking to Dorothy. She must be done with her chores, she thought. Sophronia began chanting as she jumped rope.

I had a little bird
His name was Enza
I opened up the window,
And in flew Enza…

Alafair turned back to Shaw. "Maybe when I go home for good in few days, I'll leave Fronie here to be the maid and nanny until Alice gets her strength back."

Shaw liked the irony. "That is a good plan. Let her see what real work is like. What do you think, Alice?"

"If that makes y'all feel better about leaving, it suits me. Fronie has been a good helper. Besides, I'll agree to anything that gets me my Linda back."

Shaw said he wanted to visit with Walter for a while, perhaps until Alafair returned from her trip to the farm. Alafair knew it was a ploy to enable Shaw to assess the children's ability to get along without her. If all went well, they could finally make plans to end the family quarantine and return to their own lives.

Alafair nearly ran the two blocks to the livery stable to retrieve her mare. She made a flying stop at the post office, where she found a card from Charlie, a letter for Ruth from Trent, one from Kurt to Mary, and two for Martha from Streeter in Washington City. There had been nothing from Gee Dub for a while, which worried her, even though Shaw told her he was surely too busy with his new lieutenant duties to write. She rode the half-mile north to the MacKenzie house first, and found Ruth well, in good spirits, and relieved that Miz Beckie was up and about and querulous as ever.

Alafair's mare, Missy, realized their destination as soon as she reached the turnoff that led toward the farm. The horse spontaneously broke into a trot, as full of joy at going home as Alafair was. The roadblocks leading into town were gone now but the roads were deserted. The outbreak may have abated, but it wasn't over yet. No one was taking any chances.

The fall weather was warm and sunny, the roads dry, the traffic light. It was a perfect day for a ride in the country.

Alafair greedily took in the scenery as she approached the house, riding up the long drive from the section line road. Nothing had changed. The white clapboard house was surrounded by a picket fence. The old stone well, capped off long ago, stood in its place in the front yard. The lightning-blasted hackberry tree and the honey locusts shading the house had turned yellow and were dropping their leaves. All was as she had left it, yet Alafair felt like she had not seen home in years. As she dismounted, the hounds Crook and Buttercup and the children's old yellow shepherd, Charlie Dog, rushed to meet her, barking wildly and trying their best to lick her to death. She was surprised to see her four-year-old granddaughter, Zeltha, bound down the porch steps to join the melee.

Alafair scooped her up. "I didn't expect to see you, sugarplum! Why aren't you at Aunt Mary's house?" Zeltha was squeezing her neck so tightly that it was hard to ask the question.

"Mama come and fetched us to keep her company here at your house, Grandma. We have go back to Aunt Mary's when Daddy and Grandpa come in for supper."

"We? All you kids?"

"Me and Tuck. He's around to the garden with Mama."

So Phoebe's resolve to keep her distance from her quarantined children had weakened. Alafair was not surprised. She found Phoebe in the huge truck garden at the side of the house, cutting winter squash off the vines. Tucker Day squatted close by her side, busily digging in the dirt with a stick.

The garden flowed by and around the intervening storage sheds, cribs, smokehouse, and sties like a river of black soil and greenery. Stepping stones and winding footpaths cut across and through the beds. At first glance, there didn't seem to be any rhyme or reason to the layout, just a riot of plants growing willy-nilly, falling over one another and spilling over the bricks, rocks, and planks that were meant to be retaining devices. But there was actually a well-thought-out plan to how things grew.

With so many children to feed, Alafair had always kept a very large garden. But since the beginning of the war, and the institution of the government's strict rules on the purchase and consumption of food, the vegetable garden she had planted in the spring of that year was mind-boggling. Shaw was probably teasing when he accused her of trying to raise enough to feed the entire United States Army, but she didn't see the humor.

When she caught sight of her mother, Phoebe straightened, a knife in one hand and a basket in the other. Her mild, hazel eyes widened. "Mama, what in the world! Are y'all home at last?"

Alafair hugged Phoebe with one arm, since Zeltha still occupied the other. "Afraid not, honey. Alice and Walter are much better, but Dorothy Thomason is still there, and Alice wants Linda to come home today. So I'll be staying on in town for another day or two, until I feel like Alice can handle things on her own. Your daddy has been keeping me up on how things are going out here, but I just was itching to see the rest of my tribe. Let me look at you. Mercy, you are a sight for sore eyes! Tuck, give your grandma a hug. "

Phoebe and the children led Alafair back into her own house, where Phoebe played hostess while she brought her mother up to date on the state of her domain.

After tea and biscuits and honey, they walked together down the path to Mary Lucas' front door, where Alafair was assailed by more children and more dogs.

It seemed her youngsters had grown half a foot since the middle of September. Grace was all legs, and Chase Kemp came up to her shoulder. Mary was as cheerful as ever, but Blanche was looking harried. She perked up considerably when Alafair told her that Sophronia was in big trouble for running off. One thing had not changed; her toddler grandchildren still besieged her for hugs and kisses and explored her pockets for treats like a pint-sized army of marauders.

Mary had allowed the older children to expand their range beyond the limits of her fenced front yard. Grace and her cousin Chase were eager to show Alafair the lean-to they had built in the woods behind the house. Blanche told her mother that she had been paying daily visits to the homestead, ostensibly to help Phoebe in the garden. Alafair thought it more likely that she did it so she could enjoy a daily few minutes of peace.

Alafair stayed at Mary's house, full of bright, healthy, and energetic youngsters, for as long as she could. Phoebe's husband, John Lee, joined them eventually, and they all sat together on the porch and ate pie and drank sweet tea and read Kurt's letters aloud.

But eventually the shadows moved from west to east, and Mary bundled up Linda's clothes in a saddle bag and plopped Linda herself on the saddle in front of Alafair, and grandmother and granddaughter headed back to town.

Linda was a good passenger, excited to go home, and she babbled constantly as they rode. Alafair made interested noises and listened with half an ear as she concentrated on making her plans to return to her own house. She wondered if she could get permission from Scott to take Dorothy home with her if the aunt did not show up in good time. Sophronia would need to stay in town and help Alice, and while she hated to separate the girls, she would feel better about Dorothy if she could keep an eye on her. Maybe Blanche would like to trade places with Sophronia and take care of Alice and Walter for a while.

By the time she got back to Alice's house, she had planned everyone's life to her satisfaction and was feeling light as air. Linda's reunion with her parents was a heart-swelling delight to see. Even Dorothy was smiling when Alafair left to return her horse to the stable and deliver Streeter's letter to Martha.

Chapter Twenty-two

How Alafair Got Distracted From the Matter at Hand

It was late in the afternoon by the time Alafair walked up the stairs leading to the apartment over the McCoy Land and Title Company.

The front door was unlocked, so she stepped in. "Martha? Martha, it's Mama, honey."

No one answered. Alafair puffed with disappointment. She had hoped that Martha had heeded Carney's advice and taken the day off to rest. The apartment was neat and quiet, so much so that it appeared to be unlived-in. Considering how busy Martha had been over the past few weeks, that was hardly surprising. Alafair tossed the letters on the settee where Martha would see them as soon as she got home, and turned to go. A faint scraping noise stopped her in her tracks.

There it was again. She cocked her head toward the sound. It was coming from the kitchen. It wasn't Martha's cat. He was sitting on the window sill with an inscrutable expression.

Alafair walked into the kitchen expecting nothing, which intensified her shock when she saw Martha prone on the floor, weakly scrabbling to try and get to her feet.

Alafair gasped and fell to her knees beside Martha, her heart banging against her chest.

"Mama." Martha sighed with relief at the sight of her mother. She closed her eyes and went limp.

Later, Alafair wondered how she had mustered the strength to get Martha's leaden form up off the floor and into her bed. Though when she remembered the feeling that came over her when she saw her baby on the floor, she realized that she probably could have lifted a battleship. It did not occur to Alafair to regret that she would not be going home after all, not for the foreseeable future. She did not waste time wishing that things were other than they were.

Martha was hot and flushed, and shaking so hard with ague that the bed rattled. Alafair managed to get her undressed and under the covers with a hot water bottle before she rushed into the little parlor and snatched up the telephone. The party line was engaged, but Alafair recognized the voice on the other end.

"June, get off the line. I'm sorry but this is an emergency."

After one second of shocked silence, there was a click and the line opened up. Alafair never heard whomever June had been talking to. She frantically clicked the drop hook until the operator answered.

"Kate, I just came up here to Martha's and found her on the floor. She's real sick. Will you ring Alice for me? Martha's real bad. Do you know where that doctor is?"

"I don't, Alafair, but I'll see if somebody at the schoolhouse knows. We'll find him, don't you worry."

It was fortunate that Alice Kelley was sitting in a chair right next to the telephone table. She had been out of bed for several hours, and she didn't think she would have had the energy to walk across the room to answer the telephone when it rang.

Linda was playing on the floor at Alice's feet. Sophronia and Dorothy were huddled together on the settee with a book between them, ostensibly reading aloud to one another. Judging from their secretive manner, Alice guessed that the conversation had more to do with girlish matters than with literature. Walter had volunteered to go outside and feed the chickens. It was the first time he had been out of the house in many days.

Alice grabbed the earpiece off the hook. "Oh, hey, Mama. I was wondering what had become of you. Where are you?"

The silence grew ominous as Alice listened to her mother's reply. Ominous enough to draw the attention of the girls on the settee. Alice straightened in her chair, her expression filled with worry. "All right, Ma. Daddy was here just a bit ago, but he left to go visit Ruth. I'll ring over there right away. We'll find Doctor Carney as fast as we can. No, you don't worry about us. We're up to taking care of ourselves. Do what you need to. Daddy'll be there directly."

She broke the connection and looked over at the girls on the settee, who were looking back, wide-eyed with dread. Linda had gotten up from the floor and was giving her mother comforting pats on the knee. "What's wrong?" Sophronia said.

Alice was already clicking the drop hook on the telephone to summon the operator. She held up a finger to stall Sophronia and pressed the earpiece to her ear. "Miz Smith, connect me to Miz MacKenzie's house, please. My father is over there and I need to speak with him." She put a hand over the mouthpiece and turned back to the older girls. "Mama says Martha has taken ill."

Dorothy sank back into a cushion, but Sophronia stood, alarmed. Almost fifteen years older than Sophronia, Martha had always been the general of their little battalion of Tucker children. Though they were too far apart in age to have grown up as playmates, Martha had always been like a second mother to Sophronia. Besides, she had recently saved Sophronia from being eaten alive by their parents. "Is Martha going to be all right?"

Alafair had said that Martha was deathly ill, but Alice didn't see the point of frightening her little sister any more than she had to. "Oh, I imagine so. But Martha will need somebody to nurse her. Mama'll have to stay over there now, at least until Martha gets to feeling better."

Sophronia looked like she was ready to run out the front door and confront the flu with her bare fists. "What can I do?"

Alice eyed her with amusement and more than a little admiration for her spunk. "Me and Walter and Dorothy are weak as kittens, and now we have Linda to tend to. Reckon it's up to you to take care of us, now." Her attention turned to the voice on the telephone. "Oh, Ruth, hey. I need to talk to Daddy."

Sophronia's heart was pounding. She figured that the situation was probably worse than Alice was willing to say. She had thought that since Alice and Walter were better, the crisis had passed, that soon she would be able to go home and resume her life. She glanced back at Dorothy, still so fragile, and felt her own spine stiffen with resolve. It was a good thing she was here to help.

◇◇◇

Shaw got to Alafair before the doctor did. She was sitting in a chair at Martha's bedside when she heard his boots pounding up the stairs. She knew instantly who was coming. The front door banged opened and he appeared in the bedroom door.

"How is she?" he said, at the same time she said, "I'm so glad you're here!"

He walked into the room and put a hand on Alafair's shoulder. Martha was only a shape under the piles of quilts and blankets, but he could hear her noisy rasps of breath plain enough. "Alice told me what happened. We found the doctor, and he'll be here directly."

"Oh, thank the Lord! She's real sick, Shaw, way sicker than Alice was. An hour ago she was coughing so hard I thought she'd break a rib. I gave her a spoonful of sugar with a couple drops of coal oil on it and that helped. Her head and her bones hurt so bad that she can't hardly move. She's delirious with the fever and all. I finally give her some laudanum. It seems like she's easier." Alafair paused, suddenly on the brink of tears. "I fear she may die, Shaw."

She felt his grip tighten on her shoulder. Martha groaned, stirred, and started coughing again, a braying cough that contorted her body. Her parents flew into action, one on each side of the bed, and pulled her up into a sitting position so she could breathe. It helped the coughing somewhat, but she began to bring up bloody sputum, then a gush of blood from her nose.

"Shaw! Towel! Alum! Kitchen!" Alafair gestured toward the kitchen with one hand. Shaw snatched a small container of alum from the kitchen cabinet and Alafair sprinkled the white powder on a cotton dishtowel. She pressed the towel to Martha's hemorrhaging nose, both parents too involved to realize for a moment that Doctor Carney had arrived.

"Out! Out!" Carney roared with such authority that Alafair leaped to her feet and was out of the room with Shaw quite before she knew what had happened.

"Mrs. Tucker," Carney yelled after them, "bring me more towels and a basin of hot water." Through the bedroom door they could see that Carney was holding Martha upright with one hand and digging through his bag with the other. Alafair jumped to do his bidding.

Carney banished the parents from the sick room and slammed the door behind them. Shaw and Alafair collapsed together on Martha's settee, clinging to one another for dear life. Alafair was relieved and terrified at once. She didn't particularly trust Carney's methods, but his projected confidence bolstered Alafair's hope that he could save Martha.

Carney himself was not so sure. The hemorrhaging was unusual, but it was not unheard-of. He had had to deal with it a few times since he had been in Boynton. Most of the time the patients survived. Sometimes they didn't.

He wished he hadn't run Martha's parents out of the bedroom so precipitously. It had just been a knee-jerk reaction on his part. He had become too sensitive to desperate relatives hanging over his shoulder with unwanted advice and criticism, and he was more than aware that Mrs. Tucker was not shy about offering either. But at the moment, as he tried to hold Martha up in a sitting position with one hand and manipulate his stethoscope with the other, he could have used her help.

Martha's head hung over her knees, her face obscured by her long, loose hair, as Carney pressed the chestpiece to her back. Her heartbeat was irregular and weak, and her lungs were gurgling. Her breath was coming in wheezy gasps. She was filling with fluid. Drowning.

After dealing with this cruel plague for so long and the torment it inflicted on its sufferers, Carney had trained himself to keep his emotions in check. But to his surprise, he felt a lump rise in his throat. Because of his own discontent, he had bullied and berated her and the other nurses. Nor had he praised her competence and dedication as often as he should have. He had been in the trenches with Martha McCoy and her heroic squad of volunteers. They were all scarred veterans of the same bloody battle, and that was a bond between them that no one who had not lived through it could understand.

Influenza had overtaken her like a prairie wildfire, and if he didn't do something radical, and soon, the pneumonia would kill her. He glanced at the closed bedroom door, beyond which Martha's parents were waiting for him to work magic.

He had a vial of his own pneumonia vaccine in his bag. He knew from experience that even the most effective vaccines only worked part of the time, and Martha was probably too far gone for anything to work at this point. And his vaccine was experimental and untested on any human other than himself.

He would not let her die if he could help it.

Neither Alafair nor Shaw spoke for the time Carney was shut up in the bedroom. They sat and listened to Martha hacking her lungs out, continually at first, then in fits. Then silence. Finally Carney slipped out of the room. He had taken off his coat and rolled up his sleeves, and was wiping his hands on a dishtowel. The front of his shirt was bloody. They stood up to receive the verdict, still holding on to one another.

Carney had schooled his expression to remain neutral, but it was obvious that he did not want to tell them what he was about to tell them.

He took a breath and came out with it. "I am sorry…"

Alafair clapped her hands to her face. "Is she gone?"

"No, no. The bleeding is alarming, I know," Carney said, "but I have seen these hemorrhages before and they are not necessarily fatal. It is under control for the moment. The alum you put on the towel helped. But she is becoming cyanotic, and I am afraid that when cyanosis sets in, death is practically inevitable. I gave her a shot of morphia a few minutes ago and she is sleeping. She is comfortable…"

Alafair didn't hear the last part. The doctor had just told her that there was nothing to lose now. She turned and ran to the kitchen and grabbed two onions and a knife before heading for the bedroom, full steam ahead. She pulled up, startled, when Carney didn't move out of the way.

"Mrs. Tucker, that is not going to help. I have done all that can be done, but I want you to be prepared. I have tended dozens of cases over the last weeks and I am afraid that no one has yet survived once the lungs began to fill up. That is what makes them turn blue."

"Let me by," she said.

Carney blocked the door with his body. "Madam, please do not cause her any more torment. Let her rest. The best thing you can do is comfort Mrs. McCoy in what may be her last moments. She is in need of a change of gown…"

Alafair didn't take her eyes off of Carney's face. "Let me by."

Carney placed one fist on his hip, taken aback by her intransigence. "Madam, get hold of yourself. Onions are not going to help your daughter."

She was suddenly deaf and blind with fury.

"Get out of my way." This time the voice that came out of her mouth sounded nothing like a gentle, concerned mother. It hardly sounded human. Her eyes had gone black with rage and she reached out with her free hand as though she intended to claw his face. For one horrified moment, Carney believed in witches. He gasped and flung himself back against the wall to let her pass. He could have sworn he saw her vanish from where she was standing and materialize beside Martha's bed without taking a step.

He shook himself, ashamed that superstition had overcome intellect even for an instant. Where had that sudden fear come from? He was a rational man. Some forgotten incident from his childhood, something about his own mother?

Incensed at the thought that Alafair might cause Martha unnecessary discomfort, he would have confronted her, but he was prevented by a hand on his shoulder.

He had forgotten about Shaw. Carney took a relieved breath. The husband would sort his woman out. But Shaw's expression was not one of masculine solidarity. It was more like a combination of disgust and pity.

"You've wandered deep into unknown country, partner, and there ain't no map from here on out. So if you want to keep your dignity, I suggest you stand back and leave the woman to her task."

Carney was stunned. "You cannot possibly believe…"

"You said yourself you can't do anything more. Nothing in life is guaranteed, Doc, but if Martha can be saved, I'll put my money on Alafair being the one to do it."

"Mr. Tucker, if your daughter dies from some poisonous backwoods potion, be it on your head. I can no longer take responsibility."

"You may have more education that all of us put together, son, but you've got a lot to learn. Now, you can either sit down and be quiet and see what happens, or you can gather up your marbles and go."

"I will tell Mrs. McCoy's husband what you have done."

"Go ahead, but don't expect a prompt response. He's in Washington City winning the war for us."

"I cannot watch. I am leaving." Carney was standing in the parlor in his bloody shirt, his posture rigid and his hands on his hips, with a look on his face that would curdle milk. But he did not leave. He stood there staring over Shaw's shoulder into the bedroom, watching Alafair.

He wanted to storm out, but he was captivated by the woman's strange...he didn't know what to call it...ritual? What on earth was she doing?

She was rummaging around in the chest of drawers near the window. She pulled out a pair of white cotton socks, then sat down in a chair next to the bed and commenced cutting the onions into thick slices. Alafair stood up and threw the bed covers onto the floor. Martha lay on her back with her arms outflung, her white nightgown streaked and spotted with her own blood. Her lips were a dull, leaden color, her eyes sunken. From where he stood, Carney could not see her chest rise and fall. He wondered if Alafair thought she could raise the dead.

Carney forgot to be angry as he watched Alafair stuff the onion slices into the socks and carefully pull them onto Martha's feet. Her actions were so unrelated to his reality that as far as he was concerned, she might as well have been performing an interpretive dance while her daughter died of pneumonia.

Alafair retrieved the quilts from the floor and covered Martha up again, then strode out of the bedroom, past Shaw, and toward the kitchen. As she passed Carney she spared him a glance.

"Are you still here?"

He didn't answer. He watched her take a basket of fresh eggs off the cabinet, return to the bedroom and begin placing eggs on the floor, in the corners.

"What is she doing?" Carney's question was more or less directed at Shaw.

Shaw had removed himself to one side of the bedroom door and was watching his wife's movements with his arms crossed over his chest. He looked tense. "I saw my mother do that once, when my father had the fever."

Carney blinked at him. "Did it work?"

Shaw said nothing, but shook his head.

Alafair stuck her head into the parlor. "Shaw, run over to Alice's and fetch that jug of Miz Carrizal's remedy."

Shaw grabbed his hat and left without argument. What else

was there to do? Carney stepped out of his way but otherwise stood where he was, far too curious to either leave or take action.

Alafair was changing Martha's gown now, and she was doing it without removing the quilts that covered her. She tossed the ruined gown onto the floor and proceeded to change the bloody sheets in the same inexplicable fashion. She passed by Carney half a dozen times as she went back and forth between the bedroom and the kitchen, mixing up strange potions. Garlic, he saw, and more onions and weird things that looked like weeds. She smeared flour and hot water and mustard on a piece of brown paper. She put ground coffee in a saucer on the bedside table and set fire to a wad of camphor gum in the middle of it.

Carney didn't understand or approve of one thing she was doing, but he recognized the look on her face. He had seen it every time he had looked in the mirror over the past month. Desperation.

She was trying every remedy she had ever known or heard of, and how could he fault her for that? He had just done the same thing. He had been doing the same thing for all his patients for weeks.

Chapter Twenty-three

How Doctor Carney Did the Best He Could

Carney badly wanted to see what else Alafair was going to come up with. But he had too many other patients who needed him to be able to hang around for no other reason than to satisfy his curiosity. Twenty minutes after Alafair had gone into action, Shaw returned with a glass jar full of a slimy green concoction that looked like swamp water and Carney decided it was time for him to go.

He spent the evening and half the night doing what he had been doing for weeks; going from house to house, knocking on doors, asking after those he knew were suffering and if anyone else had taken ill since the last time he had come by. He administered codeine for coughing and aspirin for the aches, and sometimes morphine if the pain was bad enough. He didn't have an oxygen tank for those whose lungs were failing, but he did have digitalis to stimulate a weakening heart.

There was little else for him to do besides give advice and reassure the hollow-eyed caregiver that the loved one was doing well. Or if he was not doing well, that everything possible was being done for him.

He was tempted to ask one of the remaining Red Cross ladies to make the call at the Kelley house tonight, but he squared his shoulders and did his duty. He was surprised and gratified when

Alice herself answered the door, pale and thin, but dressed and obviously on the mend.

She wasted no time on a greeting. "Dr. Carney, how is my sister?"

"Mrs. McCoy is very ill."

"Will she live?"

He wasn't going to lie to her, but he had no desire to pronounce Martha dead before the fact. "We will know more in the morning. Your parents are with her and your mother is doing everything that she can."

That answer seemed to satisfy Alice, and she stood aside to let Carney come in.

"I am glad to see that you are up and about, Mrs. Kelley. How does the rest of your household fare?"

"All much better, Doctor, thank you. Though neither Walter or me can walk ten feet without we have to rest. Dorothy is better, too. She is heartsick, though. Poor little thing. You want to have a look at all the invalids? Walter is in the dining room."

By the time Carney staggered back to his hotel room it was nearly midnight, his leg was aching, and he had not eaten anything since breakfast. He was exhausted and starving, but in a slightly better frame of mind than he had been earlier. Aside from Martha McCoy, he had heard of no new cases of the flu in town today, and no one had died. Yet.

He limped down Seaman Street toward the hotel, and as he passed the McCoy Land and Title Company he looked up to see a light on in the apartment above. He paused briefly, but he didn't have the energy to climb the stairs. He would have to wait until morning to find out if Martha McCoy survived.

Carney set his alarm clock for five a.m. and fell asleep as soon as his head hit the pillow. The next morning his first house call was to the apartment above the offices of McCoy Land and Title Company. Alafair answered the door. She looked haggard and sunken-eyed. Before Carney could speak, she read his expression of dismay and smiled. She did not keep him in suspense.

"Martha is doing better. She isn't gurgling anymore and her color is better. Her fever is down."

Carney let out a breath he did not realize he was holding. "Thank goodness. I would like to have a look at her and listen to her lungs…" he raised an eyebrow, "…if that is all right with you?"

Alafair was mildly surprised as his diffidence. She gestured Carney inside. "Come in, son. Won't do any good for you to just stand there looking all beflustered."

She led him into the bedroom and stood aside while he took off his coat and rolled up his sleeves. Martha was lying on her back, covered with so many quilts that Carney could barely see the top of her head. Alafair had gotten rid of all trace of the bloody chaos of the night before. The room was clean and ordered, and smelled of burnt camphor, sage, garlic, vinegar, carbolic soap, and the strong odor of cooked onion.

Carney pulled back the quilt and Martha stirred. Her breathing was raspy but even. Her sickly pallor contrasted alarmingly with the red of her swollen eyes, but her fever had broken. The doctor glanced at Alafair, incredulous. He would have bet money that she would not make it through the night.

Alafair anticipated his question. "Her temperature broke just before dawn."

Martha roused and cracked open one rheumy eye when he placed the stethoscope against her chest. "I will not be able to make it in to work today, Doctor." Her voice was a feeble whisper.

"Go back to sleep, Mrs. McCoy. We will attempt to manage without you."

Carney listened to her lungs and heart, took her pulse, peered into her eyes and throat. She was unable to stay alert and made no sense when she tried to respond to his comments. He could hear that there was still some fluid in her lungs. But she was much better than she had been the night before.

Carney felt his heart pick up speed. The vaccination had worked. He sank into the nearest chair, so relieved that he could barely breathe. He had been afraid to use his experimental serum on so many of his seriously ill patients, for fear of making things worse for them, but Martha had been so ill that nothing could have made it worse.

"She is still quite ill, but unless she relapses, I believe she will live." Carney couldn't have said that with any assurance last night. "She is still in danger, of course. The fever will continue to come up in the evenings. She will need constant watching for several days." He paused, then as though he could not believe it himself, he repeated, "But I think she will live."

"It was the onions," Alafair said.

Carney's brow knit. "What?"

"The onions that I bound to her feet last night. That's what drew out the fever."

Carney took a moment to digest Alafair's statement. It was so ridiculous that he almost laughed in her face, but he caught himself. It would be pointless to antagonize the poor woman. She had been desperate, too.

Before he could come up with some inoffensive reply, she picked up a bowl that was sitting on the bedside table and handed it to him. Startled, he took it. Something limp and stringy and coal-black lay in the bottom. It smelled burnt, like charcoal. Carney's hair rose and he thrust the bowl back at her. "What is it?"

"Onion," she said. "The fever fried them."

Chapter Twenty-four

How Alafair Returned to the Matter at Hand

Whether she owed her life to Carney's influenza vaccine or to her mother's onion poultice, Martha did live. Every day Carney made the trip up the stairs to check on her. His visits rarely lasted for more than a few minutes. Now that she was recovering, there was little that he could do for her that her mother was not already doing. Ten days after her collapse, Martha was still weak, but her fever was gone, her lungs were clear, and she was able to get out of bed and sit up in a chair for an hour at a time.

When Carney called early one chilly October morning, he found Martha sitting at the table as Alafair bustled around the small kitchen. Carney tried to maintain a stern professional demeanor when he listened to Martha's lungs, but it was hard not to smile with relief at how much better she looked. He straightened and removed the stethoscope from his ears. "I must say, considering that I was counting you among the departed only a few days ago, you are coming along remarkably well, Mrs. McCoy."

"I feel like I've been dragged through a knothole, Doctor. But after the way I felt earlier this week, I can't complain. Hattie tells me that there hasn't been a new case of influenza in town for the past four days." Hattie Tucker had recovered enough to take over management of the Red Cross volunteers, which was not much of a task anymore, considering that there were only three women left standing after the epidemic swept through their ranks.

"That is true. However, I expect there will be the odd case here and there, and perhaps another minor outbreak over the winter. I understand your sister, Mrs. Kelley, felt well enough to pay you a visit yesterday."

"Yes, her and Walter both came up to sit with me and give Mama a break. We figured that since they've already had the influenza it would be safe enough. Alice was worried about carrying the disease home on her clothes. But I told her I expect I'm not contagious."

Alafair turned away from the counter to face them. "Is she contagious, Doctor?

"No fever, so I would say no, she is not."

"Thank goodness! Alice said she would come up again this afternoon to sit with Martha for a spell. You suppose it would be all right for her to bring Linda with her? And do you think I could run out to the farm for a bit and see my young'uns without infecting them?"

"Oh, I think so. There is no guarantee that all danger is past, of course. But judging by the smell of medicinals in here, I am guessing there is not a bacterium left alive in this apartment, Mrs. Tucker."

He was teasing her, or making fun of her, but Alafair didn't care. She was so homesick for her children that she could have burst into tears at the happy prospect of seeing them again. She waited a moment for the lump in her throat to dissolve before she spoke. "Have you had breakfast, honey?"

It took a moment for Carney to realize she was talking to him. "Thank you, ma'am, but I have many calls to make. I should be on my way."

Alafair paid no mind to his words and gestured for him to take a chair. "You need a good breakfast to keep up your strength. Martha can only manage broth and gruel yet, but I'm frying up some eggs and bacon for myself." She poured a mug of coffee and plunked it on the table in front of him. He bowed to the inevitable and sat down, trying to ignore Martha's amused expression.

He spoke to Alafair's back as she cracked eggs into the skillet. "Mrs. McCoy and her nurse brigade have done yeoman's duty during this outbreak. Considering how many influenza sufferers she tended over the course of the epidemic, I am surprised she did not become ill long ago."

Alafair smiled at that. "You and me could say the same about ourselves, Doc."

Carney lifted a shoulder in half a shrug. "Do not ask me to explain why some fall ill and some do not. Especially considering how we caretakers have not had a moment to take care of ourselves. I have not had a complete night's sleep in nearly a month, and that is very detrimental to one's immunity."

"You do the best you can. I nap when my ailing youngsters are napping and when I'm awake I'm cleaning or dosing them or feeding them, like when I had little babies. But I do get a lot of thinking done when I'm washing dishes or scrubbing the floor." Alafair paused to flip an egg, then said, "Doc, did you ever find any proof that Lewis Hulce was poisoned?"

Carney blinked at the conversational change of direction. "No, I found no evidence of arsenic in Lewis' body."

"So he could he have died of the influenza after all?"

"Well, yes, ma'am, death by pneumonia was my first diagnosis based on the appearance of the body. But his lungs were clear. There was damage to his heart. There was some foaming in the bronchia, as though he had been struggling to breathe…"

Alafair considered this. "Could he have been smothered?"

The implication startled Carney. "That seems extremely unlikely. Who could have done such a thing? His poisoned and dying mother? His twelve-year-old sister? They were the only other people in the house."

Alafair set a plate piled with eggs and bacon and fried potatoes on the table in front of him. Martha turned a mild shade of green and moved to the other side of the table. Alafair didn't seem to notice.

Carney took a bite of potato. It was fried to a crisp, heavy and greasy and delicious. He was hungrier than he had realized. "Perhaps the fever killed Mr. Hulce," he said, as he reached for the salt. "Perhaps a heart attack due to the shock of his mother's horrific death."

Martha dabbled her spoon in the broth, but didn't taste it. The odor of bacon had killed her appetite. "Last I heard, the theory was that Homer Thomason killed his wife for the insurance money by sending her a poisoned cake, and that Lewis was either poisoned by accident or was meant to be his stepfather's second victim."

"That was the theory," Alafair agreed. "But Lewis wasn't poisoned, after all. So that can't be it. Something is not right."

Carney was puzzled. "How so, ma'am?"

"I begin to think that Homer Thomason didn't kill anybody."

She made the pronouncement with such certainty that Carney blinked in surprise. He shot Martha an incredulous glance along his shoulder before he said, "But it was you who suspected poison in the first place, Mrs. Tucker, and you who discovered that Mr. Thomason had motives for killing both his wife and stepson."

"But where did that cake come from?" Alafair picked up her own coffee mug and sat down next to Martha. "Yes, Homer had dinner sent to his family from Burrows' Café, but Anita says she did not send the cake. And Homer was in Muskogee, so he didn't deliver it himself."

Carney gestured at her with his fork. "The law contends that he hired an accomplice to deliver the poisoned cake."

"What accomplice? Who on earth made a poisoned cake and walked right up to Nola's front door and handed it to her, bold as brass? Scott asked the neighbors if they saw anybody go to the Thomasons' door besides Anita's delivery boys, which they didn't. Now the neighbors may have missed something, but Scott interviewed the boys, too, and none of them admitted to anybody paying them to take a cake to the Thomason house. Dorothy don't know how the cake got there, and we'll never be able to ask Nola. Doc, you saw Homer's face when he finally came back from Muskogee after Nola died. He looked like somebody had just clobbered him in the face with a two-by-four. He loved her, I'd swear to it. Just because there was an insurance policy on her doesn't mean he killed her for the money. I have one on Shaw and I guarantee I don't aim to do him in some night. So here's the question, then. If it wasn't Homer, then who poisoned Nola, and what...or who...killed Lewis?"

"He was not poisoned," Carney assured her, again. "Nor was it pneumonia. It must have been shock. He was weakened by the disease, and when he realized that his mother was dead, the shock stopped his heart."

"Maybe it was Raven Mocker, after all," Martha said.

Alafair was annoyed that Martha would joke about something so serious, and she frowned at her. But Martha's expression was anything but jovial. The hair rose at the back of Alafair's neck. "Don't even say it, honey."

Carney was confused. "What do you mean?"

Martha shook her head. "Never mind, Doctor. Ma, maybe Homer really intended to murder Lewis and not his wife. Maybe it was an accident that Nola ate the cake instead of Lewis."

"I might agree with that notion if the cake hadn't been full of strawberries."

"What are you going on about, Ma? What about strawberries?"

"Dorothy says Lewis was allergic to strawberries, same as she is. Surely Homer would know that his wife's son wouldn't eat them, so why try to poison him with a strawberry cake?"

"Well, then," Carney said, "someone knew that Mrs. Thomason was the only one in the house who was likely to eat that cake. That brings us right back to Homer Thomason."

They fell silent for a long moment, thinking, before Martha said, "Ma, did Cousin Scott ever get around to interviewing JoNell Reed?"

Chapter Twenty-five

How Alafair Really Did Figure It Out

Alafair put on her hat and walked the five blocks from Martha's apartment to JoNell Reed's home near the railroad station. JoNell lived with her mother and two older sisters in a little gray frame house with brick-red shutters. The yard was covered with dead grass, but trimmed and neat, with a fallow garden off to the side. There was no porch, but in front of the door was a small brick-paved area with a couple of slat-back chairs on it. Perfect for sitting out of an evening.

Next to the front door, a large piece of butcher paper marked with a red 'X' hung precariously by one corner. The other corner had come loose. The sign had been there for a while.

Alafair almost abandoned her plan when she saw that the quarantine sign was still up. Not that she was afraid of infection. She had already been too well exposed for far too long to worry about it now. But the epidemic had been more cruel to some families than to others, and she had no desire to intrude on anyone's grief. A couple of weeks ago JoNell had been too ill to talk to Scott. But she had not heard that JoNell or any of the other Reeds had died, so she took a breath and knocked on the door. A small, round woman answered almost immediately.

"I saw you coming up the walk," the woman said. "Are you from the Red Cross? Is Miz McCoy sick? I haven't seen her in while."

"I'm Miz Shaw Tucker, Martha McCoy's mother. Martha did come down with the grippe, but she doing all right now. Truth is I'm here to talk to JoNell, if she's up to it."

The woman pushed the door open. "Come on in."

Alafair walked into the tiny parlor and sat down. Like the yard, the house was spare but neat. Plain wooden furniture was covered with homemade cushions and pillows, doilies and throws. A brightly colored, hand-woven rag rug in the center of the room was lit by a stream of afternoon sunlight coming through the front window.

"I'm JoNell's mother," the woman said. "It's a mite chilly today. Can I get you a cup of tea? I'm out of coffee, but I still have some of the mint that I dried in the summer."

"Thank you, Miz Reed, but I don't want to take up your time. I reckon y'all must have got over the flu and are immune now, considering how you invited me in so cordial."

Mrs. Reed perched herself on the edge of a chair opposite Alafair and folded her hands in her lap. "Yes, the grippe ran through this house like wildfire and we were all so sick we were like to die. But my husband and me and my girls are all just about over it now, praise Jesus. And praise Miz McCoy and the Red Cross volunteers. There were a few days there when we were all down, and if it wasn't for them we'd have starved to death for sure. And your family?"

"We've all made it through, as well, thank you for asking. So JoNell is better, too? Is she to home?"

"Is this about Lewis?" Mrs. Reed's tone was not unfriendly, but Alafair figured it was time to get to the point.

"Yes, ma'am, it is. About him and his whole family. I know that Deputy Tucker was by here a while ago wanting to talk to JoNell, but she was in no condition."

"That's true. She was near to raving with fever. She's better now. I'll tell you, though, she's in no mood to talk about Lewis. Finding him and his folks like that near to did her in."

"Did you hear that Homer Thomason has been arrested for poisoning his family?" Alafair didn't mention that she was the one who fingered him.

"I did hear that. I also heard that the doctor thinks Lewis died from the effects of the influenza and not from poison."

"Doctor Carney did some tests and that is what he concluded."

"You know, Lewis was here for supper just two days before he came down with the grippe. JoNell cooked for him. It was the first time she ever cooked a whole meal by herself, but she did a pretty fair job of it."

"Is that so, now? Was that after Mr. Thomason blacked Lewis' eye? Did you know about that? I believe Lewis came down sick at his ma's house a couple of days after that."

"Yes, so I heard. Or rather, I saw. He dropped by the next morning after the fight to take JoNell out for a phosphate. He had a mighty impressive shiner, and he wasn't shy about letting us know who give it to him. It was a few days later, after Lewis died, when JoNell got sick, then the rest of us one by one. I figure he's the one infected us."

"Well, it's hard to tell why some come down with it hard, or how they get infected. I'm not surprised Lewis got sick, what with his job at the pharmacy and all the half-ailing folks coming to him for medicine."

"Miz Tucker, I know that you're the one who heard JoNell hollering and came over next door to help her out. I'm obliged to you for your kindness. But what do you think JoNell can tell you? If the sheriff hasn't been back here to talk to her again, he must think there's nothing more to know."

Alafair caught her bottom lip between her teeth while she considered how to put this. "I did go over there when JoNell raised the alarm," she said. "I saw the same thing she did, and it's no wonder she doesn't want to talk about it. Mr. Thomason swears up and down that he didn't do it, of course. But I've been thinking on it for a spell, Miz Reed, and it just don't add up. Maybe the poisoning was all a horrible accident, or maybe it was murder. Now, if Mr. Thomason really did kill his family, then he deserves whatever he gets. But if he did not, I'd hate to see an innocent man hanged for something he didn't do."

Mrs. Reed made a noncommittal noise before returning to the matter that concerned her. "And why do you think JoNell might know something?"

"Maybe she doesn't," Alafair admitted. "But she's the only one who was there that day, the only one involved, even if only a little bit, who Scott or Slim never talked to. What if she saw something, or heard something that turns out to be important? Surely she ought to have the chance to tell her story."

Mrs. Reed leaned back and propped her forearms on the arms of her chair. "She hasn't said a thing to me about what happened. When she came home that night she was near to crazy with grief over Lewis dying. I only found out that the mother died when Deputy Tucker came over to try and talk to her. JoNell is not much acquainted with the ways of the world, and she treats every little thing that don't go her way like it's the end of everything. I sometimes find myself wearied by her carrying-on, so truth is I've never encouraged her to tell me what happened."

Alafair took advantage of the opening. "May I ask her? It could be important."

"I would like to know myself," Mrs. Reed admitted. "Her sisters have both gone to my mother-in-law's house, but JoNell is in her bedroom. She hasn't hardly come out but to eat a bite since she got well." She stood up. "I'll go along with you."

She led Alafair into the back bedroom. It was a plain affair, furnished only with a pine clothes press and three small iron bedsteads for the sisters. Alafair made passing notice of the hand-tufted cotton bedspreads. Someday, if the opportunity arose, she might ask Mrs. Reed where she came by them. JoNell was sitting on the bed closest to the single window, staring out into the yard. When her mother opened the bedroom door, JoNell looked back over her shoulder to see who had intruded.

Her eyes widened when she recognized Alafair. She turned away quickly.

She looks older, Alafair thought. The rosy color had leached out of her cheeks, leaving her ivory pale. Her eyes were shadowed and she had lost much of her baby fat, as well. But Alafair could tell by her expression that grief had matured her far more than had the illness.

Mrs. Reed sat down on the opposite side of the bed and put a hand on JoNell's back. "Honey, you remember Miz Tucker, don't you?"

"I do," JoNell said. She didn't turn around. "You were very kind to me, Miz Tucker. I didn't know what to do."

Alafair sat down on another one of the sisters' beds. "It was a fearful thing, sugar. I'm real sorry you had to go through that. Your mama tells me that you had a bad case of the grippe but that you're feeling better now. I'm glad to hear it."

JoNell turned to looked at Alafair from under lowered eyelids. Shy, Alafair thought, maybe even a bit embarrassed at the way she had behaved that day. "I don't have the flu anymore, Miz Tucker, but I don't believe I'll ever feel better." Mrs. Reed put a sympathetic arm around her daughter and JoNell leaned into her embrace.

"I came by today to see if you'd be willing to tell me about that day, darlin'," Alafair said.

"There's nothing more to tell, ma'am. I believe you probably know more than me. I just walked into the house and saw Lewis. I ran looking for Miz Thomason and found her dead, and ran outside screaming. That's when you come over. I hadn't been there but five minutes all told."

"JoNell, I'm not as concerned about that awful day as I am about the days leading up to it. You know that Lewis and his stepdaddy had a knock-down fight just a couple days before Lewis got sick. Did he tell you how that came about? Did he tell you how he felt about it?"

JoNell sighed. "Yes, he told me all about it. He had no love for Mr. Thomason, that's for sure. He thought Mr. Thomason didn't treat his mother right. I swan, he downright couldn't hardly think of nothing else. Sometimes it got me all flusterated.

I told him that his ma was a grown up woman and if she didn't want to stay with her husband, there wasn't anybody making her. Mr. Thomason never did beat on her that I knew about, or even talk mean to her except about Lewis. But Lewis thought she only stayed married to him because she didn't have no other means of support."

Alafair was taken aback. "Did his mother tell him that?"

JoNell shrugged. "I don't know. That's what Lewis said, though. He told me that as soon as he made enough money he was going to talk her into taking Dorothy and moving in with him and me in our big house that we were going to get in Oklahoma City when we got married."

"Did he tell you what him and Mr. Thomason fought about?"

"Not really. He just said Mr. Thomason didn't want him to come around anymore because it upset Mrs. Thomason. But then the strangest thing…we were sitting at the counter with our sodas when I told him for the hundredth time that he ought to try and get along with his stepfather, unless he wanted to get banned from his mother's home and have to go to meeting her somewhere else. Always before he just got mad at me for saying it, but this time he agreed with me. That's why he went over to his mother's house the night he got sick. He told me that the fight had upset his mother so he was going to try to make it up with his stepdaddy, at least until he was rich enough to rescue her," she said. "He was even going to take a peace offering. He so much loved the spice cake I had made for him that he asked me to make a cake just big enough for one, specially to give to Mr. Thomason."

Mrs. Reed was surprised. "I didn't know that, honey. When did you make a cake for Lewis?"

"Over at his place. He just has the cutest little oven. Don't look shocked, Mama. Nobody ever saw me go to visit Lewis' apartment. Besides, he was always a perfect gentleman." Her gaze wandered off into space as she remembered. She didn't notice the aghast expression on Alafair's face. "Only instead of a spice cake, he asked if I could make a white cake with strawberries in it. I was surprised, because Lewis couldn't even touch strawberries without he got the hives. He said fresh strawberry cake was Homer's favorite, but his ma wouldn't make it because him and Dorothy couldn't eat it."

"Strawberries?" Mrs. Reed said. "Where did he think you were going to get fresh strawberries at this time of year?"

"That's what I told him. I said I could use some of your homemade jam, Mama, but, no, he had to have whole strawberries chunked up in the batter. That's why I made it at his apartment. He already had bought all the ingredients. Mr. Williams at the drug store had some whole strawberries frozen in his little freezer for ice cream and flips and the like. I made the prettiest little cake, Mama. Lewis told me to use all the sugar I wanted, so I made enough vanilla buttercream frosting for three cakes, I think. I offered to frost the cake, but Lewis said he'd do it, because he wanted to spell out 'I'm sorry' on the top with some special colored sugar he had bought just for the occasion."

Alafair could hardly breathe, but she managed to say, "Did you see the cake after he finished it?"

"No, I had to go home. Next thing I knew Lewis had been struck with the grippe and was at death's door. Mama wouldn't let me go over there to see him." She shot her mother a rueful look. "She didn't want me to get infected, but it didn't make any difference because I got the flu myself a couple days after Lewis died. I never saw my darling alive again." Her eyes flooded and tears spilled down her cheeks, but there were no hysterics.

Alafair stood up. "JoNell, thank you. Honey, I think Sheriff Tucker may be wanting to talk to you right quick. I'm real sorry that you lost your sweetheart."

Mrs. Reed showed Alafair to the door. "Miz Tucker, are you all right? You look like you've seen a ghost. I hope you aren't finally coming down with the flu."

Alafair readjusted her hat pin to give herself a moment to think. "No, it's just that I feel bad for JoNell. I'm afraid she's going to be hearing some mighty unpleasant things about Lewis and his family over the next few weeks."

Mrs. Reed leaned in confidentially. "I'm sorry Lewis died so bad, but the truth is I think she's well shet of him. That family had such ill feeling for one another. I'll tell you, it gave me second thoughts about letting JoNell step out with Lewis anymore. He was spiteful and underhanded and too old for her, anyway."

"Whyever did you let her see him, then?" Alafair blurted. She immediately wished she hadn't said it. It wasn't her business. And she knew from experience that it was not that easy to keep your children in line.

Mrs. Reed was not insulted. "I figured if I didn't press her, she'd come to her senses eventually. Besides, if I had forbid her, JoNell would have had a hissy fit, and I just don't have the strength anymore."

Alafair intended to go straight to Scott and present her new information, but her route from the Reed house to the jailhouse took her right by the big red brick building on Main Street that held several businesses—Burrows' Café, the hardware store, Kelley's Barber shop, four or five offices, and a few small apartments upstairs and down. Including the street-level apartment of the late Lewis Hulce.

It had not occurred to Alafair that Lewis' apartment was on her route, not until she passed by the front door. But the sight of that door, right on the street, caused her to consider that there may be something inside that would help corroborate JoNell's story. She was also reminded that her own son-in-law, Walter Kelley, owned the entire building, including that very door and the apartment therein.

She stopped so abruptly in the middle of the sidewalk that a woman walking behind her nearly knocked her over. The resultant apologies took long enough for Alafair to decide that since her daughter's husband owned the building, the apartment practically belonged to her and it was perfectly all right for her to go in and make herself at home.

The door was not locked. Alafair hadn't expected it to be. No one locked his front door in this town.

The single room was dark and musty from having been shut up for weeks, but it was orderly and neat, the bed made and everything in its place. There was not space for much more than a bed and a chifferobe in the front, and at the back, a tiny kitchenette containing one built-in cabinet, a sink, and a two-burner gas stove with a minuscule oven. A door at the back of the room led to the courtyard behind the building, where Walter had installed a small bathhouse with running water and a real flush toilet for his tenants.

Alafair made a beeline for the kitchenette and looked through the cabinet, careful not to disturb anything. The cabinet was almost empty. There was a sack of dried beans and a one pound can with a bit of powdered sugar at the bottom, which she sniffed suspiciously before wetting a finger and tasting a grain or two. It tasted like sugar, but she had heard that arsenic was tasteless. She put the can back, wondering if she should ask Doctor Carney to run his tests on the contents. There was no flour in the kitchen, no baking soda, not even salt. If JoNell had made the cake in this room, she had left no trace of it.

The pilot light on the stove was still lit, thank goodness. She would have to remember to mention to Walter that the gas needed to be turned off until he found a new tenant. A little wooden ice chest sat on the floor between the stove and the cabinet. The ice would be long melted, so she prepared herself for the smell of rotten food when she lifted the lid. All she found was that the metal-lined box was half full of water with a few globs of melted butter floating in it.

Butter and powdered sugar. Cream them together, and with a little milk and vanilla you have yourself a buttercream cake frosting.

Which may have been suggestive, but hardly proved anything. Alafair puffed and headed for the front door. It was almost as an afterthought that she opened the door to the chifferobe as she passed and saw the box with the skull and crossbones sitting on the top shelf, just peeking out from behind a folded blanket.

Chapter Twenty-six

How Alafair Saw That Justice Was Done

Wesley M. Cotton, prosecuting attorney for the district court of Muskogee County, laid his fountain pen on the desk and leaned back in his chair. "I'll have to interview both Miss Reed and Dorothy Thomason in order to corroborate this new information. After this amendment to your statement, Mrs. Tucker, as well the amended statement from Constable Scott Tucker, I believe we will be able to release Mr. Thomason from custody until the formal inquest is completed. I understand that the attending physician is prepared to corroborate the evidence, as well? In fact, I thought Doctor Carney was supposed to come to Muskogee with you today."

Shaw nodded. "Yes, he intended to drive in with us today, Mr. Cotton, but I'm afraid he wasn't feeling well this morning and decided not to come in case he's infectious."

Cotton's eyes widened. "Influenza?"

"An abundance of caution, I believe. But he asked us to tell you that he'll either write up his findings or take the train into Muskogee to speak to you in person, whichever you require, as soon as he possibly can."

Cotton nodded. He had already suffered his own bout of the illness and wasn't overly afraid of re-infection himself, but he appreciated Carney's adherence to the rules of hygiene. "All right, have him contact me when he feels he can." He stood up, and his visitors followed suit.

"If you would like to stop by the county jail and give the news to Mr. Thomason yourself before I ask the judge to set his bond, you are welcome to do so."

"Thank you, Lawyer Cotton," Alafair said. "I reckon Mr. Thomason would not welcome the sight of me right now."

After reviewing the amended depositions, the District Attorney dropped the charges against Homer Thomason, so the hearing was only a formality. Thomason had asked Lawyer Meriwether to see that Dorothy was in the courtroom on the day of the hearing. As soon as he was released, Thomason intended to leave for Sallisaw with his daughter and never again return to Boynton. Lawyer Meriwether agreed to take care of selling the house and disposing of the furniture.

When Meriwether gave her the news, Alafair volunteered to go to the Thomason house to retrieve Dorothy's clothing and pack for her trip to her new home. Dorothy took the news of her imminent departure with the dispassion that had become normal for her since her mother's death. To Alafair's surprise, Dorothy asked if she could come with her to pick out some special items she wanted to take to Sallisaw. Alafair was worried about the effect it would have on Dorothy to go back into the house where she had suffered such trauma, but she didn't refuse to allow it. Alafair was relieved when Sophronia asked to come along.

Alafair left the girls at Alice's house to play with Linda for half an hour while she slipped next door to clean the kitchen, make up Dorothy's bed, and tidy the bedrooms so that the house would look as normal as possible.

When she was done, she fetched Dorothy and Sophronia, and the three of them walked to the Thomason house in silence. Alafair kept a weather eye on Dorothy, looking for signs of upset, but Dorothy headed directly for her own bedroom without a glance at the kitchen floor where her mother had lain. She sat down on the flowered quilt that covered her bed and heaved a great sigh.

"Are you all right, sugar?" Alafair asked.

"Can I sit here for a spell before I pack my clothes? I want to remember a while before I go away forever."

"Sure you can, honey. Fronie, when Dorothy is ready, you help her fold her things. I put the suitcase under the window there. I'll tell you what, Dorothy, I'll just go into your daddy's room and pack his clothes, as well. He'll be glad to have some clean shirts." Alafair left the girls alone, careful to leave the bedroom door open so that she could easily hear if they needed her.

Sophronia took a seat on the bed next to her friend. "This is a nice room. I wish I had a room of my own. I have to share with my sisters."

"I wish I had sisters. I never had to share. I guess when we go stay with Aunt Molly and my cousins, I will." She looked around the room, fingered the flowers on the bedspread. "I do like my room," she admitted. "But I don't like this house anymore."

"I reckon not. Not after what happened."

"No. Not after what happened."

"I'm sorry you're leaving, though. I'll miss you."

"I'll miss you, too." Dorothy paused, took a breath to speak and thought better of it, then finally said, "You've been a real friend to me, Fronie. And now we'll never see one another ever more."

Sophronia could tell that Dorothy wanted to tell her something. She stood and walked to the open bedroom door to check on Alafair's whereabouts. She could hear her mother in the front of the house, rummaging through drawers. She resumed her seat at Dorothy's side. "You can tell me."

Dorothy smiled at being so transparent. When she spoke, her voice was just above a whisper. "It all happened just like I said. Except I didn't just hear them dying. I saw the whole thing."

"Oh, Dorothy!"

"When I heard Mama choking I got up and ran into the kitchen. It was so awful. She was upchucking everywhere, and there was blood coming out of everywhere. Lewis got out of bed. He was so sick he couldn't hardly walk, or talk to make sense. Mama fell down and we were neither of us strong enough to help her get up."

Dorothy paused, thoughtful. She was calm as she related the tale, but Sophronia could not hold back the tears. She could not stand the thought of how awful it would be to see your mother die. Dorothy watched her friend weep for a moment before she said, "It wasn't a shadow, neither."

It took a moment for Sophronia to remember what Dorothy had told her about a shadow. "What do you mean? You didn't really see any shadow pass by your bedroom door on the day that…it happened?"

Dorothy leaned in close to murmur in her ear. "It wasn't a shadow. It was my friend. Don't tell anybody."

"The shadow was your friend? What friend?"

"My friend, Mr. Escoe, who gave me the bird necklace."

"Your friend the old kitten man? He came into your house?" Sophonia exclaimed so loudly that Dorothy shushed her.

"Quiet now. I don't want him to get in trouble. But it was him, Fronie. He's the one who killed Lewis."

"Oh, my goodness! What did he do?"

"He killed Lewis," Dorothy repeated, patient. "It scared me at first, how he did it. But now I'm glad he did. Now I know that Lewis tried to poison Papa but poisoned Mama instead, so he deserved to be killed. Mama died, and I was crying so hard my friend must have heard me all the way from his house. Lewis was begging Mama to wake up because it was all a mistake. I didn't know what he meant then, but my friend must have. Mr. Escoe is magic. He didn't even touch Lewis. His feet made music when he walked in. He raised up his hands and hollered, 'You sinner!' He said, 'You're going to burn in…' Well, he said Lewis would burn in the hot place. and he pointed at Lewis and Lewis dropped down dead."

Sophronia covered her mouth with both hands, her hazel eyes, dappled gold-green like the forest floor, were wide with shock.

Dorothy took a breath and let it out. "Then he took my hand and brought me back here to my room. He tucked me in and went away. He never did say another word. It was a long time before…"

She swallowed her words when she noticed Alafair standing in the bedroom door.

"Oh, Mama." Sophronia sounded breathless.

Dorothy stood up. "Did you hear? Please don't let him get in trouble, Miz Tucker, oh, please."

Alafair put the pile of shirts she was holding down on a chair, and sat down between the two girls on the bed. "Yes, I heard. Dorothy, Mr. Escoe didn't touch Lewis at all?"

"Not even once. He's magic."

"Ma, is he the Raven Mocker?"

Alafair put an arm around Sophronia's shoulders. "Gracious! How did you remember Raven Mocker? Dorothy, Miz Gale's daddy isn't magic, honey. He didn't kill Lewis. Doctor Carney says Lewis was sick and weak, and his heart just stopped. The shock and guilt over what he did must have made his heart stop. It wasn't Mr. Escoe."

She could tell by Dorothy's skeptical look and Sophronia's expression of fear that her logical explanation was less than convincing. She remembered only too well the terror instilled in her own heart when her grandmother told her about the evil ones who roamed the earth. That was why on this very day, thirty years later, at the dawn of the twentieth century, there was a line of salt across the threshold next door. Alafair knew for a fact that there was much more to heaven and earth than met the eye. But she did not want her children to live in fear. She stood up. "Come on, girls, let's go pay Miz Gale's daddy a visit."

Dorothy looked eager to see her savior, but Sophronia did not like the idea at all. "But Mama, what if he…?"

Alafair did not let her finish. "Best to find out the truth about what you don't understand, honey. It's hardly ever what you thought it was at first."

◇◇◇

Dorothy stood right beside Alafair as she knocked on the Gales' front door, but Sophronia hung back at the edge of the porch. Alafair saw the curtain in the front window twitch before Mrs. Gale opened the door. She made no move to let them in. Her sour expression told Alafair that she was not in the market for company.

"Miz Gale, I'm Miz Tucker, Alice Kelley's mother. I've been taking care of her and Walter while they recuperate from the grippe." She beckoned Sophronia forward. "This here is my daughter Sophronia, and you know Dorothy Thomason from the house behind yours."

Mrs. Gale eyed them with suspicion. "I saw the quarantine sign on Alice's door last time I had to go to the market. The Thomasons' door too. I don't mean to be unneighborly, but we've managed to keep from getting the influenza to now, and I'd just as soon not have visitors until this epidemic is well over and done with."

Alafair was not deterred. "A wise precaution. But everybody in both those houses is over their sickness, and Dr. Carney says we're not catching at all anymore. It's just that young Dorothy here will be moving away from Boynton directly and has a yearning to say goodbye to your daddy before she goes. She tells me that they are particular friends."

Mrs. Gale's forehead puckered and she stepped closer to the screen. "Y'all are leaving, Dorothy?"

"Yes, ma'am. Since my mama died there's no reason to stay here."

"Oh, I'm sorry to hear that. I didn't know your mama died. I've been sticking close to home and have not heard any news in a long spell."

There are advantages to living in isolation, Alafair thought.

Mrs. Gale's hand reached toward the screen door, but before she pushed it open, she said, "You're sure y'all aren't infectious anymore?"

Alafair had not had the flu, and neither had Sophronia. If they were by some chance incubating the illness, and Mrs. Gale came down with it after their visit, Alafair would feel bad about it. But not bad enough to alter her plan. "As pure as springtime, Miz Gale."

"Well, I reckon it'll be all right, then." She opened the screen and stood back. "Y'all can come on in for a minute."

Mrs. Gale led Alafair and the girls to the back of the house, into a sunny sitting room filled with plants. A gray tiger-striped cat lounged on a throw rug, basking in a beam of sunshine, while three half-grown kittens romped beside her.

The kittens rushed to wind themselves around the newcomers' ankles. Sophronia recognized her yellow playmate and picked him up with an exclamation of delight. She didn't notice the frail old man sitting quietly in a chair beside the window, not until Dorothy said, "Hey, Mr. Escoe."

He did not look much like the cheerful man who had heaved a kitten at Sophronia weeks earlier. He didn't respond to Dorothy's greeting, or look away from the window. His face was slack and his eyes dull. Alafair noticed that he was wearing a shell shaker, an anklet made of small box turtle shells filled with pebbles to make them rattle. Dorothy put a tender hand on his bald dome, but he seemed unaware of it.

Alafair gave Mrs. Gale a questioning look, and she shrugged. "Papa has his good days and his bad days. His mind is just about gone now. He's well into the twilight, I fear." Mrs. Gale's smile was sad. "I wish you could have known him a few years ago, Miz Tucker. He was a Holiness pastor, a snake handler who the Lord never let get bit once. He was the best preacher, so full of fire. He saved many a soul. He could smell a sinner a mile away."

He still can, Alafair thought, but before she could comment, Mrs. Gale said, "He loved to be around children. Dorothy here was always a favorite of his."

"Dorothy tells me she feels the same." Alafair gestured toward the old man. "Why is he wearing a shell shaker?"

Mrs. Gale looked abashed. Shell shakers were usually only worn by Cherokee women, and then only during ceremonies. "Oh, that. Well, those were my mother-in-law's. She made them, oh, must be fifty years ago now. She loved the stomp dancing. Daddy would fuss if he had enough wit to know he's wearing them. I put them on him just so I'll hear when he has a notion to get up. He likes to wander, you know."

Chapter Twenty-seven

How the War Ended

Emmett Carney had come down with influenza on the day he was scheduled to accompany Alafair and Shaw Tucker to Muskogee and give his deposition to the district court. He had shown up at the Red Cross staging area in the schoolhouse at six o'clock that morning to lay out the day's battle plan for the nurses, just as he had every morning for the previous month. Hattie Tucker had taken one look at him and relieved him of command on the spot. Carney endured his bout of illness from Ann Addison's spare bedroom, where he was tended by a parade of volunteer nurses and Mrs. Addison herself, when she could spare the time.

Carney was disappointed that he had come down with the flu, but not surprised. He had never expected that his vaccine was a miracle drug. After Martha McCoy's recovery, he had held out hope that he might escape, but too many patients, too much exposure, too little rest, had proven too potent a combination for any preventive to overcome for long.

He wasn't sure how long he had been ill. Several days, at least. He knew that his case of the flu was run-of-the mill. Still, there were a couple of days that he felt so rough that he doubted he would recover.

He woke from a long sleep one November afternoon to discover that he felt better. He gingerly turned his head toward the
window. His headache was still there, but for the first time since
he became ill, he did not feel as though someone had taken an
axe to his skull. In fact, all the body aches had abated somewhat.
He released a gusty sigh. He was going to live after all. As an
experiment, he moved his head in the opposite direction and
was surprised to see Alafair Tucker sitting in a rocker beside his
bed, crocheting.

He made a croaking noise, then cleared his throat. "Mrs.
Tucker, is that you?"

She lowered the needlework into her lap. "Yes it is, Doctor
Carney."

"How long have you been here? Where is Mrs. Addison?"

"Ann got called away for a birthing. I'm in town visiting my
daughters and I said I'd tend you for a spell. I've been here a while.
I'm glad to see you're back amongst us. How are you feeling?"

He hesitated, taking stock before answering. "Like I have just
risen from the dead. Thirsty."

"That's good." She poured a glass of water from the pitcher
on the bedside table and helped him struggle upright enough to
drink it. "You've been sweating to beat the band. Your nightshirt
is soaked. Drink this down and we'll get you cleaned up and into
some dry clothes and change your sheets. Do you need to pee?"

"No. I do not feel like I will ever need to urinate again."

"Here, drink some more water while I find you some clean
linens."

He lay back on the pillow and stared at the ceiling, too wrung
out to think. His head felt sore and tender. Alafair returned
with a load of bed linen under one arm and a steaming basin
of water in her hands.

"I can change my own nightshirt," Carney said.

She put the basin on the bedside table. "I don't think so."

"Mrs. Tucker, I am not an infant." He nodded at the pile
of sheets and blankets. "I will sit in a chair while you do that."

She stepped back and regarded him with a raised eyebrow. "All right then. Go ahead on."

He tried to sit up, but when the room began to spin, he dropped back on the pillow. Alafair said nothing. Her expression didn't change as she flung the coverlet off of him. "I promise not to offend your modesty, Doctor."

Carney was too weak to argue. "I have no modesty anymore, Mrs. Tucker."

She managed to undress him without making him sit up fully, then gently washed him down with warm, lemon-scented water. Her firm, competent, gentle ministration felt so good that he fell asleep in the midst of it. When he awoke he was clad in a clean nightshirt and lying under soft, dry sheets and an herb-scented quilt. Alafair was back in her chair, crocheting lace trim onto a child's dress.

He gazed at her from under half-closed lids for some moments before she noticed that he was awake.

"I suppose your preventives worked better than mine, after all," he said.

Alafair shrugged. "They didn't keep Martha from coming down bad with the grippe."

"But you seem to have escaped."

"Luck, I reckon."

"Mrs. Addison believes that some people remain uninfected by sheer dint of will."

That made Alafair laugh. "Well, Miz Doc would know."

"How did Mr. Thomason's hearing go?"

"The District Attorney dropped the charges against Mr. Thomason. Mr. Meriwether read our statements to the judge, but it was JoNell Reed's testimony that did the trick. The evidence against Lewis Hulce was too convincing. We'll have to leave it to God to punish Lewis, though."

"Mr. Thomason is free?"

"They let him go right then and there. Him and Dorothy got on a train to Sallisaw an hour later. Fronie will miss her friend, and I reckon I will, too. Poor little gal, losing her mother like that." She placed her crocheting on the bedside table. "Ann has some some broth a-simmering in the kitchen if you feel like you could eat something."

"I am sorry, Mrs. Tucker."

She blinked at him. "What for, Doctor Carney?"

"For being such an intolerable ass."

She pressed her lips together in an effort not to laugh. "You did what you figured was right. And you did real good. But I accept your apology, Doctor."

"I still do not believe in herbs and rattles and magic, though."

"I know you don't. And I don't believe science is the answer to everything."

"We shall have to agree to disagree."

"We shall. You sound stronger. You want some of that soup?"

Before he could reply, the quiet was broken by the peal of the big bell at the Methodist church up the hill, joined shortly by the higher-pitched ringing of the bell at the Baptist church on the next block. In the distance, the faint echo of bells tolling at two or three other churches in town added to the chorus.

"Is it Sunday?" Carney sounded surprised.

"It's Monday. November 11th."

"Why are the church bells ringing?"

Alafair glanced at the clock on the dresser. "Well, Doctor Carney, as of this minute the war is over."

Carney smiled. "Yes, Mrs. Tucker, I believe that it is."

Alafair's Recipes for the Sick

Our foremothers were well versed in the medicinal qualities of food.

Garlic has antibiotic properties, and was used during the 1918 flu outbreak as a treatment. One early twentieth-century recipe for a garlic soup to be fed to a flu sufferer was made by simmering twenty-four cloves of garlic in a quart of water for an hour. The Romans believed that garlic gave one strength, and gladiators chewed raw garlic cloves before a match for just that purpose.

Ginger is a traditional and effective cure for nausea. Commercial ginger pills to prevent seasickness and nausea are available at pharmacies to this day. Ginger tea can be made by boiling a slice of fresh ginger in a cup of water until the water turns golden. Sweeten it with honey, and sip it hot.

Onion, like garlic, is antibiotic as well. The following is an anecdotal story about the curative power of onion, told to the author by the person to whom it happened. When the author's friend was a young boy, he developed such a severe case of pneumonia that the doctor told his mother to prepare herself for his imminent demise. In an act of desperation, his mother sliced up a raw onion and bound it to the bottoms of his feet with strips of sheet, then put cotton socks on him. In the morning, his fever had broken, his lungs had cleared, and the onion poultice had turned black. The author makes no judgment, but she does like this story very much.

Rice

Well-cooked, soft rice is easy to digest. The rule of thumb for cooking raw rice (not instant), is two parts liquid to one part rice, boil until liquid is absorbed and rice is soft. However, for particularly distressed digestive systems, Alafair was known to simmer one part rice in seven parts liquid—milk and/or water—for forty minutes to an hour, until almost all the liquid was absorbed, creating a wonderfully creamy and practically pre-digested dish for the invalid. Serve warm with warm milk or cream and sugar, and a dot of butter, if desired.

Chicken Soup

Remove the giblets and wash a two- or three-pound broiler chicken inside and out. Put the whole, uncut chicken in a large pot and cover with water. Add about ½ tsp of salt per pound. and pepper if desired. Bring the water to a boil, then reduce heat, cover and simmer 1½ hours, or until the chicken is tender. Remove the chicken from the broth and remove the meat from the bones with a fork. Cut the meat into bite-sized pieces. As the broth cools, the chicken fat will rise to the top. Skim the fat off. You should have four or five cups of broth. Return the chicken meat to the broth, along with noodles, chopped onion or chopped carrot, a clove of minced garlic, or other vegetables or herbs as desired. Heat until boiling, then reduce heat and simmer ten or fifteen minutes more, until noodles/vegetables are tender.

Milk Toast

Lightly toast a slice of bread, butter both sides and sprinkle with a little salt. Put the toast in a dish and pour a half-cup of boiling whole milk over it. Serve warm. Dry burned toast (just charred on top) is excellent for an upset stomach and diarrhea.

Historical Notes

The Influenza Pandemic of 1918-1919

How many people died of influenza during the pandemic of 1918-1919?

According to the U.S. Department of Health and Human Services, no one knows for sure how many died in the flu pandemic, but modern estimates put the number at somewhere between thirty and fifty million people worldwide. The U.S. Center for Disease Control estimates that more than six hundred thousand of those were Americans. In May of 2015, The U.S. Department of Veterans Affairs listed just over fifty-three thousand American battle deaths in World War I, which means that twelve times as many Americans died from complications of the flu than died in battle.

Why was the 1918 outbreak so deadly?

Most who came down with the flu that year recovered, but in a large minority of sufferers, the infection took an ominous and unusual turn; horrible burning pain in the bones and joints, fever so high that patients became delirious, hemorrhaging from the nose and mouth, a cough bad enough to crack ribs, vomiting and diarrhea. The worst and most deadly complication was a virulent type of bacterial pneumonia; the bronchia and lungs would fill with fluid and the patient would drown. The lack of oxygen made the skin turn a leaden blue color, sometimes so dark that hospital personnel could not tell the sufferer's race. This is why it was called the "blue death" or the "purple plague."

During ordinary flu outbreaks, people who die of the disease tend to be the weak, very young, or elderly, but the 1918 epidemic killed an unusual number of healthy young people. Some medical professionals believe that healthy people sometimes experienced such an immune system overreaction to the pathogen that their organs were damaged and their lungs clogged with immune cells, inhibiting their ability to breathe.

Why didn't Alafair or Shaw contract the illness?

There may be something to Mrs. Addison's assertion that some people escape illness by sheer willpower. Or, perhaps some of Alafair's remedies actually worked. A more likely answer is that those who survived the virulent outbreak of "Russian flu" that swept the country in 1890 tended to be less susceptible to the "Spanish flu" in 1918, according to the U.S. Department of Health and Human Services.

Which was more effective during the pandemic? Alafair's remedies or Doctor Carney's vaccine?

Home Remedies

In early twentieth-century America, every housewife had her arsenal of remedies for common ailments, and many of were quite effective. As Alafair told Martha, if the old remedies didn't work they wouldn't have been in use since the beginning of time. Even so, there was a lot of strange, bothersome, and useless lore out there, and it is likely that more than a few people died from an unfortunate combination of ingredients such as turpentine, coal oil, and mercury in the home remedies they were given. There has been recent speculation among scientists that many who died during the epidemic were killed by aspirin poisoning rather than the disease (Dr. Karen M. Starko, *Journal of Clinical*

Infectious Diseases, vol. 49-no.9, 2009). Desperate caregivers may have figured that if a little aspirin was good for fever and aches, then whole handfuls every hour was even better.

Medical Science

In the early part of the twentieth century, scientific research was making such amazing strides that the medical community worldwide was seized with unreasonable optimism that eventually science would be able to cure all diseases. Their helplessness in the face of the influenza pandemic of 1918 put an end to that notion. Before the advent of antibiotics in the middle of the century, researchers were heavily into the idea of what we now call *immunotherapy*. In 1918, the medical community was convinced that if they could come up with an effective vaccine, they could control the epidemic. They were on the right track, but a useful flu vaccine was not developed until 1938. The influenza virus mutates so quickly that to this day it is difficult to concoct a vaccine that totally protects from whatever strain is rife in any particular year.

Children's Rhymes

Children's games and jump-rope rhymes have been passed down from child to child, without reference to adults, for generations. The rhymes and games that Sophronia and her friends play date from far before her time and will be played and recited by her own children and grandchildren. The origins of many of the rhymes are lost in time, but a few did arise or were modified around the time of the 1918 flu epidemic, including "I had a little bird."

"This old man" may date from the Irish potato famine of the 1840s.

"The Lady with the Alligator Purse" evolved from a similar British rhyme, through a rhyme that was popular in Appalachia in the late nineteenth century. Some folk historians believe that the "lady" is Susan B. Anthony, who always carried an alligator-skin bag.

To receive a free catalog of Poisoned Pen Press titles, please provide your name, address, and e-mail address in one of the following ways:

Phone: 1-800-421-3976
Facsimile: 1-480-949-1707
Email: info@poisonedpenpress.com
Website: www.poisonedpenpress.com

Poisoned Pen Press
6962 E. First Ave. Ste 103
Scottsdale, AZ 85251